A WALKER P9-DDN-983
CAN'T AFFORD TO GET LONELY

You start to feeling like you just got to talk to some human face or you're going to bust, and then what happens? You greet some stranger and he blows your head off. You put in with some woodsy family and they slit your throat in the night and make spoons out of your bones and leather bags out of your skin and your muscle ends up in the smokehouse getting its final cure. It led to no good wishing for company, so Jamie never did.

That's why he was setting by himself in a tree over the chainlink fence that marked the border of I-40 when he heard some folks singing, so loud he could hear them before he saw them. Singing, if you can believe it, right on the road, right on the *freeway*, which is the same as to say they were out of their minds. The idea of making noise while traveling on I-40 was so brazen that Jamie first thought they must be mobbers. But no, Winston and Greensboro had a right smart highway patrol on horseback, and these folks was coming *from* Winston heading west—no way could they be mobbers. They was just too dumb to live, that's all; normal citizens, refugees or something, people who still thought the world was safe for singing in.

From "West" by Orson Scott Card

ORSON SCOTT CARD ★ DAVID DRAKE
LOIS McMASTER BUJOLD

FREE LANCERS

CREATED BY
ELIZABETH
MITCHELL

BAEN
BOOKS

FREE LANCERS

This is a work of fiction. All the characters and events portrayed in this book are fictional, and any resemblance to real people or incidents is purely coincidental.

Copyright © 1987 by Baen Publishing Enterprises

All rights reserved, including the right to reproduce this book or portions thereof in any form.

A Baen Books Original

Baen Publishing Enterprises
260 Fifth Avenue
New York, N.Y. 10001

First printing, September 1987

ISBN: 0-671-65352-0

Cover art by Larry Elmore

Printed in the United States of America

Distributed by
SIMON & SCHUSTER
1230 Avenue of the Americas
New York, N.Y. 10020

CONTENTS

WEST
Orson Scott Card

Scott Card just received his second Nebula Award, for the novel Speaker for the Dead. *The story that follows here will appear in longer form as part of his collection* Tales of the Mormon Sea.

"West" is mostly the tale of Jamie Teague, whose greatest pride is his self-sufficiency. But he is a man driven by personal demons which are beyond his power to dispel without help.   —E.M.

It was a good scavenging trip eastward to the coast that summer, and Jamie Teague had a pack full of stuff before he even got to Marine City. Things were peaceful there, and he might have stayed, he was that welcome. But along about the start of August, Jamie said his good-byes and headed back west. Had to reach the mountains before the snows came.

He made fair time on his return trip. It was only September, he was already just west of Winston—but Jamie was so hungry that kudzu was starting to look like salad to him.

Not that hunger was anything new. Every time he took this months-long trip from his cabin in the Great Smokies to the coast and back, there were days here and there with nothing to eat. Jamie was a champion scavenger, but most houses and all the old grocery stores had their food cleaned out long since. Besides, what good was it to scavenge food? Any canned stuff you found nowadays was likely to be bad. What Jamie looked for was metal stuff folks didn't make no more. Hammers. Needles. Nails. Saws. One time he found this little out-of-the-way hardware store near Checowinity that had a whole crate of screws, a good size, too, and not a speck of rust. Near killed him carrying the whole mess of it back, but he couldn't leave any; he didn't get to the coast that often, and somebody was bound to find anything he left behind.

This trip hadn't been as good as that time, but it was still good, considering most of the country was pretty well picked-over by now. He found him some needles. Two fishing reels and a dozen spools of resilient line. A lot of ordinary stuff, besides. And things he couldn't put in his pack: that long visit in Marine City on the coast; them nice folks north of Kenansville who took him in and listened to his tales. The Kenansville folks even invited him to stay with them, and fed him near to busting on country ham and sausage biscuits in the cool of those hot August mornings. But Jamie Teague knew what came of staying around the same folks too long, and so he pushed on. Now the memory of those meals made him feel all wishful, here on the fringes of Winston, near three days without eating.

He'd been hungry lots of times before, and he'd get hungry lots of times again, but that didn't mean it didn't matter to him. That didn't mean he didn't get kind of faint along about midday. That didn't mean he couldn't get himself up a tree and just sit there, resting, looking down onto I-40 and listening to the birds bullshitting each other about how it was a fine day, twitter twit, a real fine day.

Tomorrow there'd be plenty to eat. Tomorrow he'd be west of Winston and into wild country, where he could kill him a squirrel with a stone's throw. There just wasn't much to eat these days in the country he just walked through, between Greensboro and Winston. Seems like everybody who ever owned a gun or a slingshot had gone out killing squirrels and possums and rabbits till there wasn't a one left.

That was one of the problems with this part of Carolina still being civilized with a government and all. Near half the people were still alive, probably. That meant maybe a quarter million in Guilford and

Forsyth counties. No way could such a crowd keep themselves in meat just on what they could farm nearby, not without gasoline for the tractors and fertilizer for the fields.

Greensboro and Winston didn't know they were doomed, not yet. They still thought they were the lucky ones, missing most of the ugliness that just tore apart all the big cities and left whole states nothing but wasteland. But Jamie Teague had been a ways northward in his travels, and heard stories from even farther north, and what he learned was this: After the bleeding was over, the survivors had land and tools enough to feed themselves. There was a life, if they could fend off the vagabonds and mobbers, and if the winter didn't kill them, and if they didn't get one of them diseases that was still mutating themselves here and there, and if they wasn't too close to a place where one of the bombs hit. There was enough. They could live.

Here, though, there just wasn't enough. The trees that once made this country beautiful were going fast, cut up for firewood, and bit by bit the folks here were either going to freeze or starve or kill each other off till the population was down. Things would get pretty ugly.

From some stories he heard, Jamie figured things were getting pretty ugly already.

Which is why he skirted his way around Greensboro to the north, keeping his eyes peeled so he saw most folks before they saw him. No, he saw *everybody* before they saw him, and made sure they never saw him at all. That's how a body stayed alive these days. Especially a traveling man, a walking man like him. In some places, being a stranger nowadays was the same as having a death sentence from which you might get an appeal but probably not. Being invisible except when he wanted to be seen had kept Jamie alive right through the worst times of the last five years, the whole world going to hell. He'd learned to walk through the woods so quiet he could pretty near pet the squirrels; and he was so good with throwing rocks that he never fired his rifle at all, not for food, anyway. A rock was all he needed for possum, coon, rabbit, squirrel, or porcupine, and anything bigger would be more meat than he could carry. A walking man can't take a deer along, and he can't stay in one place long enough to smoke it or jerk it or salt it or nothing. So Jamie just didn't look for bigger game. A squirrel was meat enough for him. Wild berries and untended orchards and canned goods in abandoned houses did for the rest of his diet on the road.

Most of all a walking man can't afford to get lonely. You start to feeling like you just got to talk to some human face or you're going to bust, and then what happens? You greet some stranger and he blows your head off. You put in with some woodsy family and they slit your throat in the night and make spoons out of your bones and leather bags out of your skin and your muscle ends up in the smokehouse getting its final cure. It led to no good wishing for company, so Jamie never did.

That's why he was setting by himself in a tree over the chainlink fence that marked the border of I-40 when he heard some folks singing, so loud he could hear them before he saw them. Singing, if you can believe it, right on the road, right on the *freeway,* which is the same as to say they were out of their minds. The idea of making noise while traveling on I-40 was so brazen that Jamie first thought they must be mobbers. But no, Winston and Greensboro had a right smart highway patrol on horseback, and these folks was coming *from* Winston heading west—no way could they be mobbers. They was just too dumb to live, that's all, normal citizens, refugees or something, people who still thought the world was safe for singing in.

When they came into sight, they were as weird a

group as Jamie'd seen since the plague started. Right up front walked a big fat white woman looking like silage in a tent, and she was leading the others in some song. Two men, one white and one black, were each pulling wagons made of bicycles framed together with two-by-fours, loaded with stuff and covered with tarps. There was two black girls about eighteen maybe, and a blond white woman about thirty-five, and a half-dozen little white kids. Looked like a poster pleading for racial unity from back before the plague.

These days you just didn't see blacks and whites together much. People looked out for their own. There wasn't a lot of race *hatred*, they just didn't have much to do with each other. Like Marine City, where Jamie was just coming back from. There was black Marine City and white Marine City. They all pretended to be part of the same town, but they had separate police and separate courts and you just didn't go into the other folks' part of town. You just didn't. It was pretty much that way anywhere Jamie went.

Yet here they were, black and white, walking along together like they were kin. Jamie knew right off that they couldn't have been traveling together for long—they acted like they still trusted each other, and didn't mind being together. That's how it was for the first few days of traveling in the same company, and how it was again after a few years. And seeing how careless they was, Jamie knew for a fact that they'd never live a week, let alone the years it'd take to get that long-time trust. Besides, thought Jamie, with a bitter taste in his mouth, some folks you can't trust no matter how long you're together, even if it's all your whole life.

The fat lady was singing loud, in between panting—no way was she getting enough breath—and the kids sang along, but the grownups didn't sing.

"Pioneer children sang as they walked and walked and walked and walked."

The song went on like that, the same thing over and over. And when the fat lady stopped singing "walked and walked," some of the kids would smart-mouth and keep going, "walked and walked and walked and walked and walked and walked" until Jamie was sure somebody'd give them a smack and tell them to shut up. But nobody did. The adults just kept going, paying no mind. Pulling their bicycle carts, or carrying packs.

Not one gun. Not one rifle or pistol, nothing at all.

This was a group of walking dead people, Jamie knew that as sure as he knew that the kids were all off pitch in their singing. They were coming to the last border of civilization between here and the Cher-okee Reservation. They were going to sing their way right off the edge of the world.

Jamie didn't have any quarrel with himself about what to do. He didn't give no second thought to it. He just knew that their dying might be in his reach to stop, and so he reached out to stop it.

Or rather *stepped* out. He slung his rifle over his shoulder and slid out along the limb that hung over the chain-link fence, then dropped. He scooped up his pack and shrugged it on, then walked on down the embankment. Five years ago it was mowed nice and smooth all year. Now it was half grown with saplings, and it wasn't easy getting through it. By the time he reached the freeway they were a hundred yards on, still singing. A different song this time—"Give said the little stream, give oh give, give oh give"—but it amounted to the same thing. He could hear them, but they hadn't even heard him rustling through the underbrush, noisy as can be.

"Good evening," he said.

Now they stopped singing. Those carts stopped moving and the kids were scooped up and most of them were scrambling for the edge of the road be-fore the sound of Jamie's voice had quit ringing in the air. At least they knew enough to be frightened, though by the time a mobber was talking to you, there was no way you could escape just by running. And not one of them had pulled out any kind of gun, even now.

"Hold on," said Jamie. "If I meant to kill you, you'd be dead already. I've been watching you for five minutes. And *hearing* you for ten."

They stopped moving toward the shoulder.

"Besides, folks, you were running toward the median strip. That's like a chicken running from the farmer and jumping in the cookpot to hide."

They all stayed where they were, except for the black man, who came back out to the middle of the westbound lane. The fat lady was still there, her hand resting on one of the bicycle carts. She didn't look frightened like the others, neither. She didn't look like she knew how to be scared.

Jamie went on talking, knowing how his easy relaxed voice would calm them down. "See, the mobbers, when they set up to bushwhack folks, they never attack you from just one side. You run to the median strip, and you can count on finding even more of them down there waiting to catch you."

"Seems you know a lot about mobbers," said the black man.

"I'm alive and I'm on the road and I'm alone," said Jamie. "Of course I know about mobbers. The ones who didn't learn about them real fast are all dead. Like you folks."

"We aren't dead," said the fat woman.

"Well, now, I guess that's a matter of opinion," said Jamie. "You look dead to me. Oh, still walking, maybe. Still singing at the top of your voices. But forgive me if I'm wrong, I kept thinking you were singing, 'Come and kill us, anybody, come and take away our stuff!' "

"We were singing 'Give said the little stream,' " said one of the kids, a blonde girl about ten years old maybe.

"What he means is we should've kept our mouths shut," said one of the teenage black girls. The skinny one.

"Which is what I said back at the Kernersville exit," said the one who looked like her bra was about to bust from pressure.

The black man shot them a glare. They looked disgusted, but they shut up.

"My name's Jamie Teague, and I thought I'd give you some advice that would keep you alive maybe five miles farther."

"We're still safe enough here. We're in Winston."

"You just passed the Silas Creek Parkway. The Winston Highway Patrol doesn't come out this far too often. And once you pass the 421 exit, they don't come out here at all."

"But bushwhackers wouldn't be this close in to Winston, would they?" said the fat woman.

People were so dumb sometimes. "What do you think, they wait out in the middle of the wilderness, hoping for some group of travelers who managed to fight off every other band of bushwhackers between here and there? The easy pickings all get picked close in to town. Didn't the highway patrol tell you that?"

The black man looked at the fat woman.

"No they didn't," he said.

"Well then," said Jamie, "I think you must've offended them somehow, cause they know the interchange at 421 is just about the most dangerous spot to walk through, and they let you head right for it."

The fat woman's face went even uglier. "No doubt they were *Christians*," she said. She didn't spit, but she might as well have.

A sudden thought came to Jamie. "Aren't you folks Christians?"

"We always thought we were," said the white guy. He was still at the side of the road, his arm around the blonde woman. He talked quiet, but he looked strong. It was almost a relief to have the white guy talk. It was weird to have a black man do most of the talking when a white man was in the group. Not that Jamie thought it *ought* to be the other way. He'd just never seen a group of both colors where a black man was the spokesman.

Now the black man interrupted. "Thank you for your advice, Mr.—Teague, was it?"

"It wasn't advice. It was the facts. The only safe way out of town for a group your size, since you need a road for them bikes, is to go back to Silas Creek Parkway, go north to Country Club Road, and head west on that. You can hook onto 421 farther west, and it won't be so dangerous."

"But we're going on I-40 all the way," said the fat woman.

"All the way to hell, maybe. Where do you plan to go?" asked Jamie.

"None of your business," said the blonde woman. Her voice snapped out like a whip. She was a suspicious one.

"Every overpass on the interstate is taken by one group of mobbers or another," said Jamie. "It's shelter for them, and easy to find their way back to after raping and killing their way through the countryside. Even if every one of you had a machine gun and those carts were full of ammo, you'd be out of bullets before Hickory and dead before Morganton."

"How do we know that's true?" asked the blonde woman.

"Because I told you," said Jamie. "And I told you because it was plain you didn't know. Anybody who knows that stuff and still uses the freeway must *want* to die."

There was a pause, just a bit of a second where nobody answered, and it came into Jamie's head that maybe they did. Maybe they actually kind of half-way hoped to die. These were definitely crazy people. But then, who wasn't, these days? Anybody still alive had seen terrible things, enough to push sanity right out of their heads. Jamie figured sanity was barely hanging onto most folks by their ears or hair, ready to drop off at the first sign of danger, leaving them all loony as—

"We don't want to die," said the white man.

"Though the Lord may have his own private plans for us," said the fat woman.

"Maybe so," said Jamie. "But I haven't seen the Lord doing many miracles lately."

"Me neither," said the blonde woman. Oh, she was bitter.

"I've seen a lot of them," said the white man, who must be her husband.

"Let me tell you about miracles," said Jamie. He was enjoying this—he hadn't talked so much in ten days, not since he left Kenansville, and before that Marine City, or Camp Lejeune, as they used to call it. And Jamie *was* a talker. "If you folks keep going the way you're going, the next ten miles will use up your whole lifetime quota of miracles, and you'll be killed by mile eleven."

The black man was believing him now. "So we go back to Silas Creek Parkway, head north to Country Club, and go on out of town that way?"

"I figure."

"It's a trap," said the blonde woman. "He's got a gang of mobbers on Country Club, and he wants to steer us that way to get bushwhacked."

"Ma'am," said Jamie, "I suppose that's possible. But what's also possible is this." Jamie unshouldered his gun and had it pointing right at the black man in a movement so fast nobody even twitched before he had the gun set to shoot. "Bang," said Jamie. Then he pointed the gun at each of the grownups in turn. "Bang, bang, bang, bang," he said. "I don't need no gang."

Jamie didn't expect their reaction. One of the children burst into tears. One of them was shaking. A couple of kids ran over and hid behind the fat woman.

All of them had such a look of horror in their faces, staring at Jamie like they expected him to mow them all down, kids and all. The grownups were worse, if anything. They looked like they almost welcomed the gun, as if they expected it, like it was a relief that death was finally here. The black man closed his eyes, like he was expecting the bullet to be a lover's kiss.

Only the fat woman didn't get weird on him. "Don't point a gun at us again, boy," she said coldly. "Not unless you mean to use it."

"Sorry," said Jamie. He shouldered the rifle again. "I was just trying to show you how easy it is to—"

"We know how easy," said the fat woman. "And we're taking your advice. It was decent of you to warn us."

"The Lord has seen your kindness," said the black man, "and he'll reward you for it."

"Maybe so," said Jamie, to be polite.

"Even if you do it unto the least of these my brethren," said the black man.

"Which is definitely us," said the fat woman.

"Yeah, well, good luck, then." Jamie turned his back on them and headed for the shoulder of the road.

"Wait a minute," said the white man. "Where you going?"

"That's none of our business," said the black man. "He doesn't have to tell us that."

"I just thought if he was going west, like us, that maybe we could go along together."

Jamie turned back to face him. "No way," he said.

"Why not?" asked the blonde woman, as if she was offended.

Jamie didn't answer.

"Cause he thinks we're so dumb we'll get killed anyway," said the white man, "and he doesn't want to get killed along with us. Right?"

Jamie still didn't say anything, but that was an answer, too.

"You know your way around here," said the white guy. "I thought maybe we could hire you to guide us. Partway, anyhow."

Hire him! What money would they use? What coin was worth anything now? "I don't think so," said Jamie.

"Me neither," said the fat woman.

"We don't trust in the arm of flesh," said the black man, sounding pious. Was he their minister, then?

"Yeah, the Lord is our Shepherd," said the fat woman. She *didn't* say it piously. The black man glared at her.

The white man gave it one more try. "Well it occurs to me that maybe the Lord has shepherded us to meet this guy. He's got a gun and he's traveled a lot and he knows what he's doing, which is more than we can claim. We'd be stupid not to have him with us, if we can."

"You can't," said Jamie. Warning them was one thing. Dying with them was something else. He turned his back again and walked back into the scrub forest alongside the road.

He heard them behind him. "Where'd he go? Like he just disappeared."

Yeah, and that was with Jamie not even half trying to hide himself. These folks would never even see the bushwhackers that got them. City people.

Once he was up in the tall trees, though, he didn't just head out west on his own path. Without really deciding to, he climbed back into the same tree as before, to see what these people decided to do. Sure enough, they were turning their carts east.

Fine. Jamie was shut of them. He'd done what he could.

So why was he walking eastward, too, parallel to their path? The Lord is their shepherd, not me, thought Jamie. But he had some misgiving, some fear that he couldn't rightly name; and having taken *some* responsibility for them, he felt more.

They didn't even make it back to Silas Creek Parkway. There were twenty highway patrolmen, dismounted and guns at the ready. Jamie had never seen so many all in one place. Were they expecting an invasion of mobbers?

No. They were expecting this little group of travelers. This was what they had come for. Jamie couldn't hear what was said, but he got the message right enough, from the gestures, the attitudes, the gathering despair in the little group of refugees. The highway patrol wasn't letting them back into Winston, not even long enough to take the parkway north to Country Club and out. It made Jamie feel sick inside. He had no doubt that the patrol knew what I-40 was like, knew what would surely happen at the 421 interchange. The highway patrol was planning on having the mobbers do murder for them. For some reason, the highway patrol wanted these people dead. They had probably assembled there to go out and collect the bodies and make a report.

Some favor Jamie had done them. There had been some feeling of hope before as they sang; now the hope was gone, there was no spring in the children's step. They knew now that they were heading for death, and they had seen the faces of the people who wanted them dead.

They had seen such faces before, though, Jamie was sure of it. The adults among them had not been shocked when Jamie pointed a gun at them, and they showed no anger now at the highway patrol. They were convinced already that they had no help, no friends, not from the civilized towns and certainly not from bushwhackers. No wonder the blonde woman had been so suspicious of him.

But the white guy had shown some hope in the help of a stranger on the road. He had thought he could strike a deal with Jamie Teague. It made Jamie feel kind of good and kind of bad all at once, that the guy had found some hope in him. And so, as they headed west again, Jamie found himself paralleling them again, and this time going faster, getting ahead of them, crossing the freeway back and forth, as if he were scouting their path on either side.

I *am* scouting their path, he realized.

So it was that Jamie came to the 421 interchange, silently and carefully, moving through the thick woods. He spotted two bushwhacker lookouts, one of them asleep and the other one not very alert. And now he had to decide. Should he kill them? He could, easily enough—these two, anyway. And heaven knows bushwhackers probably did enough murder in a year to give them all the death penalty twice over. The real question in his mind was, do I want to get into a pitched battle with these bushwhackers, or is there another way. It wasn't like he was going to get any help from these people—not a weapon in the bunch, and not a fighter, probably, even if they had a gun. If there was any fighting, he'd have to do it all.

He didn't kill them. He didn't decide not to, he just decided he had time to go get a look at the bushwhacker town under the overpass and then come back and kill these two if need be.

The bushwhacker town was like most he'd seen, made of old cars pushed together to make narrow streets, enough of them to stretch four car lengths beyond the overpass. Outdoor shade from cloths stretched between cars here and there, a few naked children running around shouting, some slovenly women cussing at them or cooking at a fire, and men lolling around sleeping or whittling or whatever, all with guns close to hand. A quick count put the fighting force here above twenty. There was no hope of Jamie taking them on by himself. By surprise he might kill even a half dozen—he was that good a shot, and that quick—but that'd still leave plenty to chase him down in the woods while others stayed and had their way with the refugees coming up the road. Jamie wasn't against killing scum like this, not in principle, but he did figure on its only being worth doing when you had a chance of winning.

Right then he should have just gone on, figuring there was nothing else he could do for them. They were just some more statistics, some more people killed by the destruction of society. The fall of civilization was bound to mash some people, and it wasn't his fault or his job to stop it.

Trouble was that these folks he had seen up close. These folks weren't just numbers. Weren't just the corpses he was always running across in abandoned farmhouses or old dead cars or out in the woods somewhere. They had faces. He had heard their children singing. He had bent them out of their path once, and it was his duty to find some way to do it again.

How did he know that? Nobody had ever told him any such duty. He just knew that this is what a decent person does—he helps if he can. And since he wanted so bad to be a decent person, even though he knew as sharp as ever that he was surely the most inhuman soul as ever walked the face of the earth, he turned around, snuck past the sleeping lookout again, and returned to the refugees before they even got back to the place where he first met them.

Not that he figured on joining up with them, not really. He might lead them west to the Blue Ridge, since he was going there anyway, but after that they'd be on their own. Go their separate ways. He'd have done his part and more by then, and it was none of his business what happened to them after that.

Tina held her peace. Didn't say a thing. But she thought things, oh yes, she told herself a sermon like Mother used to before she died—of a stroke, back before the world fell apart, thank heaven. It was Mother's voice in her head. No use getting mad about it. No use letting it eat your stomach out from the inside, give you colitis, make you do crazy things.

No use yelling at those sanctimonious snot-faced highway patrolmen with their snappy uniforms and manure-spouting horses and shiny pistols at their belts. No use saying, You aren't any different than the filth who massacred babies on Pinetop Road. You think you're better cause you don't pull the trigger yourselves? That just means that besides being killers, you're cowards too.

No use saying any of that.

But Tina knew everybody knew what she thought, even if she did hold her tongue. Long ago she discovered that all her bad feelings got written out in big bold letters on her face. Tender feelings not so much. Soft feelings, they were invisible. But let her feel the tiniest scrap of anger, and people would start shying away from her. "Tina's on the warpath," they'd say. "Tina's mad, I hope not at me." Sometimes she didn't like being so transparent, but this time she was glad. Because she saw how each one of those patrolmen looked at her while their commander was telling his lies, how each one met her eyes and then looked away, looked at the ground, or even tried to look meaner and tougher, it all came to the same thing. They knew what they were doing.

And Tina capped it by turning her back on the commander while he was still explaining about how he doesn't make the ordinances, the city council does—she turned her back and walked away. Walked slow, because folks her size don't exactly scamper, but *walked* nonetheless. The little orphaned kids from her Primary, Scotty and Mick and Valerie and Cheri Ann, they turned and followed her at once, and when they went, so did the Cinn kids, Nat and Donna. And then their parents, Pete and Annalee; and then those two black girls from the Bennett Ward, Marie and Rona; and only then, when everybody else was walking west, only then did Brother Deaver give up trying to persuade that apprentice Hitler to let them pass.

Tina felt guilty about that. To walk off and embarrass Brother Deaver like that. His authority was scanty enough as it was, being second counselor in a bishopric that didn't exist anymore, what with the bishop and the first counselor dead. No need for her to undermine it. But then she'd always had trouble supporting the priesthood. Not in her heart—she was always obedient and supportive. She just kept accidentally doing things that made the men look somewhat indecisive in comparison. Like this time. She hadn't really figured that anybody would follow her. She just couldn't stand it anymore herself, and the only way to show her contempt for the highway patrolmen was to turn away while they were talking. To leave while it was still her choice to leave, instead of when they got fed up and leveled their guns at them and frightened the children. It was the right time to leave, and if Brother Deaver didn't notice that, well, was it Tina's fault?

Her legs hurt. No, that was too vague. With every step, her hip joints crackled, her ankles stabbed, her knees weakened, her soles stung, her arches sagged, her back twisted, her shoulders knotted tighter. Why, this is an honest-to-goodness exercise program, she realized, walking the twenty-five miles from the Guilford College Exit to the place we're going to die. I thought my muscles were in good shape from all that custodial work at the meetinghouse, all the waxing and washing and polishing and chair-moving and table-folding. I had no idea that walking twenty-five miles would make me feel like a mouse that got played with by a half-blind cat.

Tina stopped dead in the middle of the road.

Everybody else stopped, too.

"What's wrong?" asked Peter.

"You see something?" asked Rona.

"I'm tired," said Tina. "I ache all over, and I'm tired, and I want to rest."

"But it's only three in the afternoon," said Brother Deaver. "We got three good hours of walking left."

"You in some hurry to get to the 421 turn-off?" asked Tina.

"It might not be what that man said, you know," said Annalee Cinn. She always had to take the contrary view; Tina didn't mind, she was used to it.

Besides, Peter had a way of contradicting her without making her mad—which was, Tina figured, why they got married. The world couldn't have handled Annalee Davenport unless somebody stood near her all the time to contradict her without making her mad.

"I thought so, too, honey," said Peter, "till that cop sent us back. *He* knows 421 is death to us."

"The *real* number of the Beast," said Rona. Tina winced. Whoever persuaded Rona to read Revelation ought to be . . .

"Now you know you didn't think he might be lying," said Annalee. "You wanted to have him join us."

"Well I can see why he didn't," said Tina. "Everybody talks real sorry about what happened, but they all wish the mobbers had finished the job so they didn't have all these leftover Mormons to worry about."

"Don't call them mobbers," said Brother Deaver. "That makes them sound like outsiders. That's just what they want you to think—that nobody from Greensboro—"

"Don't talk about them at all," said Donna Cinn. For an eleven-year-old, she was pretty plainspoken. No sirs and ma'ams from her. But she spoke plain sense.

"Donna's right," said Tina. "And so am I. We might as well rest here by the side of the road. I could use some setting time."

"Me too," said Scotty.

It was the voice of the youngest child that decided

them. So it was they were sitting in the grass of the median strip, under the shade of a tulip tree, when Jamie came back.

"This isn't such a big tree," said Annalee. "Remember when they divided the First Ward into Guilford and Summit?"

It was a question that didn't need answering. There used to be so many Saints in Greensboro that the parking lot was completely full every Sunday. Now they could fit in the shade of a single tulip tree.

"There's still three hundred families in Bennett Ward," said Rona.

Which was true. But it was a sore point, all the same. The black part of town was just fine. Nobody was going to make *them* leave. Who would've thought, back when they formed a whole ward in the black part of town, that six years later it'd be the only congregation left in Greensboro, with most whites dead and all the white survivors, with only a handful of blacks like Deaver himself, gone off on a hopeless journey to Utah. It was hard to know whether the blacks who stayed behind were the smartest or the most fearful and faithless; not for me to judge, anyway, Deaver decided.

"They're in Bennett Ward," said Brother Deaver. "And we're here."

"I know that," said Rona.

Everybody knew that. They also knew what it meant. That the black Saints from Bennett Ward were going to stick it out in Greensboro; that out of all of them, only these two girls, for heaven only knew what reason, only Rona Harrison and Marie Speaks had volunteered to journey west. Tina hadn't decided whether this meant they were faithful or crazy. Or both. Tina well knew it was possible to be both.

Anyway, it was in the silence after Rona last spoke that they noticed Jamie Teague was standing there again. He'd come up from the south side of the road, and was standing there in plain sight, watching.

Pete jumped to his feet, and Brother Deaver was mad as hops. "Don't go sneaking up on folks like that!"

"Hold your voice down," said Teague softly.

Tina didn't like the way he always spoke so soft. Like a gangster. Like he didn't have to try to talk loud enough—it was *your* business to hear him.

"What did you come back for?" asked Annalee. Sounding hard and suspicious. I hope Teague doesn't think she really means that.

"I saw the patrol turn you away," said Teague.

"That was an hour ago," said Brother Deaver. "More."

"I also went ahead to see if maybe the mobbers at 421 weren't too much to fight through."

"And?" asked Pete.

"More than twenty men, and who knows whether their women shoot, too."

Tina could hear the others sigh, even though they didn't voice it; she could hear the breath go out of them like the air hissing out of a pop-top can. Twenty men. That was how many guns they'd have pointing at them. All these days, and we'll face the guns after all.

"So what I'm thinking is, do you plan to stay here till one of them wanders up here and finds you? Or what?"

Nobody had an answer, so nobody said anything.

"What I'm trying to figure," said Teague, "is whether you folks want to die, or whether it's worth the trouble trying to help you get out of this alive?"

"And what I'm trying to figure is what difference it makes to you," said Annalee.

"Shut your mouth, Annalee," said Tina, gently. "I want to know what you have in mind, Mr. Teague."

"Well it isn't like you're in a car or anything, right? You don't have to wait for an exit to get off the freeway."

"We do with these carts," said Pete.

"Are those carts worth dying for?"

"All our food's on there," said Brother Deaver.

"They come apart," said Tina.

The others look at her.

"My husband designed them so you could just take them apart," she said. "For fording rivers. He figured at least one bridge was bound to be out."

"Your husband's a smart man," said Teague. But there was a question in his eyes.

"My husband's dead," said Tina. "But we both knew from the first plagues that we'd end up making this trip, and without gasoline, either. I suppose most Mormons have thought some time or other that there'd come a time when they had to make their way to Utah."

"Or Jackson County," said Annalee.

"Somewhere," said Tina. "He figured the carts wouldn't be much good if we couldn't ford a river with them. Only in this case, I guess we're fording a freeway."

"More like a portage around a rapids," said Teague.

"I like that," said Pete. "These carts are boats, the freeway's a river, and the overpasses are waterfalls."

"A metaphor," said Brother Deaver. He was smiling. He always got some kind of thrill out of knowing a fancy name for things.

Just like that, and Teague had got them out of despair and into hoping again. Made them all wonder why nobody had thought of taking apart the carts and just walking into the woods. Maybe it was because they were city people who thought of freeways as things you couldn't get off of except at places with an arrow and the word EXIT. But Tina thought it was probably because they all expected to die; some of them were maybe even disappointed they weren't already dead. Or not disappointed, exactly. Ashamed. Living just didn't have all that much attraction to them. Even the children. They weren't ready to walk on and greet death with hymns and rejoicing,

but they might well have sat there waiting for death to
stumble over them. Till Teague came back.

They moved the carts as far into the underbrush
on the north side of the road as they could, then
unloaded them and carried all the bundles up to the
chain-link fence. Teague carried heavy wire-clippers
with him—this wasn't his first time going through a
fence, obviously—and he made them notice how he
cut low. "You got to crawl through," he said, "but
then they can't see the cut from the road, and they're
less likely to follow you."

"You think they aim to follow us?" asked Marie,
scared.

"Not the highway patrol," said Teague. "I don't
think they care. But if the mobbers see a new break
in the fence—"

"We'll crawl," said Tina. And if she was willing to
crawl through, nobody else could complain about it.

Once the cart was unloaded, they carefully dis-
mantled the two-by-four frames that bound each pair
of bikes together. Teague wouldn't let them do it,
though, till he had looked carefully at every lashpoint.
Tina liked him better and better. He wasn't in such a
hurry that he got himself into a mess. He took the
time to make sure he could make things work right
later on.

She also noticed that he did none of the unloading
and carrying. Instead he watched constantly, looking
up and down the freeway and into the woods. One
time he ran up the hill, skinnied under the chain-
link fence, and climbed a tree fast as a squirrel. He
was back down a minute later. "False alarm," he
said.

"Story of my life," said Pete.

"Pete's a fireman," said Annalee.

"Was," said Brother Deaver.

"I am a fireman," said Pete. "Till I die I'm a
fireman." He spoke fiercely.

Brother Deaver backed off. "I meant no harm."

Teague lost his temper for a second. "I don't give a flying—"

He didn't finish, cause right then he caught Tina's eye and she looked at him just like a misbehaving child in Primary. She had a look that could tame the wildest brat. She used it on bishops and stake presidents too sometimes, and they calmed down even quicker than the kids.

Brother Deaver felt the need to say the obvious. "I hope you'll continue to watch your language around the children."

Teague never took his gaze from Tina's eyes. "I know I'll sure as heck watch my language around *her*."

"Tina Monk," she said.

"*Sister* Monk," said Brother Deaver.

"Tell those kids not to make a path up there," said Teague. "Walk in different places through that open grassy place."

The bikes and two-by-fours got through fine. So did everybody except Teague and Tina. And there she stood, looking at that little bitty hole and feeling exactly how thick she was from front to back. How tired she was. How she wasn't in the mood to shinny through there with everybody watching. How she wasn't altogether sure she could do it without help. She imagined Brother Deaver or Pete Cinn grabbing two hands onto her wrists and pulling and pulling and finally collapsing in exhaustion. She shuddered.

"Well, go on," she said to Teague. "I'll come on later."

Brother Deaver and Pete Cinn started to argue with her, but Annalee shut them up and made them pull stuff over the crest of the hill.

"Sister Monk," she said, "We aren't going nowhere without you, so you might as well make up your mind and get through there."

"The only way I'll get through is if you cut that

fence from top to bottom and I walk through," she said.

"Can't do that," said Teague. "Might as well put up a flashing neon sign."

"Good-bye and God bless you all," said Tina. She started walking down the hill.

Teague fell in step right beside her. "Maybe you're a dumb lady, after all, ma'am, and that's fine with me. But when I scared those little ones, it was you they went to."

"I can't shimmy under that fence, not uphill," she said.

"You're about wore out, I guess," said Teague.

"I'm about a hundred and fifty pounds too heavy, is what."

"I'll push you."

"If you lay a hand on me I'll break it off."

He laid his hand on her shoulder. "OK, I've touched it. Skin with a lot of fat under it. So what. Get up there and I'll push you under the fence."

She shuddered at the touch of his hand, but she also knew he was right. There were lots of reasons to die, but dying because you couldn't stand the humiliation of some man pushing his hands into your fat and shoving you up a hill—that wasn't a good enough reason.

"If you get a hernia, don't expect me to knit you a truss," she said.

Back at the fence, she made Annalee go up the hill. "You keep everybody on that side. I don't want anybody watching this."

Tina noted with satisfaction that Annalee may be contrary sometimes, but not when it counts. As soon as she was on her way up the slope, Tina sat down with her back toward the fence, then lay down.

"On your stomach," said Teague.

"I plan to dig in with my heels."

"And then how do I push you without giving offense, ma'am? Crawl through and grab saplings on the other side."

She rolled over. He immediately shoved his hands into her thighs and started pushing. It was a hard shove he had—the boy was strong. And it didn't feel humiliating. It felt plain irresistible. He was moving her at a good clip without her even helping. And uphill, too.

"Maybe I've been losing weight," she panted. With all her weight on her lungs, she didn't have much breath.

"Shut up, ma'am, and grab onto something."

She shut up and grabbed a sapling and pulled. With all her strength, sliding herself forward, feeling him pressing upward on her thighs, feeling the grass tear loose under her breasts and belly, the dirt slide into her clothes, the chain-link pushing down on her back. Her arms had never pulled so hard in her life. She could hardly breathe.

"You're through."

So she was. Covered with dirt and sweat from neck to knees, but through the fence. She got up onto all fours, then rolled over to a sitting position, feeling, as always, like a rotating planet. She sat there to rest for a moment. While she did, Teague rolled the cut flap of chain-link back down and tied one corner of the bottom in place with a short piece of twine he took out of his pocket.

"Let's go," he said. He held out a hand. She took it, and he pulled her to her feet. Then he stood there, holding her wrist, looking at her face. "I don't want you carrying anything. I don't want you so much as holding hands with a little kid who gets tired."

"I'll pull my weight," she said.

"And nothing else," he said. "From the look of you, I'd say you're ten miles from a heart attack."

"Stroke," she said. "In my family, it's strokes."

"I mean it," Teague insisted. "And if you get tired, you make everybody stop and rest."

"I'm not going to slow them down just because I'm—"

"Fat," he said.

"Right," she said.

"I'll tell you, ma'am. They need you, and they need you alive. You pull nothing, you carry nothing, you drink whenever you're thirsty, and you rest whenever you're tired."

"And I tell you that I'm in better shape than you think. I was custodian at the church, I worked my body all day every day, and furthermore I never smoked a single cigarette or drank a drop of liquor from the day I was born."

"You're telling me why you ain't dead already," said Teague. "I'm telling you how not to be dead tomorrow. You watch. You stay alive on this trip of yours, you'll thin out."

"Don't tell me what to do."

"Walk up this hill."

She turned around and start walking up. Briskly, to show him she could do it. Ten paces later, her right leg just gave out. Gave right out, and she stumbled and fell on her face. Not a bad fall, since she was going uphill anyway. He helped her up, and she let him half-pull her the rest of the way. It was plain that she had used herself up, at least for one day. They made their camp right there on the far side of the hill, just a hundred yards farther on than the gap where they came through. Teague wouldn't let them light a fire, and he spent most of the time till dusk scouting around or climbing trees and looking.

It was a warm night, so they slept right there in the woods on the far side of the hill, out of sight of the road, out of sight of everything. Yet they could hear, not all that far off, the crackling of a fire and folks laughing and talking. Couldn't make out the words, but they were having fun.

"Mobbers?" whispered Pete.

"Barbecue," said Teague.

Citizens of Winston. Protected by the law. A couple of miles away, mobbers hoping to kill and strip passersby. And in between them, quiet, listening, Tina Monk, breathing heavily, the pain in her unaccustomed muscles making it impossible to sleep, her weariness making it unbearable to be awake. Laughter. Pleasant company. Someone had all those things tonight, all those things that come with peace. How dare they have peace, when their highway patrolmen sent a dozen souls to what they thought was certain death? You are responsible, you laughers, you friends and lovers, you are the ones in whose name those stolid killers acted. You.

Then she slept and dreamed of crawling through tight places. Cramming her bulk into a narrow shaft, her clothing climbing up her body as she thrust herself farther in, farther, until she could put the cover on. Then lying there in the heat, the close air, hearing shooting, the sound of it echoing, amplified through the air conditioning system; and screams. Every bullet meant for kin of hers. Brothers and sisters, all of them, screaming in pain and terror while Tina Monk, building custodian, Primary president, choir leader, cowered in the air conditioning system trying to keep her breathing soft enough that no one would find her. They shot her husband at the top of the stairs down into the furnace room. When she finally opened the door, it was Tom's body she had to shove out of the way in order to open it, Tom's blood that made prints of her shoes as she walked up the stairs. His sweet and patient face, she saw it now in her mind as she slept her dark unquiet sleep.

Herman Deaver knew that he had no authority. Bishop Coward could say he was in charge, as the only high priest in the group, but it wasn't spiritual leadership they needed. This wasn't a prophetic journey; there was no Lehi to wake up with dreams that told them where to go; there was no divine gift of a liahona with pointers on it to show the way. There wasn't even a trace of manna on the ground in the morning, just dew soaking them, making the morning stiff and clinging and miserable.

I can explain, very clearly, how Shakespeare's *Hamlet* is in fact not contemplating suicide in the "To Be or Not to Be" soliloquy, but rather deciding whether to endure suffering as a Christian or take vengeful action. What Herman Deaver could not explain, to himself or anyone else, was why he, a high priest, a temple-going Saint, a professor of literature, why he was so terribly sorry to be alive. I apologize. My mistake. An oversight. An error of scheduling. If only you had sent a reminder. To be or not to be was not the question at all. Hamlet did not care about vengeance or justice. What he wanted was his father back. Good intentions—but he took away his friend Laertes' father instead. Now we're alike, eh what? Even Stephen. Get up, Deaver. Set an example, even if you aren't the leader. You're the chaplain now, that's what you are, so at least keep morale up by being perky and chipper and energetic. Ignore that pain from your burning prostate. It isn't agony yet. Not till you take the first leak of the day.

"The boys' lavatory is that stand of bushes over there," said Sister Monk.

Since his eyes were closed, Deaver didn't know if she meant him or not. But he took it as if she did, and struggled to his feet, squinting to see as the first sunlight slanted through the branches. It burned, it burned, it burned; the sunlight, his prostate, the urine tearing at him as it passed out of his body and sizzled on last year's leaves. When I was young I never thought it would be such agony to do this. I never thought at all. I can feel all my bones.

This much courtesy they still had: they didn't start

the meeting till he was back. Or perhaps they hadn't noticed yet that he wasn't in charge. That Peter, so young and strong, that he was more listened to; that Tina Monk, always forceful and now more so than ever, that she now made decisions in her simple forthright way. Perhaps they thought of this as "giving counsel." But the decision was made before he spoke. He didn't mind this. He welcomed it. Decisions were not his strong suit. Teaching was his strong suit. They could make decisions; then he would explain to them why it was a good idea. That's the skill of the scholarly critic. Explaining after the fact why somebody was great, who everybody already agrees was great. The metaphor of the freeway as river, with portages around the rapids, that was far easier for him to comprehend than the way this gentile, Teague, made sense of what he saw when he stared at the uninterrupted wall of forest green.

"We need you," Pete was saying. "We got no right to ask it, but we need you to guide us or we'll never get there."

"Get where?" Ah, a sensible question. Of course Teague goes straight to the point. Get where? To heaven, to the celestial glory, Jamie Teague. To life eternal, where we will know the only true God, and Jesus Christ, whom he has sent.

"To Utah," said Tina. Oh yes. The *immediate* destination. The *short-term* destination. How far-sighted of me. Over-sighted.

"You're crazy," said Teague.

"Probably," said Tina.

"Not really," said Pete. "Where else can people like us go?"

"That's two thousand miles away. For all you know, all kinds of bombs landed there. It might be hot as D.C."

"There was still radio for a while. Utah wasn't hit bad."

"Or wiped out by plague."

"There'll be something," said Pete.

"You hope."

"We *know*." Pete grinned. "We may not look like much to you, but out there Mormons are in charge. I promise you that wherever there's four Mormons, there'll be a government. A president, two counselors, and somebody to bring refreshments."

Deaver laughed. He remembered that jokes like that were funny. Some others joined in. Mostly children who didn't get the joke, but that was good. It was good for the children to laugh.

Deaver couldn't help but be hurt, though, when Teague looked for confirmation, not to him, but to Sister Monk.

"It's true," she said. "We've been preparing for this for years. We knew it was coming. We tried to warn everybody. Put no trust in the arm of flesh. Your weapons will mean nothing. Only trust in the Lord, and he will save you."

"How's he been doing so far for you folks?" asked Teague.

It was a bitter and terrible question, so Deaver knew that he was the only one who could answer it. "You understand that the promise refers to large groups. America as a whole. The Church as a whole. Many individuals will suffer and die."

Teague only now seemed to realize that he had maybe given offense. "I'm sorry," he said.

"It's a natural question," said Deaver. "In the Book of Mormon, the prophets Alma and Amulek were forced to watch as their enemies threw whole families of the faithful into a fire and burned them alive. Why doesn't God reach out and save these people, Amulek asked. And Alma said, Death tastes sweet to them; why should the Lord prevent it? But the wicked must be allowed to do their wickedness, so that everyone will know that their terrible punishment is just. Then Amulek said, Maybe they'll kill us, too. And Alma said, If they do, then we'll die.

But I think the Lord won't allow it. Our work is not yet done."

Deaver could feel their eyes on him, could hear how their breathing had become quiet. The children especially, they listened to him, they watched his lips as he spoke. He knew that they understood what the story meant to them. Our work is not yet done, that's why we're alive.

But don't ask me what our work *is*. Don't ask me what we're supposed to accomplish, if by some miracle we survive a two-thousand-mile journey through hell until we reach the kingdom of God in the mountains.

Teague did not break the silence; Deaver knew from that that he was a sensitive man, despite his youth, despite the fact that he was a gentile. For the first time it occurred to him that Teague might even be a potential convert. Wouldn't that be a miracle, to baptize a new member here in the wilderness!

"The Church will be strong in Utah," said Tina Monk. "And you can bet we won't be much safer anywhere else than we were in Greensboro and Winston."

"You're Mormons, right?" said Teague.

"You mean you only just now guessed that?" said Annalee. She was always disrespectful and sharp-tongued. Deaver heard that marriage had mellowed her. He was grateful he never knew her before.

"You never said right out," said Teague.

"Does it make a difference?" asked Deaver. Will you not help us, now that you know we are—what is the term?—the cult of the anti-Christ? The secret worshippers of Satan? Secular Humanists masquerading as Christians in order to seduce impressionable young people and lead them into unspeakable abominations?"

"It does if you're going to Utah," said Teague.

"I-40 to Memphis," said Pete. "Then up to St.

Louis and I-70 to Denver. After that, who knows?
They might even have trains running, or buses."

"Or a weekly space shuttle flight," said Teague.

"Don't underestimate the resourcefulness of the
Mormon people," said Deaver.

"Don't underestimate how much trouble a few
nukes, some biological warfare, and the collapse of
civilization can cause," said Teague. "Not to mention
how the climate's changed. How do you know Utah
isn't buried under glaciers?"

"They don't form that fast," said Pete.

"Two thousand miles," said Teague. "With winters
colder and longer now than they used to be—how far
you think you'll get before September?"

"We didn't expect to do it in one year," said
Deaver.

"We need you," said Pete. "We'll hire you."

Teague laughed. "And pay me what?"

"A house and a job in Utah," said Pete.

"You can guarantee that?" said Teague. "You guarantee that I'll have a little plot of ground? A house
with hot and cold running water? A nice little job to
go to? Eight to five? What about location—I don't
want to have to commute more than fifteen minutes
to—"

"Shut up," said Tina.

Teague shut up.

"We can promise you that there's peace in the
mountains of Utah. We can promise you that if you
lead us there, you'll be rewarded as best they can. We
can promise you that in Utah, you can reap what you
plant, you can keep what you make, you can count
on being as safe tomorrow as you are today. Where
else in all this world are those things true?"

"I'm not about to become a Mormon," said Teague.

"No one expects it," said Sister Monk.

"They'll just expect you to be a good man," said
Deaver.

"Then forget it," said Teague.

"A *good* man," said Deaver. "Not a perfect one."

"How bad can a man be and still be good?"

"You have to be good enough to take a helpless group like us two thousand miles, with no promise of payment beyond our word."

Deaver saw, with satisfaction, that Teague was being won over. He halfway suspected that Teague *wanted* to be won over. After all, he had already invested a lot of time and effort in helping them get off the freeway. He was risking a lot, too—if the highway patrol caught them here, they'd no doubt be in trouble. And the fact that there wasn't any shooting last night—the patrol might well notice that and come looking for them.

Maybe Teague thought of that at the same time, because he stood up suddenly. "I'll think about it. But for now we've got to get moving. It'll be slow going for a while, till we can put the carts back together on a road. Put the heaviest stuff on bikes. I hope those things have airless tires."

"Of course," said Tina. "My husband never considered anything else. What good would bikes be on a cross-country trip, if they're always going flat?"

"The little kids will carry the two-by-fours."

Annalee started to protest. "They're too heavy for—"

"They'll rest a lot," said Teague. "We're going to do this all in one trip. Grown-ups will be carrying a lot more."

It turned out that Scotty, Mick, Cheri Ann, and Valerie could only handle four of the two-by-fours, but Pete thought of using the others to make a kind of sedan chair, which he and Deaver bore on their shoulders, with a much heavier burden on the two-by-fours between them than they could possibly have carried on their backs.

Sister Monk started to pick up a bundle of dried food.

"Put it down," said Teague.

"It's light," said Sister Monk.

Teague didn't say another word. Just stared at her, and she stared back. To Deaver's surprise, it was Sister Monk who gave in. He'd never seen such a thing in all his years in the Church. Sister Monk backed down to no man, or woman either. But she backed down to this Jamie Teague.

It was the first time Deaver realized what Teague must have seen right off—that Sister Monk wasn't doing so well, physically speaking. Deaver was so used to her being fat, and having that mean nothing so far as her being a hard worker in the Church, that it didn't occur to him that this journey was different. But now that Teague's insistence on her carrying nothing had brought the matter to Deaver's attention, he could see how flushed and weak she looked, how her walk was none too steady even in the morning after a night of sleep. For the first time it occurred to Deaver that she might not make it through the trip.

It made him angry, to realize how much he had unconsciously been depending on this woman. Wasn't he the one with the authority? Wasn't he supposed to lead? Yet he was depending on *her*. Well, he wouldn't, that's all. Nobody's indispensible. If we can get along without—

No, he wouldn't start listing the indispensible people who were dead, bulldozed into the mass grave in the parking lot of the stake center on Pinetop Road. There was no point in a census now. They were gone, and this meager handful of Saints was still alive. That meant that the Church was still alive, and would go on, sustained by faith and the Lord and, with any luck, this stranger who came out of nowhere offering help unasked. An angel would have been more useful, but if this Jamie Teague was all the Lord had to offer in the way of help, he'd have to do. If it was, in fact, the Lord who sent him.

They made it in one trip. One long trip, with frequent stops. Teague wasn't actually with them most of the way. He ranged ahead, leaving south and returning from the north. Sister Monk actually led them, spotting the marks Teague had made on tree trunks, showing which way to go. At the end of the day they were back on the road. U.S. 421 this time, a four-lane expressway, with the overpass some miles behind them. Exhausted as they were, Teague made them rebuild the carts before they gnawed on their jerky and went to sleep. "You'll want to be underway at dawn," he said. "Not sitting around in the open building carts. That was just one overpass."

So they rebuilt the carts, and he finally let them build a very small fire so they could boil up some soup and give the children a decent meal. Hungry as they were, the kids could hardly keep their eyes open long enough to eat. And when they were asleep, Teague laid out his conditions for traveling with them.

"I'm not good enough to take you two thousand miles," he said, looking Deaver in the eye. "I only promise to take you as far as the Great Smokies. I haven't traveled west of there anyway, only between the mountains and the sea, so I don't know any more about the country than you do. But I've got a cabin there that's good for the winter. It's where I live. I know my neighbors there, I've got trade goods from my traveling to buy food, and we've kept it free of mobbers. It's as much as I can promise, but I think I can teach you a few things along the way, give you a better chance next spring."

"If that's as far as you go with us," said Pete, "then we can't pay you anything at all. We got nothing you need, until we get to Utah."

Teague pulled up a tuft of grass, started splitting the blades up the middle, one by one. "You got something I need."

"What is it?" demanded Annalee.

Teague looked at her coldly.

Deaver offered an explanation. "Maybe we're people he thinks are going to die if he doesn't help us. Maybe he needs not to see us dead."

Deaver saw Teague's expression change again. An unreadable look, hiding some strange unnameable emotion. Am I right? Is Teague's motive altruistic? Or is there something else, so shameful Teague can't hardly admit it? Does he plain to betray us at some terrible time? Never mind. If the Lord means us to thrive, he'll protect us from such treason. And if he doesn't, I'd rather die by trusting a man who may not be as good as he seems than by being so suspicious I refuse a true friend.

Sister Monk changed the subject. "You by yourself, Jamie Teague, you can generally avoid trouble, I imagine. You can pretty much be invisible out in the woods, and stay off the roads. But with us, trouble's *going* to come. We'll be on the roads most of the time, too many of us and too clumsy to hide. Somebody's going to spot us."

"Might be," said Teague.

"You got the gun, Jamie Teague. But do you figure you can kill a man with it?"

"Reckon so," said Teague.

A pause.

"*Have* you ever killed anybody?" asked Pete. There was awe in his voice, as if having killed somebody was a magical act that would endow this stranger with supernatural power.

"Reckon so," said Teague.

"I don't believe it," snapped Annalee.

"We want him as a guide anyway," said Deaver, "not a soldier."

"Where we're going I don't think there's a difference," said Sister Monk. "You're an English professor. Pete's a fireman, trained to save lives, to risk his own life—but none of us has ever killed anybody, I think."

"Wish I had," murmured Pete.

Sister Monk ignored him. "And what if the only

way to save us was to sneak up on somebody and kill them. From behind, without even giving them a fair chance. Could you do that, Jamie Teague?"

Teague nodded.

"How do we know that?" said Annalee.

Teague waved her off with a gesture of impatience. "I killed my mother and father," he said. "I can kill anybody."

"My God," said Rona Harrison.

Deaver turned to snap at the girl about not taking the name of the Lord in vain. But then it occurred to him that with Teague confessing to patricide, saying "My God" seemed pretty tame by comparison.

"Well now," said Pete.

"Isn't that what you wanted to hear?" asked Teague. "Didn't you want to know whether I was bloodthirsty enough to do the killing you need done to save your lives? Don't you want to know that your hired soldier has references?"

"I wasn't trying to pry into things you don't want to talk about," said Sister Monk.

"They deserved it," said Teague. "The court gave me a suspended sentence because everybody agreed they deserved it."

"Did they abuse you?" asked Annalee. Finally she was curious instead of suspicious. A mind like a grocery store newspaper, thought Deaver.

"Annalee," said Sister Monk sharply. "We've all stepped too far."

"I've answered the question you need to know," said Teague. "I can kill when I need to. But *I* decide when I need to. I give orders, I don't take them. That clear? If I tell you to get off the road, you get—no arguments. Right? Cause I don't aim to stick around and kill all comers just cause you aren't willing to do what it takes to avoid a fight."

"Brother Teague," said Deaver. He pretended not to notice how startled Teague was to be addressed as *Brother*. "We will gladly accept your authority about how and when to travel, and on what path. And I assure you that it is the desire of our hearts to kill no one, to harm no one, to leave things undisturbed wherever we go."

"I don't want you killing anybody for *me* anyhow," said Marie Speaks.

Everybody looked at her—she'd been talking like a teenager so long that nobody expected her to have an opinion on something serious like this.

"I die myself first, you got that?"

"You crazy," said Rona. "You lost your mind, girl."

"Killing a bushwhacker isn't murder," said Pete.

"Neither is killing a Mormon," said Marie. "So I hear." Then she got up and walked over to where the little ones were sleeping.

"She's crazy," said Rona.

"She's Christian," said Deaver.

"So am I," said Pete, "but I know there's times when the Lord lets good people fight back. Think of Captain Moroni and the title of liberty. Think of Helaman and the two thousand young men."

"Think about sleeping," said Teague. "I'm not taking first watch tonight, I'm too tired."

"Me," said Pete.

"No, me," said Deaver.

"You, Mr. Deaver," said Teague. "Your timepiece there still work, or is it on your wrist from nostalgia?"

"It's solar," said Deaver. "It works fine."

"Watch till midnight. Then wake Pete. Pete, you wake me at three."

Then Teague got up and went to the bushes they had designated as the boys' lavatory that night.

"Murder's the unforgiveable sin," said Annalee. "I don't want a murderer telling us what to do."

"Judge not lest ye be judged," said Deaver. "Let him or her who is without sin cast the first stone."

That was the end of the discussion, as Deaver knew it would be. There wasn't a one of them who didn't feel guilty for one reason or another. For just being alive with so many others dead, if nothing else. Maybe Marie had learned the right lesson from it after all. Maybe killing was never worth it.

But Deaver heard the people breathing around him, he looked and watched the children's chests rising and falling with each breath, and then he imagined somebody coming and raising a knife to them, or pointing a gun at them. That's not the same thing as somebody raising a weapon against me personally. I might have the courage to let the blow fall and not defend myself. But there's not a chance in the world that I'd let them harm a hair on those children's heads. I'd blast the bushwhackers to hell and back if I thought they'd harm the children. Now maybe that's murderousness, maybe that's a secret lust for blood in my heart. But I don't think so. I think that's the indignation of God. I think that's what Christ felt when he said it was better to tie a millstone around your neck and jump into the sea than to raise your hand to harm a child.

Teague killed his mama and his daddy. That was a hard one. Not mine to judge. But I'll be watching that boy differently now. Watching real close. We didn't escape one band of murderers just to fall in with a worse one now. Bad enough to kill strangers because you don't like their religion. But to kill your own mama and daddy.

Deaver shuddered, and stared into the darkness beyond the flickering firelight.

The fifth day after Teague joined them, they were heading toward Wilkesboro. Travel was getting into a regular rhythm now, and nobody was half as sore as they were the third day. And it wasn't so scary anymore. A few times Teague had come rushing back from scouting ahead and made them get off the road, but this wasn't freeway now and most times they could run the bikes up behind some bushes without dismantling the carts. The only portage was crossing I-77. Mostly it was just walking, one foot after the other.

One of those times in hiding, Rona made Marie peek through the bushes and watch the horsemen going by. They looked like a rough crew, and to Marie it looked like one of them had three human heads hanging from his saddle. Three black human heads, and it made her shudder.

"Canteens," Teague said, but Marie knew better. She knew lots of things folks didn't think she knew. So now, on the afternoon of the fifth day out of Winston, when Marie was feeling hot and tired and wanted a little entertainment, she got a meanness on her and started doing a number on Rona.

"You got your eye on him," said Marie.

"Do not," said Rona. She sounded outraged. This was working fine.

"You say his name in your sleep."

"Nightmares is what."

"You were thinking of him just now when you smiled."

"Was not. And I didn't smile."

"Then how do you know who I'm talking about?"

"You're a queen bitch, that's what you are," said Rona.

"Don't you talk to me with words like that," said Marie. She was the one supposed to be needling, not the other way around.

"Stop acting like a bitch and people won't call you one," said Rona.

"At least I don't get the hots for murderers," said Marie. That got her back.

"He isn't."

"Said he was himself."

"He had good reason."

"Oh yeah?"

"They used to torture him."

"He say that?"

"I know it."

"Murder is the unforgiveable sin," said Marie. "He'll be in hell forever, so you just don't even bother thinking about marrying him."

"Shut your mouth! I'm not thinking about marrying him!"

"And he's white and he's not a Mormon and he'll never never never take you to the temple."

"Maybe I don't care."

"If you don't care about the temple, why are you going to Utah?"

Rona looked at her strangely. "Well it ain't to go to the *temple*."

Marie didn't know what to make of that, and didn't want to find out what Rona meant. But the meanness wasn't gone out of her yet. So she turned back to the old topic. "He's going to hell no matter what."

"No he's *not*!" And Rona gave Marie a shove that nearly knocked her on her butt.

"Hey!"

"What's going on here!" It was Brother Deaver, of course. None of the white folks ever told them off about anything. "Haven't we got things bad enough without you two tailing into each other?"

"I didn't tail into *her*," said Marie.

"Saying he was going to hell!"

Marie felt Brother Deaver's hand on the back of her neck. "The Lord is the judge of men's souls," he said softly.

Marie squirmed to get free of his grasp. She was eighteen now, not some kid that grownups could grab onto whenever they wanted.

"So if you can't keep your heart free of condemnation, Marie, I think you'd better learn to keep your mouth shut. Do you understand me, girl?"

She finally broke free. "You got no right to tell a black girl what to do!" she said—loudly now, so that others farther back could hear. "You just teach your own white kids and leave me alone!"

It was a terrible thing to say, she knew it and she

was sorry. But it also got him to shut up and leave
her alone, which was what she wanted, wasn't it?
Besides, he *did* marry a white woman, which was the
same thing as saying black women were trash. Well,
see what it got him—all of them shot dead along with
all the other white Mormons, while he was at A&T,
where the white Christian Soldiers didn't dare to go.
That's the only reason he wanted her to forgive Teague
for being a murderer—because he felt like a murderer, too, him being alive because he was black,
while his wife and kids were shot down and bulldozed into a parking lot grave. He wanted everybody
to be nice and forgiving. Well she knew the law of
heaven, didn't she? She wasn't just a Sunday School
Mormon, she studied the doctrine and read all the
time, and she knew that Christ's atonement had no
force over them as murdered. Though truth to tell,
his face looked stricken like he was about to die, and
just from her cruel hard words against him. She
might even have apologized on the spot, except that
right then they heard horses' hoofs and all hell broke
loose.

The mobbers came up a side road, just sauntering
like they didn't expect trouble. Must have come up
since Teague passed that road in his scouting. There
was only two of them, and for a minute Marie hoped
they'd think this group was too much for them. But
the mobbers sized them up quick and didn't even
pause a minute. They had guns out before they got
to 421.

"We don't mean you no harm," Brother Deaver
said, or started to say, anyway, when the one mobber
got off his horse and whipped him across the face
with his pistol, knocking him down.

"That's *our* speech," said the mobber, "and we do
all the talking, got it? Everybody lie down—on your
bellies."

"Look at what they got in the way of women,
Zack, if that ain't pitiful."

"That blonde one—"

"Keep your hands off her," said Pete. He started to get up. The taller one with the long beard gave him a kick that looked like it might tear his head off.

"She's dessert," said the tall one. "We got dark meat for dinner."

Marie thought she was already as scared as she could be, but now when the cold barrel of a shotgun was pressed against her forehead, pressing down real heavy, she tasted terror for the first time in her life.

"Please," whispered Rona.

"Now you just hold still while I get this off you, honey, and open wide for papa, or Zack's gonna blow your girlfriend's head clean off."

"I'm a good girl!" Rona whined.

"I'll make you even better," said the long-bearded man.

"No!" Rona screamed.

Marie felt the painful motion of the gun as Zack drew a charge into the chamber. "Don't fight with them, Rona," said Marie. She knew it was a cowardly thing to say, but Rona didn't have the gun at her head.

"You little kids best close your eyes," said Zack. "Wouldn't want you finding out the facts of life too young."

Marie could hear the other one set down his shotgun and start unzipping himself, mumbling to himself about how if she gave him a disease he'd hang her head from his saddle, which told Marie that she *did* see what she thought she saw. It made her gag all over again.

"Hold still," said Zack, "or it won't go so nice for you when I—"

Suddenly the gun barrel jammed sharp into her head as Zack slumped on it; not even a second later she heard the crack of a gun going off not far away. Zack's shirt blossomed open and spattered blood;

Marie grabbed the shotgun barrel and tore it away from her face.

The other mobber muttered something and fumbled for his gun, but then another cracking sound and he was down, too.

"Teague!" Marie shouted. She got to her feet, her head bleeding. Everybody was getting up. Pete had Zack's shotgun in a second and pointed it at the two mobbers—but they were stone dead, each killed with one shot.

"Catch the horses!" Teague was shouting that. And he was right, they had to catch the horses, they could pull the carts, they could carry stuff, had to catch them, but Marie couldn't find them, not with blood pouring down into her eyes—

"Marie honey, here, are you all right?" Sister Monk was dabbing at her with a cloth. It stung like hell.

"Did he shoot Marie?" It was one of the little boys.

"Just jammed his gun in her head when he was dying is all—Donna Cinn, you get the little ones back to the side of the road." Sister Monk taking charge as usual. And as usual everybody hopped to do it. Only this time Marie didn't mind at all, didn't mind those big old hands dabbing at the blood on her face.

Then she noticed Rona making a grunting noise, and she turned to look. Brother Deaver was tugging at Rona's sleeve, but Rona wouldn't quit stomping her foot down on the bearded mobber's face. It wasn't even human anymore, but she kept stomping and now the skull broke through and her shoe sank down in a ways.

Now Teague came up, leading one horse. He handed the reins to Deaver, stepped astride the dead man's body, and took Rona in his arms and just held her, saying, "You're OK, you're OK now, you're safe."

"Took you damn long enough," said Pete. He had

the other horse, and he sounded more scared than mad.

"Came as soon as I heard the horses. Had to make sure it was only the two before I started shooting. Rona, I'm sorry, I'm sorry you got so scared, I'm sorry he treated you so bad, but I had to wait until he set his gun down, don't you see."

"It's OK, he didn't do nothing," said Annalee.

Rona screamed into Teague's shirt.

"I don't call it nothing to have her lying there with her skirt up like that," said Teague.

"I just meant he didn't—"

"If it didn't happen to you then you just shut up about what's nothing or not," said Teague.

Brother Deaver held out a little blue swatch of cloth. "Here's your underwear, Rona—"

Rona turned away. Sister Monk snatched the panties out of Brother Deaver's hand. "For heaven's sake, Brother Deaver, use some sense. He *touched* these! She isn't going to put them back on."

"Rona, I'm sorry, but we've got to get moving," said Teague. "Right now, right this second. Those gunshots are bound to call more of them—these two might have twenty more a mile behind them."

Rona turned away from him, staggered to Sister Monk. Marie didn't mind much, having Sister Monk switch from nursing her to comforting Rona. It was plain Rona was in worse shape.

Teague got the other two men to help him hoist the corpses onto the horses.

"Leave them here," said Annalee.

"Got to bury them," said Teague.

"They don't deserve it."

Pete explained, real gentle. "So nobody finds the bodies and chases after us to get even."

A minute later they were off the road and cutting along the edge of some farmer's field, half-screened by trees. Teague pushed them to go faster, and quieter, too, his voice just a whisper. Finally they were down a hill in a hollow. Teague had Brother Deaver and Brother Cinn dig a single large grave, while Annalee kept the children away from the horses.

"Bury these, too," said Teague.

That was the first time Marie noticed that both saddles had heads tied to them. They looked even worse close up than the heads Marie had seen from a distance.

"I'll take them down," said Rona. She set right to untying the thongs from the saddle.

"Me too," said Marie. She didn't even let herself wonder whether it had been a girl or a boy, a man or a woman.

Teague took his rifle and went back up the hill to keep a watch on the road.

Marie didn't puke and neither did Rona. Mostly Marie was just thinking about how grateful she was that her head wasn't on the horse. Then Marie helped Sister Monk strip the corpses and empty the pockets of everything. Three dozen shotgun shells. All kinds of matches and supplies. They stuffed it all in the saddlebags, which were already near full of stuff the mobbers no doubt stole from other folks just today. In twenty minutes both corpses were in the hole, dressed in their ragged underwear, the heads tucked around them, their limp, filthy clothes tossed in on top of them. Only Marie had noticed how Sister Monk wrapped Rona's blue panties inside one of the dead men's shirts. Rona insisted on helping then, tossing dirt onto the bodies until they were covered up.

Marie couldn't keep from speaking. "They were *poor*."

"Everybody's poor," said Pete. "But they kept alive by stealing the little that others had, and likely killing them, too."

"Feels wrong, having their victims' heads buried with them," said Sister Monk.

"The victims don't mind," said Brother Deaver,

"and we didn't have time to dig more holes. Marie, can you get up the hill real quiet and tell Brother Teague that we're done here?"

But Teague had already seen from up the hill, and he slid down the slope. "Nobody coming. These two might've been alone," he said. "It's getting late enough, maybe we ought to camp farther on down the hollow here. If I remember right there's water. The horses'll need that. We can work the rest of the afternoon rigging up some kind of harness for the horses to pull the bikes." Teague looked at the grave. "Get some dead leaves on here. Something to make the soil not look so fresh-turned. And if this happens again, save out their clothes. Dead people don't need them."

"We'd never wear them," said Brother Deaver.

"You would, if it got cold enough, and you got naked enough."

"I've never been that naked," said Brother Deaver.

Teague shrugged.

"Brother Teague," said Marie.

"Yeah?"

"I was wrong about not wanting you to kill for me."

"I know," said Teague. And that was all he said to her. "Mr. Deaver, Mr. Cinn, you got any objection to hanging onto those shotguns?"

"If *they* do, *I* don't," said Sister Cinn.

Brother Deaver and Brother Cinn kept to themselves any objections they might have had. They slung the shotguns over their shoulders. Brother Cinn dropped a few shells in his pocket; then he dropped some in Brother Deaver's pocket. Brother Deaver looked at him in surprise, then embarrassment. Marie was a little disgusted. Didn't college professors know *anything*?

Mostly, though, Marie watched Teague. That's why she was the only one who saw how Teague kept clenching and unclenching his jaw. How his hand shook a little. And late that night, she was the only one who woke up when he took a walk in the moonlight.

She got up and followed him. He stood beside the grave, looking nowhere in particular, his hands jammed in his pockets. He showed no sign of noticing she was there, but she knew he had heard her coming from the minute she got up from the ground.

"You're such a liar," said Marie. "You didn't kill your parents."

He didn't say a thing.

"You never killed a living soul before today."

"Believe what you like," he said.

"You never."

He just stood there with his hands in his pockets until she went back to the camp. She lay there wondering why a man might want other folks to think he was a murderer when he wasn't. Then she wondered why she wanted so bad to believe a man wasn't a murderer when he said right out that he was. She lay awake a long time, but she was asleep before he came back.

Day after next they came to the mountains, where the road sloped upward so steep that they had to stop and rest every twenty minutes or so. Pete was grateful they had the horses now, to pull the carts, though he didn't say so out loud; it didn't do to start saying it was a good thing to have the horses, not with Rona still so upset about how they got them.

Pete concentrated on the children, his own and the orphans. They were the ones who suffered most, he knew that. The youngest of them, Scotty Porter and Valerie Letterman, they weren't even born when the first plague struck. The famous Six Missiles had already fallen before Scotty and Valerie said their first words. He murmured to Annalee one time, "Think there's any chance of getting them into a college-prep kindergarten?" But she'd either forgotten all that craziness from the old days, or else she didn't think it was funny. She didn't think much was funny these days. Neither did Pete, for that matter. But at least he tried now and then. Sometimes, for hours, maybe even days at a time he didn't think about his father killed in the missile that got D.C., or his stepfather shot by looters, or his Mom and Annalee's folks and all their brothers and sisters and nieces and nephews crammed into the cultural hall at the stake center, not being sure what was going to happen to them, but knowing deep down all the time, knowing and being terrified. I was in plays on the stage where the guys with the guns stood. I played basketball on the floor where the bullets gouged up the wood finish and blood soaked in under the polish. I was baptized in the font behind the stage, where the men from the city hooked up the hoses to wash out the blood. The Baptists were already talking about making it a Christian library when Pete went there to lay flowers in the parking lot where he had first kissed Annalee after a dance, where now his kin and his friends lay in a jumbled heap of broken bodies under the dirt.

That was the whole world to these children. It had always been in turmoil—did they even realize that things weren't supposed to be this way? Would they ever trust anything again, now that their parents had been taken away from them?

Teague asked him once, when they were alone together, leading the horses, "Whose kids are those?"

"Donna, the big one, she's mine, and so's Nat, he's my boy."

"Any fool can see that, they're so blond," said Teague.

"Mick and Scotty Porter, Valerie Letterman, Cheri Ann Bee, they're orphans."

"Why'd you bring them along? Wasn't there anybody in Greensboro who could've took care of them?"

"That's what took us so long leaving. Fighting everybody to get the right to take them with us."

"But why? Don't you know how much faster we'd go, how much safer we'd be without them?"

Pete held himself back, kept himself from being angry, like he always tried to do and almost always succeeded. "It's like this, Teague. If we left them, they would've been raised up Baptists."

"That ain't so bad," said Teague.

Pete held himself back again, a long time, before he could answer quiet and calm. "You see, Teague, it was mostly Baptist preachers who spent fifteen years telling people how Mormons were the anti-Christ, how we had secret rituals in the temple where we worshiped Satan. How we said Jesus and the devil were brothers, and how we weren't Christians but pretended to be so we could steal away their children, how we Mormons owned everything and made sure we got rich while good Christians stayed poor. And then when bad times came, all those Baptist preachers washed their hands and said, 'We never told anybody to *kill* Mormons.' Well, that's true. They never taught murder. But they taught hate and fear, they told lies and they knew they were doing it. Now, Teague, do you see why we wouldn't let these Mormon kids get raised by people who'd tell such lies about the religion their parents died for?"

Teague thought about that for a while. "How come these kids got out alive? I heard the Christian Soldiers went through killing the wounded."

So Teague *had* heard the story. "These four went to Guilford Primary. When the Christian Soldiers were going around arresting people, they got to Guilford Primary School, and Dr. Sonja Day, the principal, she met them at the door. Didn't have a gun or anything. She just shows them the ashes of the school records, still smoldering. She says to them, 'All the children in this school are Mormon today, and me and all the faculty. If you take anybody, you take us all.' Faced them down and they finally went away."

"Guts."

"Think about it, Teague. Mormon kids were ripped out of class in fifty schools in the county. If more principals had guts—"

"One out of fifty's above average, Cinn."

"That's why America deserves all that's happened to her. That's why the Lord hasn't saved us. America turned to loving evil."

"Maybe they were just afraid," said Teague.

"Afraid or weak or evil, all three roads lead to hell."

"I know," whispered Teague.

His whisper was so deep and sore that Pete knew he'd touched some wounded place in Teague. Pete wasn't one to push deeper at a time like that. He backed off, let a man be. You don't go poking into a wound, that just gets it all infected. You keep hands off, you let it heal up, you give it time and air and gentleness.

"Teague, I wish you'd take me with you when you scout around or go hunting or whatever."

"I need you to stay with the rest. I don't figure Deaver to be much good with a shotgun."

"Maybe not," said Pete. "But if you don't go with us beyond these mountains, somebody's got to be able to do some of what you do."

"I been walking the woods for ten years now, long before the plagues started."

"I got to start sometime."

"When we get to the Blue Ridge Parkway, I'll start to take you hunting with me. But you carry no gun."

"Why not?"

"Take it or leave it. Can you throw?"

"I pitched hardball."

"A rock?"

"I suppose."

"If you can't hunt with a rock, you can't hunt. Bullets are for killing things big enough to kill *you*. Because when the bullets run out, there won't be no more."

The higher they got into the mountains, the more relaxed Teague got. After a while, he stopped having them look for sheltered, hidden places to camp in; they camped right out in the open. "Mobbers don't come up this high," said Teague.

"Why not?"

"Because when they do, they don't come back."

At the Blue Ridge Parkway, Teague laid out a whole new set of rules. "Walk spaced apart, not bunched up. Stay on the pavement or close to it. Nobody goes off alone. Don't hold anything in your hand, not even a rock. Keep your hands in plain sight all the time. If somebody comes, don't move your hands above your waist, not even to scratch your nose. Just keep walking. Above all, make plenty of noise."

"I take it we're not afraid of bushwhackers anymore," said Brother Deaver.

"These are mountain people around here, and Cherokees beyond Asheville. They don't rob people, but they also don't ask a lot of questions before they kill strangers. If they think you might, just *might* cause them any trouble, you're dead where you stand. So you make it plain that you aren't trying to sneak up on anybody and you stay visible all the time."

"We can sing again?" asked Sister Monk.

"Anything but that 'walked and walked and walked and walked' song."

It was a glorious time then. The Blue Ridge Parkway crested the hills, so they had sky all round them, and the mountains were as pretty as Pete had ever seen them. His real dad took them along the parkway most autumns when he was growing up. One year they drove it clear from Harper's Ferry down to the Cherokee Reservation. Pete and his brother griped the whole way till their dad was promising to amputate limbs if they didn't shut up, but now the trip was glorious in memory. Sometimes Pete forgot he was a grownup, walking along here, especially when he walked on ahead so he couldn't see any of them. It wasn't autumn yet, though autumn wasn't far off; still, it felt good, felt like coming home. He'd heard other folks say that, too, about the Blue Ridge. About the Appalachians in general. Felt like coming home even if they grew up in some desolate place like California or North Dakota.

Teague made good his promise. It near drove Pete crazy the first few times, when his rock always missed and Teague's almost never did. But after a while he got the knack of it. It was like pitching with a smaller strike zone. By the time they skirted around Asheville, he could clean a squirrel in two minutes and a rabbit in three. He also learned how to choose a hunting ground. You always look for a cabin and walk up singing, so they know you're coming. Then you ask the owner where it's OK to hunt, and if he'd like you to split your catch with him. To hear these mountain folks talk, you could hunt wherever you liked; but Teague would never so much as pick up a rock unless the folks had said "That holler down there" or "Along that slope there," and even though they always said "No need to bring me none," Teague always took the whole catch to them and offered them half. He wouldn't leave until they'd accepted at least one animal. "They can't claim you stole it then," said Teague. "If they took part of it, it wasn't poaching."

"What's to stop them from lying and *saying* you stole it?" asked Pete.

Teague looked at him like he was stupid. "These are mountain people."

Whenever they returned from hunting, Pete loved to hear the sound of the children singing, and the grownups too now, more and more. Most of all he loved hearing his Annalee's voice, singing and laughing. When they climbed up out of the piedmont and into the mountains it was like rising out of hell. This is what redemption feels like, he thought. This is what it's like when Christ forgives you of your sins. Like putting you on the top of a green mountain, with as many clouds below you as above; and all your bad memories just washed away with the rain, got lost in the morning fogs. All those bad memories were lowland troubles, left behind, gone. Pete had been born again.

"I never want to come down out of here," he told Annalee.

"I know," she said. "I feel like that too."

"Then let's don't go down."

She looked at him sharply. "What's got into you, Peter? You talk like Teague, you walk like Teague. If I'd wanted to marry a hillbilly I'd've gone to Appalachian State or Western Carolina."

"A man belongs up here."

"A Latter-day Saint belongs in the kingdom of God."

"Look around you, Annalee, and tell me God doesn't love this place."

"There's no safety here. You feel good cause we don't have to hide every night. But we aren't staying in the open cause we're safe and free, we're staying in the open so somebody won't shoot our heads off. We'd never belong here. But we're already citizens of Utah. Every Mormon is."

After that Pete didn't mention his desire to stay in the mountains, not to Annalee, not to anybody. He knew that after a while they'd all come around to his point of view. When you get to heaven, why go farther? That's what Pete thought.

"Sister Monk, your dress is getting longer," said Valerie Letterman one day.

"I must be getting shorter," Tina answered.

"You're getting prettier."

"Child, you're going to make a lot of friends in this world."

But Valerie was right. Walking more than two hundred miles was every bit as effective as stomach stapling in the old days. She'd already hemmed up the skirts of all her dresses twice, as her bulk evaporated. She could feel the muscles working under the flesh of her arms and legs. She could spring to her feet all at once, instead of step by step—all fours, kneel up, one foot planted, two feet squatting, and the last terrible unbending of the knees. That was ancient history now. She rolled out of her blanket—it was cold at night up here—and got right to her feet and felt like every step she was jumping several feet into the air. All the pills she'd tried, all the doctors, all the diets, all the exercises—but the only thing that worked was to walk from Greensboro to Topton.

No trouble all through the mountains. No danger that felt like danger, except a few tight minutes at the Cherokee border, till somebody came along who recognized Jamie Teague. And at last they left the paved road and climbed up a dirt track, all overgrown now that no cars ever came through, and came to a two-story house completely dwarfed by giant chestnut trees.

"I thought you called this a cabin, Jamie Teague," she said.

"My foster parents called it that," he said. "They were summer people. But as soon as I was old enough, I stayed year-round."

Tina caught up that information and remembered it. Teague had foster parents before he was old enough to decide where he was going to live. So if he was fostered out because he killed his parents, he must have killed them when he was young. Probably *very* young.

The door was not locked. Yet inside, the house was untouched by thieves or vandals. It was deep with dust and dead insects—no one had entered all

summer, least of all to clean. Yet every implement
was in its place, and Annalee immediately set everyone to work cleaning up. Tina knew she should have
joined in—she probably knew more about cleaning
than everybody else put together—but for some reason she just felt an aversion to it, just didn't want to.
And the more she thought she ought to help, the less
she felt like helping, until finally she fled the house.

"Stop," said Teague.

"Why?"

"You don't just walk outside and go where you
want," said Teague.

"Why not?"

"My neighbors don't know you yet."

"They'll know me soon enough," she said. "I've
always been a good neighbor."

"It ain't like neighbors down in the city, Mrs.
Monk."

"If you can't bring yourself to call me Sister Monk,
then at least call me Tina."

Teague grinned. "Go in there and get everybody
ready for an expedition."

The expedition was a trip to each of four neighbors' houses, singing and talking the whole way. The
houses were set so far apart you couldn't see any of
them from the others. But that didn't matter. They were
neighbors all the same. They were the reason Teague's
house was untouched. And they could be deadly.

"Mr. Bicker," said Teague. "I see you pulled a
good crop of tobacco."

"Mountain tobacco's only a speck better than chewing dog turds," said Bicker, "but I got a few leaves
curing anyway."

"Mr. Bicker, you see these folks I got with me?"

"Do I look blind?"

"I've been with these folks since Winston, and
they treated me like kin. We've been eating out of
the same pot and walking the same road, and stood
back to back a few times. They're staying the winter

with me and then they're moving on. I showed them the property line, and they all know what land is mine and what land is yours."

Bicker sniffed. "Never knowed city people could tell one tree from another."

But we can read, thought Tina, and we don't let snot trail on our upper lips. She had sense enough not to say it.

"City people or not, Mr. Bicker, they're *my* people, all of them."

"Them is colored there."

"I call that a deep suntan, Mr. Bicker. Or maybe Cherokee blood. But they'll be gone in spring, and you'll hardly notice they're around."

Bicker squinted.

"But they'll *be* around," said Teague. "Every one of them. Every last one, alive and moving around in the spring."

"Hope there's no influenza," said Bicker. Then he went back into his cabin, laughing and laughing.

Teague led them away. "Sing," he told Tina, and she led them in singing.

"This is like Christmas caroling," said Annalee's girl Donna.

"Except we didn't used to sing carols so people wouldn't shoot at us," said Tina.

"Oh, Bicker's all right," said Teague. "He'll be fine."

"Fine? He practically loaded his shotgun right in front of us."

"Oh, he's a good neighbor, Tina. You just got to know how to treat him."

"I don't call it a good neighbor when he merely agrees not to kill you before spring."

But Tina was pretty sure Teague didn't entirely know what he was talking about. After all, he'd been a boy up here, not a girl. There was one kind of neighborliness between men, which mostly consisted of not stealing from each other and not sleeping with each other's wife. Then there was the neighborliness of women, which Teague wouldn't know a thing about.

So she made sure to go along with him as ┐ he started going around trading the things he'd gotten on his trip to the coast. All kinds of tooled metal, threads and needles, buttons, pins, scissors, spoons and knives and forks. A precious pair of binoculars, for which Teague got a queen-size mattress in exchange. Bullets to fit half a dozen different guns. A bottle of vitamin C and a bottle of Extra-Strength Tylenol Caplets, both for an old lady with arthritis.

And right after he got through bartering, Tina would start in talking about how she was near helpless cooking wild game. "I make a fair broth, and I expect I can use my sweet dumpling recipe with honey for the sugar, but you must know ten dozen herbs and vegetables that I'll just step on thinking they're weeds. I don't want to be a bother, but I can trade sewing for cooking lessons. I've got a decent eye with a needle." Teague was dumfounded at first—it was obvious that in all the time he'd been trading with the menfolk, talking in words of one or two syllables and sentences of three or four words, he'd never had an inkling of how a woman goes calling, of how women help each other instead of trying to drive a bargain. "It's called civilization," she said to Teague, between visits. "Women invented it, and every time you men blow it all to bits, we just invent it again."

By Christmas she had Bicker himself coming over for supper every night, bringing his fiddle and a memory of a thousand old songs, none of which he sang on key, which nobody minded except Tina, who had been cursed with pitch so clear she could sing quarter tones in a chromatic scale. Never mind—the kids didn't have to live in fear of getting their feet shot off if they happened to stray over the line into Bicker's land. And Teague just sat there singing and laughing along with everybody else, now and then getting this look of surprise on his face, like he'd never had a notion that folks in these mountains ever did such things as this.

In only one thing did Tina follow Teague's heartfelt advice. She never told a soul, nor did anybody else, that they were Mormons. They never sang a Mormon hymn, and on Sunday mornings, when Brother Deaver and Pete Cinn broke bread and blessed the sacrament and passed it, and then they preached, why, they kept the shutters closed and never sang. It wasn't the hate from the TV preachers and the Baptist ministers of the city that they feared. It was an older kind of loathing. Put a name like *Mormon* on somebody, and he stopped being folks and started being Other. And around here, Other got ostracized at the least, and usually got burnt out before spring planting.

But it was a good winter all the same. And Tina noticed how Teague listened and finally came downstairs during church meetings, and even asked a question now and then about something from the Book of Mormon or some point of doctrine he'd never heard of before. Sometimes he shook his head like it was the craziest mess he'd ever heard of. And sometimes he kind of almost nodded. At Christmas he even told the Christmas story, pretty much following Luke.

Tina held school every day, at first just for the kids in their group, but pretty soon for whatever mountain kids could make it through the snow. She got Rona and Marie to teach sometimes, so she could divide the classes. Brother Deaver taught grammar to Donna and the older kids from the nearby cabins. The worst thing was, no paper to write on, and nothing to write *with*. They wrote with burnt sticks on the porch, then scrubbed the porch with snow and started over. Mostly, though, they did their writing and arithmetic in their heads, reciting their answers. Tina realized she was growing old when the kids regularly out-ciphered her—she just couldn't hold as many numbers at once as they could. That was when Rona became the permanent arithmetic teacher.

They didn't teach geography at all. Nobody knew geography anymore. Everything had changed.

All through the winter, Teague took Pete along to teach him more about hunting and tracking, and Pete learned pretty well, Tina gathered; at least Teague seemed to get closer to him all the time, approving of him, trusting him. At the same time, Tina noticed that Pete seemed to get more and more distant from his family. There wasn't much room for privacy, but as the only married couple, Pete and Annalee had a room to themselves. The day after Christmas Annalee told Tina that she might as well sleep on the dining room table for all the lovemaking she got anymore. "I might as well be a widow, he never even talks to me." And then: "Tina, I think he isn't planning to go on west with us."

Tina let things ride through January, watching. Annalee was right. Pete never took part in their frequent speculations about Utah. Teague would tease them all sometimes, when nobody else was around. "Nothing grows out west," he'd say. "They probably all moved on to Seattle. You'll get to Utah and nobody'll be there."

"You don't know what you're talking about, Jamie Teague," said Tina one time. "You don't know our people. If it floods we all go into the boatmaking business. If there's a hurricane we all learn to fly."

Others picked up on it. "If the corn crop fails, we learn to eat grass," said Donna.

"And when the grass gets used up, we chew up the trees!" said Mick Porter.

"And then we eat bugs!" shouted his little brother Scotty.

"And worms!" shouted Mick, even louder.

Annalee put a hand on Mick's mouth. "Let's keep

it down." Didn't want the neighbors to hear them talking about Utah.

"You can bet they're making gasoline out of shale oil," Tina said. "That's no tall tale. I bet there's still tractors plowing there, and fertilizer."

"I believe the fertilizer," said Teague. But his eyes danced a little, Tina could see that.

So she pressed her case. "And what have you got here, Jamie?"

It wasn't Teague who answered. It was Pete. "He's got everything," he said. "Safety. Good land. Enough to eat. Good neighbors. And no reason to move on, ever."

There it was, out in the open.

But Tina pretended that it was still Teague she was talking to, instead of Pete. "That's this year, Jamie. You make your trips down into the Carolinas. You go into abandoned houses, you visit places and tell stories and they give you gifts. And what do you collect to bring back here? Needles and pins, scissors and thread, tools and all the things that make life halfway livable. Think about that! Do you think those things will last forever? Nobody's making them anymore, and someday the scavenging will run out. Someday there'll be no more thread, no more needles. What'll you wear then? Some rag of homespun? Anybody spinning yet?"

"Lady down in Murphy spins and weaves real good," said Teague. Pete nodded like that answered everything.

"Enough for everybody in the hills? Jamie, don't you see that folks around here are just holding on by their fingernails? It isn't as plain to see here because you don't go to sleep in fear of mobs every night. But it's all slipping away. It's fading. And whoever stays here is going to fade, too. But out west—"

"Out west they might all be dead!" said Pete.

"Out west the temple is still standing, and the wards are all still functioning, just like they always have. They're growing crops on good land—in peace—and there'll still be hospitals and medicines. What if you marry someday, Jamie? What if your kids get some disease? A simple one like measles. And they end up blind. A kidney infection. Appendicitis, for heaven's sake. You see any more doctors growing up around here? Every year you'll slip back another fifty years."

"It's safe here," said Pete. But his voice was fainter.

"It isn't safe compared to *safety*," said Tina. "It's only safe compared to the open lands where the mob rules. And someday you know the mobbers are coming up here. They'll have killed off or run off everybody down there who isn't protected by an army. Those mobbers aren't going to settle down and learn to *farm*, you know. They won't attack the Cherokees, either. They'll come to places like this—"

"And we'll kill them all," said Pete.

"Till you run out of bullets. Then there's no more shooting from behind trees. Then you fight out in the open against ten times your number, by hand, till they sweep you under. I tell you there's only one place safe in all America, only one place that's growing upward against all the dying."

"Says you," said Pete.

"Says all the history of the Mormon people. We've been driven out and mobbed and massacred before, and all we ever do is move on and settle somewhere else. And wherever we settle there's peace and progress. We never hold still. I'm betting we don't even have to get to the mountains to find them. I'm betting they send people out to meet folks like us and help us safely in. That's what they used to do, in the covered wagon days."

All this time Tina only looked at Teague, never once at Pete. But out the corner of her eye she could see how Pete deflated when Teague nodded. "I guess you aren't crazy to try to get there after all. I just wish I had more hope of your making it."

"The Lord will protect us," said Tina.

"He was doing a slim job of it till Teague came along," said Pete.

"But Jamie came along, didn't you, Jamie? Why do you think you happened to be there when we needed you so bad?"

Teague grinned. "I reckon I'm just a regular old angel," he said.

Still, Easter came and no decision had been made. They had a church service on Easter Sunday, but nobody preached this time. They just bore testimony. It wasn't like the old days, when people used to get up and recite the same old I'm-thankful-fors and I-know-thats. This time they spoke from the heart, spoke of terrible things and wonderful things, spoke of love for each other and anger at the Lord and yet in the end spoke of faith that things would all work out.

And after a while they started talking about the thing they'd only hinted at all these months together. The thing that happened back in May, almost a year before. The terrible death of so many of the people they knew and loved and missed so bad. And the even worse thing—that they themselves had not died.

It was Cheri Ann Bee who started it off. She was seven now, and not even baptized yet, but she still bore her testimony, and at the end she said something real simple, but it about broke Tina's heart. "I'm sorry I didn't get sick that day and stay home," she said, "so I could've gone with Mommy and Daddy to visit Heavenly Father." Cheri Ann didn't cry or anything; she just plain believed that things were better with her mother and father. And as Tina sat there with tears in her eyes, she wasn't sure if she felt like crying out of pity for this girl or if she felt like crying because she herself didn't have such plain and simple faith, and lacked something of that perfect trust that death was just a matter of going to pay a call on God, who would invite you into his house to live with him.

"I'm sorry, too," said Brother Deaver, and then he *did* cry, tears running down his cheeks. "I'm sorry I went to work that day. I'm sorry that the Christian Soldiers were so afraid of provoking the black community of Greensboro that they didn't come take me out of class at A&T and let me hold my babies in my arms while they were dying."

"His kids wasn't babies," Scotty Porter whispered to Tina. "They was bigger than me."

"All children are always babies to their mama and papa," Tina answered.

"I called my mama that morning," said Annalee, and wonder of wonders, she was crying, too, looking as soft and vulnerable as a child. "I told her how Pete was keeping the kids home from school and we were making a picnic of it at the fire station. And she said, I wisht I could come. And then she said, Can't talk now, Anny Leedy, there's somebody at the door. Somebody at the door! It was *them* at the door, and there I was talking to her on the phone and I didn't even say I love you one last time or nothing."

There was silence for a while, the way there always was in testimony meetings from time to time, when nobody stood up to talk. It always used to be so tense when nobody talked, everybody feeling guilty cause the time was going to waste and hoping somebody else would get up and talk cause they didn't feel like it. This time, though, the silence was just because everybody was so full and there wasn't a thing to say.

"I knew," said Pete, finally. "I had a dream the night before. I saw the men coming to the doors. I was *shown*. That's why I kept the kids home. That's why I got us all over to the fire station."

"You never told me this," said Annalee.

"I thought it was crazy, that's why. I thought I was plain out of my mind to take a nightmare so serious. But I couldn't leave you all home, feeling like I did." Pete looked around at the others. "My station, they stood by me. They turned on the hoses and drove them back. My captain said to them, 'If you touch any fireman or any fireman's family, don't be surprised to find your own house on fire someday, and the fire engines a little slow to show up and save you.' And so they went away, and we were alive." Suddenly his face twisted up and he sobbed, great and terrible sobs.

"Petey," said Annalee. She put her arm around him, but he shrugged her off.

"God showed me a vision, don't you see? And all I could think to save was my own family. Not even my brothers and sisters! Not even my mama! I had a chance to save them all, and they're dead because I didn't give warning."

Brother Deaver tried to soothe him with words. "Pete, the Lord didn't command you in that dream to give warning. He didn't tell you to call everybody and tell them. So he probably meant to take the others to himself, and spare only a few to suffer further in this vale of tears."

Pete lifted his face from his hands, a mask of grief with reddened eyes staring out, wild and terrible. "He did tell me," said Pete. "Warn them all, he said, only I just thought it was a nightmare, I was too embarrassed to claim to have a vision, I thought they'd all think I was crazy. I'm going to hell, don't you see? I can't go to Utah. I'm rejected and cast off from the Lord."

"Even Jonah was forgiven," said Brother Deaver.

But Pete wasn't in the mood to be comforted. It was the end of the meeting, but it was a good meeting, Tina knew that. Everybody said the things they'd been holding back all along, or had those things said for them. They'd done what a testimony meeting was supposed to do. They'd confessed their sins, and now there was hope of forgiveness.

It was afternoon of Easter Sunday. The day had

warmed up right smart, and Jamie shed his jacket and felt the wind cool on his back and arms, right through his shirt, and felt the sun hot, too, right at the same time. Best kind of weather, best kind of day.

"I guess you got an earful today."

Jamie turned around. He couldn't believe he hadn't heard a big woman like Tina come lumbering up behind him. But then she wasn't so big these days. And he had a lot of noisy thoughts going round in his head.

"I figured a lot of this out before, anyway," said Jamie. "I heard tales of the Greensboro massacre."

"Is that how they tell it? That our people were massacred?"

"Sometimes," said Jamie. "Other times they call it the Purification of Greensboro. Them as says that usually allow as how other places need purification, too."

"I hope all our people are heading west. I pray they all have sense to go. We should've gone years ago."

"May be," said Jamie. But he knew this wasn't what Tina came to say.

"Jamie," said Tina.

This was it.

"Jamie, what's holding you here?"

Jamie looked around at the trees, at the bright spring grass, at the distant curls of smoke from two dozen chimneys spread out through the hills.

"You hardly speak to your neighbors, leastwise you didn't till we came here, Jamie. You got no close friends in these hills."

"They leave me alone," said Jamie Teague.

"Too bad," said Tina.

"I like it. I like being left alone."

"Don't tell me lies, Jamie."

"I was a loner before the collapse, and I'm a loner now. Whole thing made not a speck of difference to me."

"Don't tell yourself lies, either."

Jamie felt anger flash out inside him. "I don't need anybody talking like a mama to me. I had one once and I killed her dead."

"I don't believe that lie," said Tina.

"Why?" demanded Jamie. "Do you think I'm so *nice* I'd just naturally never kill a soul? Then you don't know me at all."

"I know there's times you kill," said Tina. "I just don't believe you killed your mama and papa. Because if you did, then why are you still so mad at them?"

"Leave me alone." Jamie meant it with all his heart.

But Tina didn't seem interested in leaving him alone. "You know you love us and you don't want to lose us when we leave."

"Is that what you think?"

"That's what I know. I see how good you are with the kids. What a friend you been to Peter. Don't you see that's half why he wanted to stay, to be with you? We all count on you, we all lean on you, but you count on us, too, you *need* us."

She was pushing too hard. Jamie couldn't stand it. "Back off," he said. "Just back off and leave me be."

"And when we pray, you fall silent, and your lips say Amen when the prayer is over."

"I got respect for religion, that's all."

"And today when we all confessed the blackest things that hurt us to the soul, you wanted to confess, too."

"I confessed a long time ago."

"You confessed a terrible lie. That's what I keep wondering about, Jamie Teague. What sin are you hiding that you think is so bad that it's easier to confess to killing your mama and papa?"

"Leave me alone!" shouted Jamie. Then he ran off from her, ran off up the hill, scrambling fast so he knew there was no hope of her keeping up. Didn't matter. She didn't chase him.

*   *   *

Mick Porter took his brother Scotty with him everywhere. Never let that little boy out of his sight. Have to look out for a kid like Scotty, always running off, always getting into things like he shouldn't.

In the old days it wasn't like that, of course. In the old days Mick used to complain to Mom about how Scotty always had to do everything the same as him. Mick used to wallop Scotty sometimes, and Scotty'd break down whatever Mick made out of Legos or blocks, and it got to be like a war. But that all ended. Just didn't happen no more, on account of who'd break up their fights and send them to their rooms till they could just treat each other like civilized human beings now? Mick felt like he was almost Scotty's dad. I am his only kin, and he's my only kin, so look out, everybody else, and that's all.

So Mick had Scotty tagging right along with him, gathering fallen sticks for kindling and getting in some rock-throwing practice, too. Mick wasn't up to getting squirrels, yet. He still had kind of a hard time hitting the same tree he was aiming at. Scotty, of course, had no idea about aim at all. He just felt good if the rock went more than five feet in the general direction he threw it.

Hardly a surprise, then, when Scotty threw his latest rock and it went sideways, whizzing right past Mick's nose and then going thunk, right into something soft not more than a few feet off.

"OK, I'm dead, just skin me gentle so you don't wake me up."

Mick near to swallowed his tongue he was so surprised. There was Mr. Jamie Teague, sitting right there, and until he spoke Mick hadn't even noticed him. He just held so *still* all the time.

"I hit something!" said Scotty.

"You hit my jeans," said Mr. Teague. "If I was a squirrel I might not be dead, but I'd sure be crippled."

"We can't cook *you*," said Scotty.

"Guess not," said Mr. Teague. "I'm sorry about that."

"We don't eat people anyhow," Mick told Scotty.

"I know that," Scotty said, his voice full of scorn.

Mick turned his attention to Mr. Teague. "What you doing just setting there?"

"Setting here."

"I just said that."

"And thinking."

"Of course you were thinking," said Mick. "Everybody's always thinking. You can't turn it off."

"And ain't that a damn shame, too," said Mr. Teague.

Scotty gasped and covered his mouth.

"I'm sorry," said Mr. Teague. "I grew up in a family where 'damn' was the *nice* way of saying stuff."

"I know a worser word," said Scotty.

"No you don't," said Mick.

"He might," said Mr. Teague. "You never know."

"It's another word for poop," said Scotty.

"Don't that beat all," said Mr. Teague. "Better not teach me what it is, now, Scotty. I might slip and use it in polite company."

Mick sat down near Mr. Teague's leg, and looked him in the eye. "Sister Monk says you didn't really kill your mama and daddy."

"Does she now."

"I heard her," said Scotty.

"Is she right?" asked Mick.

"I used to dream about killing them. But after they took us kids away from them, nobody ever told us where they were. Jail, I guess. I always meant to look for them and kill them when I got eighteen and could leave my foster parents, so-called, but the collapse came before I could get a fair start. So you see I meant to do it, and it wasn't my fault I didn't do it, so the way I figure it, I did it in my heart so I'm a murderer."

"No sir," said Mick. "You never did it. You got to kill somebody to be a murderer."

"Maybe so," said Mr. Teague.

"Then you'll come with us?"

Mr. Teague laughed out loud. He pulled his legs up close to his body and hugged them. They were the longest pair of legs Mick ever saw. Even longer than Daddy's legs used to be.

"You think my daddy's a skeleton now?" asked Mick.

Mr. Teague's smile went away. "Maybe," he said. "Hard to say."

"The Christian Soldiers killed him," said Mick.

"And Mommy," said Scotty.

"Those are what murderers are," said Mick.

"I know," said Mr. Teague.

"Brother Deaver says they killed our mama and daddy because we believe in a living prophet and how Jesus isn't the same person as God the Father."

"That's right, I guess."

"What did *your* mama and daddy believe?"

Mr. Teague took in a long breath. He crossed his arms on top of his knees, and then rested his chin on top of his arms. He looked right between Mick and Scotty so long that Scotty started breaking twigs and Mick began to think Mr. Teague just wasn't going to answer, or maybe even he was mad.

"Don't break them sticks, Scotty," said Mick. "We can't use it for kindling if it's all broke up."

Scotty stopped breaking twigs. Didn't sass or stick out his tongue or nothing. It was all different now.

"My mama and daddy believed in getting by," said Mr. Teague.

"Getting by what?" asked Scotty.

"Just—getting by."

"That's what you wanted to kill them about?" asked Mick.

Mr. Teague shook his head.

"You aren't making sense, you know," said Mick.

Mr. Teague grinned. "Guess not." He reached out a long arm, and with a single long finger he lifted

Mick's chin. Mick didn't like it when grown-ups started moving parts of his body around or grabbing his hand or whatever, like they thought he was a puppet. But it wasn't so bad when Mr. Teague did it, especially because he didn't act like he was planning to make Mick do something or yell at him or anything. "You love your little brother, don't you?"

Mick shrugged.

Scotty looked at him.

"Course," said Mick.

"Not when you're mad at me," said Scotty.

"I'm never mad at you anymore," said Mick.

"No," said Scotty, as if he was realizing it for the first time.

"I had a little brother," said Mr. Teague.

"Did you love him?" asked Mick.

"Yes," said Mr. Teague.

"Where is he?"

"Dead I guess," said Mr. Teague.

"Don't you know?"

"They put him in a mental hospital same time they locked up my folks. Put my little sister in a mental hospital, too. Then they farmed out me and my older brothers to foster homes. Never saw any of them again, but I reckon my little brother, being crazy like he was, I reckon he didn't last long after the collapse."

Mr. Teague was breathing kind of fast, and not looking Mick in the eye anymore. It was kind of scary, like Mr. Teague was a little crazy himself. "How'd he get crazy?" asked Mick. He wondered if the same thing was happening to Mr. Teague.

"Does he scream?" asked Scotty. "Crazy people scream."

"Sometimes he screamed. Mostly he just sat there, looking past you. He'd never look folks in the eye. It was like you wasn't even there. Like he was erasing you in his own mind. But he looked at *me*."

"How come you?"

"Because I brought him food."

"Not your mama?"

Mr. Teague shook his head. "It was when I was five. Your age, Scotty. And my little brother, he was three."

"I'm five and a half," said Scotty.

"And my little sister, she was only two."

"Was she crazy?" asked Mick.

"Not then. But she was sick. And so was my little brother. Both of them, all the time. Ever since they was born. My brother got pneumonia and cried all the time. Lots of bills to pay. My little sister was fussy, too. I used to hear Mama and Daddy yelling at each other all the time, about money, about too damn many kids. Fighting and screaming, and Mama screaming about how she just couldn't take any more, she just couldn't stand it if us kids didn't just shut *up* and let her be for just a couple of hours, that's all she wanted, just a couple of hours of silence, and she was going to have it by God or she'd kill herself, see if I don't, she said, I'm going to cut my wrists and die if you don't shut up. And me, I'd shut up all right, I kept my mouth shut. The older kids, they were in school. But my little brother, he was just sick and out of sorts and he just kept crying and whimpering and the more she yelled the more he whimpered and then my sister, she woke up from her nap and she started crying even louder than my brother did, they just screamed and screamed, and my mama screamed even louder, she just got this horrible face, and she picked up my sister and I thought she was going to throw her on the floor, but she didn't do it. She just took her and grabbed my brother by his arm and dragged him along, dragged them over to the cedar closet that had a lock on the door and she opened it up and shoved them inside and closed the door and locked it. Cry and whine all you want to but I'm not going to hear any more, do you understand me? I just can't stand it any more I'm going to have some *peace.*"

"Daddy locked me in the bathroom one time when I was bad," said Mick.

"Did they have a light in there?" asked Scotty.

"They had a light. There was a switch and my brother could stand on a box in there and turn it on, so he did. But they didn't like being in there. They screamed and yelled and cried like it was the worst thing in the world, and my brother banged on the door and rattled the handle and kicked the door and stamped his feet. But Mama just went downstairs and turned on the dishwasher and went into the living room and turned on the stereo and laid there on the couch listening to the radio until she fell asleep. Every now and then my brother and sister, they let up on their yelling, but then they'd start all over again. When the older kids got home from school they knew right off to stay away from Mom, and they didn't even ask where the little ones were. They knew you don't mess with Mom in a mood like that. Anyway, Mom got up and fixed dinner, and when Dad came home we ate, and Dad asked where the little kids were, and Mom said, Learning to be quiet. And when she said that, Dad knew not to mess with her, either. Except at the end of the meal he said, Aren't they going to eat? And so Mom slopped food onto a couple of plates and put spoons on them and then she handed me the key and said, Take them their dinner, Jamie. But if you let them out I'll kill myself, do you understand?"

"They was really in trouble I guess," said Scotty.

"When I opened the door my brother tried to get out, but I pushed him back in. He screamed and cried louder than ever, except he was hoarse by then. My sister was just setting in a corner with her face all red and covered with snot, but he kicked me

and tried to shove me out of the way, but I knocked
him down and then I knocked him down again and
then I slid their plates in with my foot and slammed
the door and locked it. My brother kicked and yelled
and screamed for a while, but then he quieted down
and I guess they ate their dinner. Later on they
screamed and yelled some more, about going to the
bathroom, but Mom just pretended not to hear, she
just shook her head. They're not getting out by yelling, they're not getting their way by yelling."

"They spent the night in there?" asked Mick.

"Next morning she gave me the key and one bowl
of oatmeal and two spoons. This time they were both
back in the corner. They'd made themselves pillows
and beds kind of, out of the rags in there, we kept
the old rags in that closet. And my sister looked like
she was afraid of getting hit, and it stunk real bad,
because she'd done her poop in a shoebox, but what
could she do, if Mom wouldn't let her out to use the
toilet? I told Mom, and she just said, Empty it and
put it back. I didn't want to, but you don't argue
with Mom when she's like that."

"Gross," said Mick.

Scotty just stared. Mick knew it was because he
messed his pants a couple of times lately, after the
Christian Soldiers killed Mama and Daddy, and so
talking about pooping in a shoebox kind of embarrassed him.

"I kept thinking, Mom's going to let them out
pretty soon. I kept thinking that. But every morning
I took them breakfast and emptied the shoebox and
the mason jar we left in there for them to piss in.
And every night I took them dinner on a plate.
Sometimes I could hear them talking in there. Sometimes they played. That was all at first though. After
a while it was always quiet, except when one of them
was sick and coughed a lot. When the bulb burned
out I told Mom but she just didn't say anything. I

said, The bulb's out in the cedar closet, but she just looked at me like she'd never even heard of a cedar closet. I finally got my big brother to change the bulb while I watched the door so they couldn't get out. That first time—other times from then on he wouldn't do it, so I had to tie my little brother's hands and feet together so I could change the bulb. When I started first grade, I'd feed them and do the box in the morning before school, and take them dinner at night, just the same thing, day after day, week after week. Most of the time my brother and sister just sat there when I opened the door, not looking at me, just staring at each other or at nothing at all. But every now and then my brother would scream and run at me like he wanted to kill me, and I'd knock him down and slam the door and lock it. I was so mean to him and so angry and so scared that somebody would find out what I was doing to my own brother and sister, how I was keeping them locked in a closet. Nobody else in the family ever even saw them after my brother changed the light bulb that time. Mom didn't even make up the plates for them, I had to do it after everybody left the kitchen. When they grew out of their clothes, I tried to sneak some of the clothes I grew out of, but then Mom would say, What happened to those pants of yours, what happened to that blue shirt, and I'd say, They're in the cedar closet, and she'd look at me that way and say, Those are perfectly good clothes and if they don't fit you anymore we'll give them away to the poor. Can you believe that?"

"We used to give old clothes to Goodwill," said Scotty.

"They were naked in there, and their skin was white and they looked like ghosts, their eyes empty and never looking at me except when my brother screamed at me and ran at me, and every time I slammed the door and locked it, I wanted to kill them, I wanted to die, I hated it. I'd go to school and look around and I knew that I was the most evil person there, because I kept my little brother and sister naked locked up in a closet. Nobody even knew I *had* a little brother and sister. And I never told them. I never even walked up to a teacher and said, Miss Erbison, or Mrs. Ryan, or whoever, any of them, I could have said, I got me a little brother and sister at home that we've kept locked in the cedar closet since they was three and two years old. If I'd've done that, maybe my brother wouldn't have gone so crazy, maybe my sister wouldn't have forgotten how to walk, maybe they could've been saved in *time*, but I was so scared of what my Mom would do, and I was too ashamed to tell anybody what a terrible person I was, they all thought I was an OK guy."

He stopped talking for a while.

"Didn't they *ever* get out?" asked Scotty.

"When I was in seventh grade. I did a report on Nazi Germany and the concentration camps. I read about the tortures they did. And I thought, That's me. I'm a Nazi. And I read about how all them Nazis, they all said, I was just following orders. Well that was me, just following orders. And then I read how after the war they put them on trial, all those Nazis, and they sentenced them to death for what they did, and then I knew I was right all along. I knew I deserved to die, and my Mom and Dad deserved to die, but my little brother and sister, they deserved to go free, they deserved to have a day of liberation. So one afternoon when my little brother got hate in his eyes and ran at me, I didn't knock him down. I stepped out of his way and let him run by me. He ran out of the closet and looked around, like he'd never seen the hall before, and I guess he never had, really, he never remembered it. And then he sat down on the top step and bumped his way down the stairs, like he always did when he was a little kid, and I realized that he'd forgotten how to walk down stairs. And then all of a sudden I thought, he's going to go in the kitchen and Mom's going to see him and get mad. And I got scared, and I thought, I got to catch him and put him back, or Mom will kill me. So I started to chase him down the stairs, but he didn't go into the kitchen, he ran right out the front door, stark naked, I never thought he'd do that, but what did he care about naked, he never wore clothes in seven years. He just ran down the street, screaming and screaming like a creature from space, and I ran after him. I would've called out to him, yelled for him to stop, but I couldn't."

"Why not?" asked Mick.

"I didn't remember his name." Brother Teague began to cry. "I couldn't even remember what his name was."

It was only then, with Brother Teague crying into his hands like a little baby, that Mick even noticed that Sister Monk and Brother Deaver had both come up sometime, they were both there listening, they probably heard the whole story. Sister Monk came over and knelt down by Brother Teague and gathered him into her arms and let him cry all over her dress. Brother Deaver bowed his head like he was praying, only silently. Scotty noticed that, too, and bowed his head, but then when nobody said a prayer he lifted his head and looked over to Mick.

Mick didn't know what to do, except that it was a terrible story, a terrible thing that happened to Brother Teague's crazy sister and brother. Mick never heard of anybody forgetting how to walk or climb down stairs, or forgetting his own brother's name. When he tried to imagine somebody locking Scotty into a closet and never letting him out, it made Mick so mad he wanted to kill them for doing that. But then he tried to imagine if it was his own mama who locked Scotty up, what then? What would he do then? His mama never would've done such a thing, but what if she did?

It was just too hard to figure out by himself. All he knew was that Brother Teague was crying like Mick never heard anybody cry before in his whole life. Finally he just had to reach over and take hold of Brother Teague's ankle, which was the only part of him that Mick could reach. Mick's hand was so small he couldn't even grab, it was like he was just pressing his hand against Brother Teague's leg.

"You shouldn't feel bad, Brother Teague," said Mick. "You're the one who let him out."

Brother Teague shook his head, still crying.

"I wish these kids hadn't heard that story," said Brother Deaver.

"Some things you can only tell to children," said Sister Monk. "It'll do them no harm."

Brother Teague pulled his face away from Sister Monk's dress. "I knew when you came. I was telling *you*. Isn't that how it's done in your testimonies?"

"That's right, Jamie," said Sister Monk. "That's how you do it."

"Now you see why I'll never be a worthy man, Mormon or not," said Brother Teague. "There's no place for me out west."

"It was your mama made you do it," said Mick.

"I was the one who pushed him back inside," said Brother Teague. His voice was awful. "I was the one who turned the key." Then he reached down inside his shirt and pulled up a key on a leather thong. A common ordinary door key. "This key," he said. "I had the key all along."

"But Brother Teague," said Mick, "you weren't eight years old yet when it all started. You weren't baptized yet. Don't you know Jesus doesn't blame children for what they do before they're eight? I turn eight next week, and when I'm baptized I'll be like I was born all over again, pure and clean, isn't that right, Brother Deaver?"

Brother Deaver nodded. "Mm-hm," he said. He was crying now, too, though Mick couldn't figure why, seeing how it was Brother Deaver himself who interviewed him for baptism and taught him half this stuff right after testimony meeting today.

Scotty must have been getting bored now that the story was over. He got up and walked over to Brother Teague and poked him on the shoulder to get his attention. "Brother Teague," he said. "Brother Teague."

Brother Teague looked up just as Sister Monk said, "Leave him be, now, you hear?"

"What do you want, Scotty?" asked Brother Teague.

"Now that we're calling you Brother Teague, does that mean you're going west with us to Utah?"

Brother Teague didn't say anything. He just rubbed his eyes and then sat there with his face covered up. Sister Monk and Brother Deaver stayed with him, but Mick couldn't figure out what was going on anymore, and besides, he had to think about the story, and anyway he needed to take a leak and he couldn't do it in the woods unless he got a lot farther away from Sister Monk. So he took Scotty by the hand and led him off to a bunch of bushes higher up the hill.

The whole next week everybody ignored Mick and Scotty and the other kids. There was no school, just packing up and getting ready to go. On Saturday they went down to a deep slow place in the river and baptized Mick in his underwear, because he didn't have any white clothes except his shorts and t-shirt, and Brother Teague had to be baptized in his most faded boxers and a t-shirt he borrowed from Brother Cinn, because Brother Teague didn't have any white clothes at all. Brother Teague came out of the water shivering just as bad as Mick did.

"Water's cold, ain't it?" said Mick.

"Isn't it," said Sister Cinn.

"Damn cold," said Brother Teague.

Funny thing was, nobody so much as blinked that Brother Teague swore, right after his baptism, too. Mick couldn't say *ain't*, but Brother Teague could cuss. Which just goes to show you that kids just can't get away with anything, Mick figured.

"That's done it," said Brother Deaver. "You're one of us now."

"Guess so," said Brother Teague. He looked as goofy as a kindergartner, with his hair all wet and sticking out and that smile on his face.

"It's just a sneaky Mormon trick," said Brother Cinn. "Once you're baptized, we don't have to pay you for leading us anymore."

"I been paid," said Brother Teague.

Next morning they had a prayer meeting and headed off west toward Chattanooga. They only made it to somewhere between St. Louis and Kansas City that summer, what with getting arrested in Memphis and nearly lynched in Cape Girardeau. Winter was hard, so far north, and the next summer, crossing the plains, they ran across a little wagon train that some mobbers had just wiped out. The only survivor was a little boy who couldn't even remember his name; Brother Teague picked him up and took him along, never letting him out of his sight the whole rest of the way. It wasn't much after that before outriders from Utah found them and led them the rest of the way home, with spare horses no less, so they could ride. Mick was sure that if Brother Teague had been a married man then, he would have adopted that new boy they found; as it was, it near broke Brother Teague's heart to turn him over to the authorities, who found a family to take care of the boy day and night, something Brother Teague just couldn't do. But that's the way of it—everybody doing his best, fitting in and helping others all he can.

Mick remembered that journey all the days of his life, you can bet on that, and whenever he saw Jamie Teague after that, like at Jamie's wedding with Marie Speaks, and once when they ran into each other at Conference, times like that they'd greet each other and laugh and tell folks that they were the very same age, they had the very same birthday. And it was true, too, because they were born again in ice cold water on that spring morning in the Appalachians.

LIBERTY PORT
David Drake

Combat injuries take some men out of the fighting only briefly, others forever. Commandant Horace Jolober will never return to the front line, but he is a leader still; and in "Liberty Port" he finds himself joining forces with Hammer's Slammers against an enemy more insidious than any they'd faced on the battlefield.
                                             —E.M.

Commandant Horace Jolober had just lowered the saddle of his mobile chair, putting himself at the height of the Facilities Inspection Committee seated across the table, when the alarm hooted and Vicki cried from the window in the next room, *"Tanks!* In the street!"

The three Placidan bureaucrats flashed Jolober looks of anger and fear, but he had no time for them now even though they were his superiors. The stump of his left leg keyed the throttle of his chair. As the fans spun up, Jolober leaned and guided his miniature air-cushion vehicle out of the room faster than another man could have walked.

Faster than a man with legs could walk.

Vicki opened the door from the bedroom as Jolober swept past her toward the inside stairs. Her face was as calm as that of the statue which it resembled in its perfection, but Jolober knew that only the strongest emotion would have made her disobey his orders to stay in his private apartments while the inspection team was here. She was afraid that he was about to be killed.

A burst of gunfire in the street suggested she just might be correct.

"Chief!" called Jolober's mastoid implant in what he thought was the voice of Karnes, his executive

84

officer. "I'm at the gate and the new arrivals, they're Hammer's, just came right through the wire! There's half a dozen tanks and they're shooting in the air!"

Could've been worse. Might yet be.

He slid onto the staircase, his stump boosting fan speed with reflexive skill. The stair treads were too narrow for Jolober's mobile chair to form an air cushion between the surface and the lip of its plenum chamber. Instead he balanced on thrust alone while the fans beneath him squealed, ramming the air hard enough to let him slope down above the staircase with the grace of a stooping hawk.

The hardware was built to handle the stress, but only flawless control kept the port commandant from up-ending and crashing down the treads in a fashion as dangerous as it would be humiliating.

Jolober was a powerful man who'd been tall besides until a tribarrel blew off both his legs above the knee. In his uniform of white cloth and lavish gold, he was dazzlingly obvious in any light. As he gunned his vehicle out into the street, the most intense light source was the rope of cyan bolts ripping skyward from the cupola of the leading tank.

The buildings on either side of the street enticed customers with displays to rival the sun, but the operators—each of them a gambler, brothel keeper, and saloon owner all in one—had their own warning systems. The lights were going out, leaving the plastic façades cold.

Lightless, the buildings faded to the appearance of the high concrete fortresses they were in fact. Repeated arches made the entrance of the China Doll, directly across the street from the commandant's offices, look spacious. The door itself was so narrow that only two men could pass it at a time, and no one could slip unnoticed past the array of sensors and guards that made sure none of those entering were armed.

Normally the facilities here at Paradise Port were

open all day. Now an armored panel clanged down across the narrow door of the China Doll, its echoes merging with similar tocsins from the other buildings.

Much good that would do if the tanks opened up with their 20-cm main guns. Even a tribarrel could blast holes in thumb-thick steel as easily as one had vaporized Jolober's knees and calves. . . .

He slid into the street, directly into the path of the lead tank. He would have liked to glance up toward the bedroom window for what he knew might be his last glimpse of Vicki, but he was afraid that he couldn't do that and still have the guts to do his duty.

For a long time after he lost his legs, the only thing which had kept Horace Jolober from suicide was the certainty that he had *always* done his duty. Not even Vicki could be allowed to take that from him.

The tanks were advancing at no more than a slow walk, though their huge size gave them the appearance of speed. They were buttoned up—hatches down, crews hidden behind the curved surfaces of iridium armor that might just possibly turn a bolt from a gun as big as the one each tank carried in its turret.

Lesser weapons had left scars on the iridium. Where light powerguns had licked the armor—and even a tribarrelled automatic was light in comparison to a tank—the metal cooled again in a slope around the point where a little had been vaporized. High-velocity bullets made smaller, deeper craters plated with material from the projectile itself.

The turret of the leading tank bore a long gouge that began in a pattern of deep, radial scars. A shoulder-fired rocket had hit at a slight angle. The jet of white-hot gas spurting from the shaped-charge warhead had burned deep enough into even the refractory iridium that it would have penetrated the turret had it struck squarely.

If either the driver or the blower captain were riding with their heads out of the hatch when the missile detonated, shrapnel from the casing had decapitated them.

Jolober wondered if the present driver even saw him, a lone man in a street that should have been cleared by the threat of one hundred and seventy tonnes of armor howling down the middle of it.

An air-cushion jeep carrying a pintle-mounted needle stunner and two men in Port Patrol uniforms was driving alongside the lead tank, bucking and pitching in the current roaring from beneath the steel skirts of the tank's plenum chamber. While the driver fought to hold the light vehicle steady, the other patrolman bellowed through the jeep's loudspeakers. He might have been on the other side of the planet for all his chance of being heard over the sound of air sucked through intakes atop the tank's hull and then pumped beneath the skirts forcefully enough to balance the huge weight of steel and iridium.

Jolober grounded his mobile chair. He crooked his left ring finger so that the surgically redirected nerve impulse keyed the microphone implanted at the base of his jaw. "Gentlemen," he said, knowing that the base unit in the Port Offices was relaying his words on the Slammers' general frequency. "You are violating the regulations which govern Port Paradise. Stop before somebody gets hurt."

The bow of the lead tank was ten meters away—and one meter less every second.

To the very end he thought they were going to hit him—by inadvertence, now, because the tank's steel skirt lifted in a desperate attempt to stop but the vehicle's mass overwhelmed the braking effect of its fans. Jolober knew that if he raised his chair from the pavement, the blast of air from the tank would knock him over and roll him along the concrete like a trashcan in a windstorm—bruised but safe.

He would rather die than lose his dignity that way in front of Vicki.

The tank's bow slewed to the left, toward the

China Doll. The skirt on that side touched the pavement with the sound of steel screaming and a fountain of sparks that sprayed across and over the building's high plastic façade.

The tank did not hit the China Doll, and it stopped short of Horace Jolober by less than the radius of its bow's curve.

The driver grounded his huge vehicle properly and cut the power to his fans. Dust scraped from the pavement, choking and chalky, swirled around Jolober and threw him into a paroxysm of coughing. He hadn't realized that he'd been holding his breath—until the danger passed and instinct filled his lungs.

The jeep pulled up beside Jolober, its fans kicking up still more dust, and the two patrolmen shouted words of concern and congratulation to their commandant. More men were appearing, patrolmen and others who had ducked into the narrow alleys between buildings when the tanks filled the street.

"Stecher," said Jolober to the sergeant in the patrol vehicle, "go back there—" he gestured toward the remainder of the column, hidden behind the armored bulk of the lead tank "—and help 'em get turned around. Get 'em back to the Refit Area where they belong."

"Sir, should I get the names?" Stecher asked.

The port commandant shook his head with certainty. "None of this happened," he told his subordinates. "I'll take care of it."

The jeep spun nimbly while Stecher spoke into his commo helmet, relaying Jolober's orders to the rest of the squad on street duty.

Metal rang again as the tank's two hatch covers slid open. Jolober was too close to the hull to see the crewmen, so he kicked his fans to life and backed a few meters.

The mobile chair had been built to his design. Its only control was the throttle with a linkage which at high-thrust settings automatically transformed the plenum chamber to a nozzle. Steering and balance were matters of how the rider shifted his body weight. Jolober prided himself that he was just as nimble as he had been before.

—Before he backed into the trench on Primavera, half wrapped in the white flag he'd waved to the oncoming tanks. The only conscious memory he retained of *that* moment was the sight of his right leg still balanced on the trench lip above him, silhouetted against the criss-crossing cyan bolts from the powerguns.

But Horace Jolober was just as much a man as he'd ever been. The way he got around proved it. And Vicki.

The driver staring out the bow hatch at him was a woman with thin features and just enough hair to show beneath her helmet. She looked scared, aware of what had just happened and aware also of just how bad it could've been.

Jolober could appreciate how she felt.

The man who lifted himself from the turret hatch was under thirty, angry, and—though Jolober couldn't remember the Slammer's collar pips precisely—a junior officer of some sort rather than a sergeant.

The dust had mostly settled by now, but vortices still spun above the muzzles of the tribarrel which the fellow had been firing skyward. "What're you doing, you bloody fool?" he shouted. "D'ye *want* to die?"

Not any more, thought Horace Jolober as he stared upward at the tanker. One of the port patrolmen had responded to the anger in the Slammer's voice by raising his needle stunner, but there was no need for that.

Jolober keyed his mike so that he didn't have to shout with the inevitable emotional loading. In a flat, certain voice he said, "If you'll step down here, Lieutenant, we can discuss the situation like officers—

which I am, and you will continue to be unless you insist on pushing things."

The tanker grimaced, then nodded his head and lifted himself the rest of the way out of the turret. "Right," he said. "Right. I . . ." His voice trailed off, but he wasn't going to say anything the port commandant hadn't heard before.

When you screw up real bad, you can either be afraid or you can flare out in anger and blame somebody else. Not because you don't know better, but because it's the only way to control your fear. It isn't pretty, but there's no pretty way to screw up bad.

The tanker dropped to the ground in front of Jolober and gave a sloppy salute. That was lack of practice, not deliberate insult, and his voice and eyes were firm as he said, "Sir. Acting Captain Tad Hoffritz reporting."

"Horace Jolober," the port commandant said. He raised his saddle to put his head at what used to be normal standing height, a few centimeters taller than Hoffritz. The Slammer's rank made it pretty clear why the disturbance had occurred. "Your boys?" Jolober asked, thumbing toward the tanks sheepishly reversing down the street under the guidance of white-uniformed patrolmen.

"Past three days they have been," Hoffritz agreed. His mouth scrunched again in an angry grimace and he said, "Look, I'm real sorry. I know how dumb that was. I just . . ."

Again, there wasn't anything new to say.

The tank's driver vaulted from her hatch with a suddenness which drew both men's attention. "Corp' ral Days," she said with a salute even more perfunctory than Hoffritz's had been. "Look sir, *I* was drivin', and if there's a problem, it's my problem."

"Daisy—" began Captain Hoffritz.

"There's no problem, Corporal," Jolober said firmly. "Go back to your vehicle. We'll need to move it in a minute or two."

Another helmeted man had popped his head from the turret—surprisingly, because this was a line tank, not a command vehicle with room for several soldiers in the fighting compartment. The driver looked at her captain, then met the worried eyes of the trooper still in the turret. She backed a pace but stayed within earshot.

"Six tanks out of seventeen," Jolober said calmly. Things *were* calm enough now that he was able to follow the cross-talk of his patrolmen, their voices stuttering at low level through the miniature speaker on his epaulet. "You've been seeing some action, then."

"Too bloody right," muttered Corporal Days.

Hoffritz rubbed the back of his neck, lowering his eyes, and said, "Well, running . . . There's four back at Refit deadlined we brought in on transporters, but—"

He looked squarely at Jolober. "But sure we had a tough time. That's why I'm CO and Chester's up there—" he nodded toward the man in the turret "—trying to work company commo without a proper command tank. And I guess I figured—"

Hoffritz might have stopped there, but the port commandant nodded him on.

"—I figured maybe it wouldn't hurt to wake up a few rear-echelon types when we came back here for refit. Sorry, sir."

"There's three other units, including a regiment of the Division Legere, on stand-down here at Paradise Port already, Captain," Jolober said. He nodded toward the soldiers in mottled fatigues who were beginning to reappear on the street. "Not rear-echelon troops, from what I've heard. And they need some relaxation just as badly as your men do."

"Yes sir," Hoffritz agreed, blank-faced. "It was real dumb. I'll sign the report as soon as you make it out."

Jolober shrugged. "There won't be a report, Captain. Repairs to the gate'll go on your regiment's damage account and be deducted from Placida's payment next month." He smiled. "Along with any chairs or glasses you break in the casinos. Now, get your vehicle into the Refit Area where it belongs. And come back and have a good time in Paradise Port. That's what we're here for."

"*Thank* you, sir," said Hoffritz, and relief dropped his age by at least five years. He clasped Jolober's hand and, still holding it, asked, "You've seen service too, haven't you, sir?"

"Fourteen years with Hampton's Legion," Jolober agreed, pleased that Hoffritz had managed not to stare at the stumps before asking the question.

"Hey, good outfit," the younger man said with enthusiasm. "We were with Hampton on Primavera, back, oh, three years ago?"

"Yes, I know," Jolober said. His face was still smiling, and the subject wasn't an emotional one any more. He felt no emotion at all . . . "One of your tanks shot—" his left hand gestured delicately at where his thighs ended "—these off on Primavera."

"Lord," Sergeant Days said distinctly.

Captain Hoffritz looked as if he had been hit with a brick. Then his face regained its animation. "*No* sir," he said. "You're mistaken. On Primavera, we were both working for the Federalists. Hampton was our infantry support."

Not the way General Hampton would have described the chain of command, thought Jolober. His smile became real again. He still felt pride in his old unit—and he could laugh at those outdated feelings in himself.

"Yes, that's right," he said aloud. "There'd been an error in transmitting map coordinates. When a company of these—" he nodded toward the great iridium monster, feeling sweat break out on his forehead and arms as he did so "—attacked my battalion, I jumped up to stop the shooting."

Jolober's smile paled to a frosty shadow of itself. "I was successful," he want on softly, "but not quite as soon as I would've liked."

"Oh, Lord and Martyrs," whispered Hoffritz. His face looked like that of a battle casualty.

"Tad, that was—" Sergeant Days began.

"Shut it *off*, Daisy!" shouted the Slammers' commo man from the turret. Days' face blanked and she nodded.

"Sir, I—" Hoffritz said.

Jolober shook his head to silence the younger man. "In a war," he said, "a lot of people get in the way of rounds. I'm luckier than some. I'm still around to tell about it."

He spoke in the calm, pleasant voice he always used in explaining the—matter—to others. For the length of time he was speaking, he could generally convince even himself.

Clapping Hoffritz on the shoulder—the physical contact brought Jolober back to present reality, reminding him that the tanker was a young man and not a demon hidden behind armor and a tribarrel—the commandant said, "Go on, move your hardware and then see what Port Paradise can show you in the way of a good time."

"Oh, *that* I know already," said Hoffritz with a wicked, man-to-man smile of his own. "When we stood down here three months back, I met a girl named Beth. I'll bet she still remembers me, and the *Lord* knows I remember her."

"Girl?" Jolober repeated. The whole situation had so disoriented him that he let his surprise show.

"Well, you know," said the tanker. "A Doll, I guess. But believe me, Beth's woman enough for *me*."

"Or for anyone," the commandant agreed. "I know just what you mean."

Stecher had returned with the jeep. The street was emptied of all armor except Hoffritz's tank, and that was an object of curiosity rather than concern for the men spilling out the doors of the reopened brothels. Jolober waved toward the patrol vehicle and said, "My men'll guide you out of here, Captain Hoffritz. Enjoy your stay."

The tank driver was already scrambling back into her hatch. She had lowered her helmet shield, so the glimpse Jolober got of her face was an unexpected, light-reflecting bubble.

Maybe Corporal Days had a problem with where the conversation had gone when the two officers started talking like two men. That was a pity, for her and probably for Captain Hoffritz as well. A tank was too small a container to hold emotional trouble among its crew.

But Horace Jolober had his own problems to occupy him as he slid toward his office at a walking pace. He had his meeting with the Facilities Inspection Committee, which wasn't going to go more smoothly because of the interruption.

A plump figure sauntering in the other direction tipped his beret to Jolober as they passed. "Ike," acknowledged the port commandant in a voice as neutral as a gun barrel that doesn't care in the least at whom it's pointed.

Red Ike could pass for human, until the rosy cast of his skin drew attention to the fact that his hands had only three fingers and a thumb. Jolober was surprised to see that Ike was walking across the street toward his own brothel, the China Doll, instead of being inside the building already. That could have meant anything, but the probability was that Red Ike had a tunnel to one of the buildings across the street to serve as a bolthole.

And since all the *real* problems at Paradise Port were a result of the alien who called himself Red Ike, Jolober could easily imagine why the fellow would want to have a bolthole.

*　　*　　*

Jolober had gone down the steps in a smooth undulation. He mounted them in a series of hops, covering two treads between pauses like a weary cricket climbing out of a well.

The chair's powerpack had more than enough charge left to swoop him up to the conference room. It was the man himself who lacked the mental energy now to balance himself on the column of driven air. He felt drained—the tribarrel, the tank . . . the memories of Primavera. If he'd needed to, sure, but . . .

But maybe he was getting old.

The Facilities Inspection Committee—staff members, actually, for three of the most powerful senators in the Placidan legislature—waited for Jolober with doubtful looks. Higgey and Wayne leaned against the conference room window, watching Hoffritz's tank reverse sedately in the street. The woman, Rodall, stood by the stairhead watching the port commandant's return.

"Why don't you have an elevator put in?" she asked. "Or at least a ramp?" Between phrases, Rodall's full features relaxed to the pout that was her normal expression.

Jolober paused beside her, noticing the whisper of air from beneath his plenum chamber was causing her to twist her feet away as if she had stepped into slime. "There aren't elevators everywhere, Mistress," he said. "Most places, there isn't even enough smooth surface to depend on ground effect alone to get you more than forty meters."

He smiled and gestured toward the conference room's window. Visible beyond the China Doll and the other buildings across the street was the reddish-brown expanse of the surrounding landscape: ropes of lava on which only lichen could grow, where a man had to hop and scramble from one ridge to another.

The Placidan government had located Paradise Port in a volcanic wasteland in order to isolate the mercenaries letting off steam between battles with Armstrong, the other power on the planet's sole continent. To a cripple in a chair which depended on wheels or unaided ground effect, the twisting lava would be as sure a barrier as sheer walls.

Jolober didn't say that so long as he could go anywhere other men went, he could pretend he was still a man. If the Placidan civilian could have understood that, she wouldn't have asked why he didn't have ramps put in.

"Well, what *was* that?" demanded Higgey—thin, intense, and already half bald in his early thirties. "Was anyone killed?"

"Nothing serious, Master Higgey," Jolober said as he slid back to the table and lowered himself to his "seated" height. "And no, no one was killed or even injured."

Thank the Lord for his mercy.

"It *looked* serious, Commandant," said the third committee member—Wayne, half again Jolober's age and a retired colonel of the Placidan regular army. "I'm surprised you permit things like that to happen."

Higgey and Rodall were seating themselves. Jolober gestured toward the third chair on the curve of the round table opposite him and said, "Colonel, your, ah—opposite numbers in Armstrong tried to stop those tanks last week with a battalion of armored infantry. They got their butts kicked until they didn't *have* butts any more."

Wayne wasn't sitting down. His face flushed and his short white moustache bristled sharply against his upper lip.

Jolober shrugged and went on in a more conciliatory tone, "Look, sir, units aren't rotated back here unless they've had a hell of a rough time in the line. I've got fifty-six patrolmen with stunners to keep order . . . which we *do*, well enough for the people using Paradise Port. We aren't here to start a major battle of our own. Placida needs these mercenaries and needs them in fighting trim."

"That's a matter of opinion," said the retired officer with his lips pressed together, but at last he sat down.

The direction of sunrise is also a matter of opinion, Jolober thought. It's about as likely to change as Placida is to survive without the mercenaries who had undertaken the war her regular army was losing.

"I requested this meeting—" requested it with the senators themselves, but he hadn't expected them to agree "—in order to discuss just that, the fighting trim of the troops who undergo rest and refit here. So that Placida gets the most value for her, ah, payment."

The committee staff would do, if Jolober could get them to understand. Paradise Port was, after all, a wasteland with a village populated by soldiers who had spent all the recent past killing and watching their friends die. It wasn't the sort of place you'd pick for a senatorial junket.

Higgey leaned forward, clasping his hands on the table top, and said, "Commandant, I'm sure that those—" he waggled a finger disdainfully toward the window "—men out there would be in better physical condition after a week of milk and religious lectures than they will after the regime they choose for themselves. There are elements—"

Wayne nodded in stern agreement, his eyes on Mistress Rodall, whose set face refused to acknowledge either of her fellows while this subject was being discussed.

"—in the electorate and government who would like to try that method, but fortunately reality has kept the idea from being attempted."

Higgey paused, pleased with his forceful delivery and the way his eyes dominated those of the much bigger man across the table. "If you've suddenly got religion, Commandant Jolober," he concluded, "I suggest you resign your current position and join the ministry."

Jolober suppressed his smile. Higgey reminded him of a lap dog, too nervous to remain either still or silent, and too small to be other than ridiculous in its posturing. "My initial message was unclear, madam, gentlemen," he explained, looking around the table. "I'm not suggesting that Placida close the brothels that are part of the recreational facilities here."

His pause was not for effect, but because his mouth had suddenly gone very dry. But it was his duty to—

"I'm recommending that the Dolls be withdrawn from Paradise Port and that the facilities be staffed with human, ah, females."

Colonel Wayne stiffened and paled.

Wayne's anger was now mirrored in the expression on Rodall's face. "Whores," she said. "So that these— *soldiers*—can disgrace and dehumanize real women for their fun."

"And kill them, one assumes," added Higgey with a touch of amusement. "I checked the records, Commandant. There've been seventeen Dolls killed during the months Paradise Port's been in operation. As it is, that's a simple damage assessment, but if they'd been human prostitutes—each one would have meant a manslaughter charge or even murder. People don't cease to have rights when they choose to sell their bodies, you know."

"When they're forced to sell their bodies, you mean," snapped Rodall. She glared at Higgey, who didn't mean anything of the sort.

"Scarcely to the benefit of your precious mercenaries," said Wayne in a distant voice. "Quite apart from the political difficulties it would cause for any senator who recommended the change."

"As a matter of fact," said Higgey, whose natural caution had tightened his visage again, "I thought you were going to use the record of violence here at Paradise Port as a reason for closing the facility.

Though I'll admit that I couldn't imagine anybody selfless enough to do away with his own job."

No, you couldn't, you little weasel, thought Horace Jolober. But politicians have different responsibilities than soldiers, and politicians' flunkies have yet another set of needs and duties.

And none of them are saints. Surely no soldier who does his job is a saint.

"Master Higgey, you've precisely located the problem," Jolober said with a nod of approval. "The violence isn't a result of the soldiers, it's because of the Dolls. It isn't accidental, it's planned. And it's time to stop it."

"It's time for us to leave, you mean," said Higgey as he shoved his chair back. "Resigning still appears to be your best course, Commandant. Though I don't suppose the ministry is the right choice for a new career, after all."

"Master Higgey," Jolober said in the voice he would have used in an argument with a fellow officer, "I know very well that no one is irreplaceable—but *you* know that I am doing as good a job here as anybody you could hire to run Paradise Port. I'm asking you to listen for a few minutes to a proposal that will make the troops you pay incrementally better able to fight for you."

"We've come this far," said Rodall.

"There are no listening devices in my quarters," Jolober explained, unasked. "I doubt that any real-time commo link out of Paradise Port is free of interception."

He didn't add that time he spent away from *his* duties was more of a risk to Placida than pulling these three out of their offices and expensive lunches could be. The tanks roaring down the street should have proved *that* even to the committee staffers.

Jolober paused, pressing his fingertips to his eyebrows in a habitual trick to help him marshal his thoughts while the others stared at him. "Mistress, masters," he said calmly after a moment, "the intention was that Paradise Port and similar facilities be staffed by independent contractors from off-planet."

"Which is where they'll return as soon as the war's over," agreed Colonel Wayne with satisfaction. "Or as soon as they put a toe wrong, any one of them."

"The war's bad enough as it is," said Rodall. "Building up Placida's stock of *that* sort of person would make peace hideous as well."

"Yes ma'am, I understand," said the port commandant. There were a lot of "that sort of person" in Placida just now, including all the mercenaries in the line—and Horace Jolober back here. "But what you have in Port Paradise isn't a group of entrepreneurs, it's a corporation—a monarchy, almost—subservient to an alien called Red Ike."

"Nonsense," said Wayne.

"We don't permit that," said Rodall.

"Red Ike owns a single unit here," said Higgey. "The China Doll. Which is all he *can* own by law, to prevent just the sort of situation you're describing."

"Red Ike provides all the Dolls," Jolober stated flatly. "Whoever owns them on paper, they're his. And *everything* here is his because he controls the Dolls."

"Well . . ." said Rodall. She was beginning to blush.

"There's no actual proof," Colonel Wayne said, shifting his eyes toward a corner of walls and ceiling. "Though I suppose the physical traits are indicative . . ."

"The government has decided it isn't in the best interests of Placida to pierce the corporate veil in this instance," said Higgey in a thin voice. "The androids in question are shipped here from a variety of off-planet suppliers."

The balding Placidan paused and added, with a tone of absolute finality, "If the question were mine to decide—which it isn't—I would recommend searching for a new port commandant rather than trying to prove the falsity of a state of affairs beneficial to us, to Placida."

"I think that really must be the final word on the subject, Commandant Jolober," Rodall agreed.

Jolober thought she sounded regretful, but the emotion was too faint for him to be sure. The three Placidans were getting up, and he had failed.

He'd failed even before the staff members arrived, because it was now quite obvious that they'd decided their course of action before the meeting. They—and their elected superiors—would rather have dismissed Jolober's arguments.

But if the arguments proved to be well founded, they would dismiss the port commandant, if necessary to end the discussion.

"I suppose I should be flattered," Jolober said as hydraulics lifted him in the saddle and pressure of his stump on the throttle let him rotate his chair away from the table. "That you came all this way to silence me instead of refusing me a meeting."

"You might recall," said Higgey, pausing at the doorway. His look was meant to be threatening, but the port commandant's bulk and dour anger cooled the Placidan's face as soon as their eyes met. "That is, we're in the middle of a war, and the definition of treason can be a little loose in such times. While you're not technically a Placidan citizen, Commandant, you—would be well advised to avoid activities which oppose the conduct of war as the government has determined to conduct it."

He stepped out of the conference room. Rodall had left ahead of him.

"Don't take it too hard, young man," said Colonel Wayne when he and Jolober were alone. "You mercenaries, you can do a lot of things the quick and easy way. It's different when you represent a government and need to consider political implications."

"I'd never understood there were negative implications, Colonel," Jolober said with the slow, careful enunciation which proved he was controlling himself rigidly, "in treating your employees fairly. Even the mercenary soldiers whom you employ."

Wayne's jaw lifted. "I beg your pardon, Commandant," he snapped. "I don't see anyone holding guns to the heads of poor innocents, forcing them to whore and gamble."

He strode to the door, his back parade-ground straight. At the door he turned precisely and delivered the broadside he had held to that point. "Besides, Commandant—if the Dolls are as dangerous to health and welfare as you say, why are you living with one yourself?"

Wayne didn't expect an answer, but what he saw in Horace Jolober's eyes suggested that his words might bring a physical reaction that he hadn't counted on. He skipped into the hall with a startled sound, banging the door behind him.

The door connecting the conference room to the port commandant's personal suite opened softly. Jolober did not look around.

Vicki put her long, slim arms around him from behind. Jolober spun, then cut power to his fans and settled his chair firmly onto the floor. He and Vicki clung to one another, legless man and Doll whose ruddy skin and beauty marked her as inhuman.

They were both crying.

Someone from Jolober's staff would poke his head into the conference room shortly to ask if the meeting was over and if the commandant wanted nonemergency calls routed through again.

The meeting was certainly over . . . but Horace Jolober had an emergency of his own. He swallowed, keyed his implant, and said brusquely, "I'm out of action till I tell you different. Unless it's another Class A flap."

The kid at the commo desk stuttered a "Yessir"

that was a syllable longer than Jolober wanted to hear. Vicki straightened, wearing a bright smile beneath the tear streaks, but the big human gathered her to his chest again and brought up the power of his fans.

Together, like a man carrying a moderate-sized woman, the couple slid around the conference table to the door of the private suite. The chair's drive units were overbuilt because men are overbuilt, capable of putting out huge bursts of hysterical strength.

Drive fans and power packs don't have hormones, so Jolober had specified—and paid for—components that would handle double the hundred kilos of his own mass, the hundred kilos left after the tribarrel had chewed him. The only problem with carrying Vicki to bed was one of balance, and the Doll remained still in his arms.

Perfectly still, as she was perfect in all the things she did.

"I'm not trying to get rid of you, darling," Jolober said as he grounded his chair.

"It's all right," Vicki whispered. "I'll go now if you like. It's all right."

She placed her fingertips on Jolober's shoulders and lifted herself by those fulcrums off his lap and onto the bed, her toes curled beneath her buttocks. A human gymnast could have done as well—but no better.

"What I *want*," Jolober said forcefully as he lifted himself out of the saddle, using the chair's handgrips, "is to do my job. And when I've done it, I'll buy you from Red Ike for whatever price he chooses to ask."

He swung himself to the bed. His arms had always been long—and strong. Now he knew that he must look like a gorilla when he got on or off his chair . . . and when the third woman he was with after the amputation giggled at him, he began to consider suicide as an alternative to sex.

Then he took the job on Placida and met Vicki.

Her tears had dried, so both of them could pretend they hadn't poured out moments before. She smiled shyly and touched the high collar of her dress, drawing her fingertip down a centimeter and opening the garment by that amount.

Vicki wasn't Jolober's ideal of beauty—wasn't what he'd *thought* his ideal was, at any rate. Big blondes, he would have said. A woman as tall as he was, with hair the color of bleached straw hanging to the middle of her back.

Vicki scarcely came up to the top of Jolober's breastbone when he was standing—at standing height in his chair—and her hair was a black fluff that was as short as a soldier would cut it to fit comfortably under a helmet. She looked buxom, but her breasts were fairly flat against her broad, powerfully muscled chest.

Jolober put his index finger against hers on the collar and slid down the touch-sensitive strip that opened the fabric. Vicki's body was without blemish or pubic hair. She was so firm that nothing sagged or flattened when her dress and the supports of memory plastic woven into it dropped away.

She shrugged her arms out of the straps and let the garment spill as a pool of sparkling shadow on the counterpane as she reached toward her lover.

Jolober, lying on his side, touched the collar of his uniform jacket.

"No need," Vicki said blocking his hand with one of hers and opening his trouser fly with the other. "Come," she added, rolling onto her back and drawing him toward her.

"But the—" Jolober murmured in surprise, leaning forward in obedience to her touch and demand. The metallic braid and medals on his stiff-fronted tunic had sharp corners to prod the Doll beneath him whether he wished or not.

"Come," she repeated. "This time."

Horace Jolober wasn't introspective enough to understand why his mistress wanted the rough punishment of his uniform. He simply obeyed.

Vicki toyed with his garments after they had finished and lay on the bed, their arms crossing. She had a trick of folding back her lower legs so that they vanished whenever she sat or reclined in the port commandant's presence.

Her fingers tweaked the back of Jolober's waistband and emerged with the hidden knife, the only weapon he carried.

"I'm at your mercy," he said, smiling. He mimed as much of a hands-up posture as he could with his right elbow supporting his torso on the mattress. "Have your way with me."

In Vicki's hand, the knife was a harmless cylinder of plastic—a weapon only to the extent that the butt of the short tube could harden a punch. The knife was of memory plastic whose normal state was a harmless block. No one who took it away from Jolober in a struggle would find it of any use as a weapon.

Only when squeezed after being cued by the pore pattern of Horace Jolober's right hand would it—

The plastic cylinder shrank in Vicki's hand, sprouting a double-edged 15-cm blade.

"*Via!*" swore Jolober. Reflex betrayed him into thinking that he had legs. He jerked upright and started to topple off the bed because the weight of his calves and feet wasn't there to balance the motion.

Vicki caught him with both arms and drew him to her. The blade collapsed into the handle when she dropped it, so that it bounced as a harmless cylinder on the counterpane between them.

"My love, I'm *sorry*," the Doll blurted fearfully. "I didn't mean—"

"No, no," Jolober said, settled now on his thighs and buttocks so that he could hug Vicki fiercely. His eyes peered secretively over her shoulder, searching for the knife that had startled him so badly. "I was surprised that it . . . How *did* you get the blade to open, dearest? It's fine, it's nothing you did wrong, but I didn't expect that, is all."

They swung apart. The mattress was a firm one, but still a bad surface for this kind of conversation. The bedclothes rumpled beneath Jolober's heavy body and almost concealed the knife in a fold of cloth. He found it, raised it with his fingertips, and handed it to Vicki. "Please do that again," he said calmly. "Extend the blade."

Sweat was evaporating from the base of Jolober's spine, where the impermeable knife usually covered the skin.

Vicki took the weapon. She was so doubtful that her face showed no expression at all. Her fingers, short but perfectly formed, gripped the baton as if it were a knife hilt—and it became one. The blade formed with avalanche swiftness, darkly translucent and patterned with veins of stress. The plastic would not take a wire edge, but it could carve a roast or, with Jolober's strength behind it, ram twenty millimeters deep into hardwood.

"Like this?" Vicki asked softly. "Just squeeze it and . . . ?"

Jolober put his hand over the Doll's and lifted the knife away between thumb and forefinger. When she loosed the hilt, the knife collapsed again into a short baton.

He squeezed—extended the blade—released it again—and slipped the knife back into its concealed sheath.

"You see, darling," Jolober said, "the plastic's been keyed to *my* body. Nobody else should be able to get the blade to form."

"I'd never use it against you," Vicki said. Her face was calm, and there was no defensiveness in her simple response.

Jolober smiled. "Of course, dearest; but there was

a manufacturing flaw or you wouldn't be able to do that."

Vicki leaned over and kissed the port commandant's lips, then bent liquidly and kissed him again. "I told you," she said as she straightened with a grin. "I'm a part of you."

"And believe me," said Jolober, rolling onto his back to cinch up his short-legged trousers, "You're not a part of me I intend to lose."

He rocked upright and gripped the handles of his chair.

Vicki slipped off the bed and braced the little vehicle with a hand on the saddle and the edge of one foot on the skirt. The help wasn't necessary—the chair's weight anchored it satisfactorily, so long as Jolober mounted swiftly and smoothly. But it *was* helpful, and it was the sort of personal attention that was as important as sex in convincing Horace Jolober that someone really cared—*could* care—for him.

"You'll do your duty, though," Vicki said. "And I wouldn't want you not to."

Jolober laughed as he settled himself and switched on his fans. He felt enormous relief now that he had proved beyond doubt—he was sure of that—how much he loved Vicki. He'd calmed her down, and that meant he was calm again too.

"Sure I'll do my job," he said as he smiled at the Doll. "That doesn't mean you and *me*'ll have a problem. Wait and see."

Vicki smiled also, but she shook her head in what Jolober thought was amused resignation. Her hairless body was too perfect to be flesh, and the skin's red pigment gave the Doll the look of a statue in blushing marble.

"Via, but you're lovely," Jolober murmured as the realization struck him anew.

"Come back soon," she said easily.

"Soon as I can," the commandant agreed as he

lifted his chair and turned toward the door. "But like you say, I've got a job to do."

If the government of Placida wouldn't give him the support he needed, by the Lord! he'd work through the mercenaries themselves.

Though his belly went cold and his stumps tingled as he realized he would again be approaching the tanks which had crippled him.

The street had the sharp edge which invariably marked it immediately after a unit rotated to Paradise Port out of combat. The troops weren't looking for sex or intoxicants—though most of them would have claimed they were.

They were looking for life. Paradise Port offered them things they thought equaled life, and the contrast between reality and hope led to anger and black despair. Only after a few days of stunning themselves with the offered pleasures did the soldiers on leave recognize another contrast: Paradise Port might not be all they'd hoped, but it was a lot better than the muck and ravening hell of combat.

Jolober slid down the street at a walking pace. Some of the soldiers on the pavement with him offered ragged salutes to the commandant's glittering uniform. He returned them sharply, a habit he had ingrained in himself after he took charge here.

Mercenary units didn't put much emphasis on saluting and similar rear-echelon forms of discipline. An officer with the reputation of being a tight-assed martinet in bivouac was likely to get hit from behind the next time he led his troops into combat.

There were regular armies on most planets—Colonel Wayne was an example—to whom actual fighting was an aberration. Economics or a simple desire for action led many planetary soldiers into mercenary units . . . where the old habits of saluting and snapping to attention surfaced when the men were drunk and depressed.

Hampton's Legion hadn't been any more interested in saluting than the Slammers were. Jolober had sharpened his technique here because it helped a few of the men he served feel more at home—when they were very far from home.

A patrol jeep passed, idling slowly through the pedestrians. Sergeant Stecher waved, somewhat uncertainly.

Jolober waved back, smiling toward his subordinate but angry at himself. He keyed his implant and said "Central, I'm back in business now, but I'm headed for the Refit Area to see Captain van Zuyle. Let anything wait that can till I'm back."

He should have cleared with his switchboard as soon as he'd . . . calmed Vicki down. Here there'd been a crisis, and as soon as it was over he'd disappeared. Must've made his patrolmen very cursed nervous, and it was sheer sloppiness that he'd let the situation go on beyond what it had to. It was his job to make things simple for the people in Paradise Port, both his staff and the port's clientele.

Maybe even for the owners of the brothels: but it was going to have to be simple on Horace Jolober's terms.

At the gate, a tank was helping the crew repairing damage. The men wore khaki coveralls—Slammers rushed from the Refit Area as soon as van Zuyle, the officer in charge there, heard what had happened. The faster you hid the evidence of a problem, the easier it was to claim the problem had never existed.

And it was to everybody's advantage that problems never exist.

Paradise Port was surrounded with a high barrier of woven plastic to keep soldiers who were drunk out of their minds from crawling into the volcanic wasteland and hurting themselves. The fence was tougher than it looked—it looked as insubstantial as moonbeams—but it had never been intended to stop vehicles.

The gate to the bivouac areas outside Paradise Port had a sturdy framework and hung between posts of solid steel. The lead tank had been wide enough to snap both gateposts off at the ground. The gate, framework and webbing, was strewn in fragments for a hundred meters along the course it had been dragged between the pavement and the tank's skirt.

As Jolober approached, he felt his self-image shrink by comparison to surroundings which included a hundred and seventy tonne fighting vehicle. The tank was backed against one edge of the gateway.

With a huge *clang!* the vehicle set another steel post, blasting it home with the apparatus used in combat to punch explosive charges into deep bunkers. The ram vaporized osmium wire with a jolt of high voltage, transmitting the shock waves to the piston head through a column of fluid. It banged home the replacement post without difficulty, even though the "ground" was a sheet of volcanic rock.

The pavement rippled beneath Jolober, and the undamped harmonics of the quivering post were a scream that could be heard for kilometers. Jolober pretended it didn't affect him as he moved past the tank. He was praying that the driver was watching his side screens—or listening to a ground guide—as the tank trembled away from the task it had completed.

One of the Slammers' non-coms gestured reassuringly toward Jolober. His lips moved as he talked into his commo helmet. The port commandant could hear nothing over the howl of the drive fans and prolonged grace notes from the vibrating post, but the tank halted where it was until he had moved past it.

A glance over his shoulder showed Jolober the tank backing into position to set the other post. It looked like a great tortoise, ancient and implacable, maneuvering to lay a clutch of eggs.

Paradise Port was for pleasure only. The barracks

housing the soldiers and the sheds to store and repair their equipment were located outside the fenced perimeter. The buildings were pre-fabs extruded from a dun plastic less colorful than the ruddy lava fields on which they were set.

The bivouac site occupied by Hammer's line companies in rotation was unusual in that the large leveled area contained only four barracks buildings and a pair of broad repair sheds. Parked vehicles filled the remainder of the space.

At the entrance to the bivouac area waited a guard shack. The soldier who stepped from it wore body armor over her khakis. Her submachine gun was slung, but her tone was businesslike as she said, "Commandant Jolober? Captain van Zuyle's on his way to meet you right now."

Hold right here till you're invited in, Jolober translated mentally with a frown.

But he couldn't blame the Slammers' officer for wanting to assert his authority *here* over that of Horace Jolober, whose writ ran only to the perimeter of Paradise Port. Van Zuyle just wanted to prove that his troopers would be punished only with his assent—or by agreement reached with authorities higher than the port commandant.

There was a flagpole attached to a gable of one of the barracks. A tall officer strode from the door at that end and hopped into the driver's seat of the jeep parked there. Another khaki-clad soldier stuck her head out the door and called something, but the officer pretended not to hear. He spun his vehicle in an angry circle, rubbing its low-side skirts, and gunned it toward the entrance.

Jolober had met van Zuyle only once. The most memorable thing about the Slammers' officer was his anger—caused by fate, but directed at whatever was nearest to hand. He'd been leading a company of combat cars when the blower ahead of his took a direct hit.

If van Zuyle'd had his face shield down—but he hadn't, because the shield made him, made most troopers, feel as though they'd stuck their head in a bucket. That dissociation, mental rather than sensory, could get you killed in combat.

The shield would have darkened instantly to block the sleet of actinics from the exploding combat car. Without its protection . . . well, the surgeons could rebuild his face, with only a slight stiffness to betray the injuries. Van Zuyle could even see—by daylight or under strong illumination.

There just wasn't any way he'd ever be fit to lead a line unit again—and he was very angry about it.

Commandant Horace Jolober could understand how van Zuyle felt—better, perhaps, than anyone else on the planet could. It didn't make his own job easier, though.

"A pleasure to see you again, Commandant," van Zuyle lied brusquely as he skidded the jeep to a halt, passenger seat beside Jolober. "If you—"

Jolober smiled grimly as the Slammers officer saw—and remembered—that the port commandant was legless and couldn't seat himself in a jeep on his air-cushion chair.

"No problem," said Jolober, gripping the jeep's side and the seat back. He lifted himself aboard the larger vehicle with an athletic twist that settled him facing front.

Of course, the maneuver was easier than it would have been if his legs were there to get in the way.

"Ah, your—" van Zuyle said, pointing toward the chair. Close up, Jolober could see a line of demarcation in his scalp. The implanted hair at the front had aged less than the gray-speckled portion which hadn't been replaced.

"No problem, Captain," Jolober repeated. He anchored his left arm around the driver's seat, gripped one of his chair's handles with the right hand, and jerked the chair into the bench seat in the rear of the open vehicle.

The jeep lurched: the air-cushion chair weighed almost as much as Jolober did without it, and he was a big man. "You learn tricks when you have to," he said evenly as he met the eyes of the Slammers officer.

And your arms get very strong when they do a lot of the work your legs used to—but he didn't say that.

"My office?" van Zuyle asked sharply.

"Is that as busy as it looks?" Jolober replied, nodding toward the door where a soldier still waited impatiently for van Zuyle to return.

"Commandant, I've had a tank company come in shot to *hell*," van Zuyle said in a voice that built toward fury. "Three vehicles are combat lossed and have to be stripped—*and* the other vehicles need more than routine maintenance—*and* half the personnel are on medic's release. Or dead. I'm trying to run a refit area with what's left, my staff of twenty-three, and the trainee replacements Central sent over who haven't *ridden* in a panzer, much less pulled maintenance on one. And you ask if I've got time to waste on you?"

"No, Captain, I didn't ask that," Jolober said with the threatening lack of emotion which came naturally to a man who had all his life been bigger and stronger than most of those around him. "Find a spot where we won't be disturbed, and we'll park there."

When the Slammers officer frowned, Jolober added, "I'm not here about Captain Hoffritz, Captain."

"Yeah," sighed van Zuyle as he lifted the jeep and steered it sedately toward a niche formed between the iridium carcases of a pair of tanks. "We're repairing things right now—" he thumbed in the direction of the gate "—and any other costs'll go on the damage chit; but I guess I owe you an apology besides."

"Life's a dangerous place," Jolober said easily. Van Zuyle wasn't stupid. He'd modified his behavior as soon as he was reminded of the incident an hour before—and the leverage it gave the port commandant if he wanted to push it.

Van Zuyle halted them in the gray shade that brought sweat to Jolober's forehead. The tanks smelled of hot metal because some of their vaporized armor had settled back onto the hulls as fine dust. Slight breezes shifted it to the nostrils of the men nearby, a memory of the blasts in which it had formed.

Plastics had burned also, leaving varied pungencies which could not conceal the odor of cooked human flesh.

The other smells of destruction were unpleasant. That last brought Jolober memories of his legs exploding in brilliant coruscance. His body tingled and sweated, and his mouth said to the Slammers officer, "Your men are being cheated and misused every time they come to Paradise Port, Captain. For political reasons, my superiors won't let me make the necessary changes. If the mercenary units serviced by Paradise Port unite and demand the changes, the government will be forced into the proper decision."

"Seems to me," said van Zuyle with his perfectly-curved eyebrows narrowing, "that somebody could claim you were acting against your employers just now."

"Placida hired me to run a liberty port," said Jolober evenly. He was being accused of the worst crime a mercenary could commit: conduct that would allow his employers to forfeit his unit's bond and brand them forever as unemployable contract-breakers.

Jolober no longer *was* a mercenary in that sense; but he understood van Zuyle's idiom, and it was in that idiom that he continued, "Placida wants and needs the troops she hires to be sent back into action in the best shape possible. Her *survival* depends on it. If I let Red Ike run this place to his benefit and not to Placida's, then I'm not doing my job."

"All right," said van Zuyle. "What's Ike got on?"

A truck, swaying with its load of cheering troopers, pulled past on its way to the gate of Paradise Port. The man in the passenger's seat of the cab was Tad Hoffritz, his face a knife-edge of expectation.

"Sure, they need refit as bad as the hardware does," muttered van Zuyle as he watched the soldiers on leave with longing eyes. "Three days straight leave, half days after that when they've pulled their duty. But Via! I could use 'em here, especially with the tanks that're such a bitch if you're not used to crawling around in 'em."

His face hardened again. "Go on," he sad, angry that Jolober knew how much he wanted to be one of the men on that truck instead of having to run a rear-echelon installation.

"Red Ike owns the Dolls like so many shots of liquor," Jolober said. He never wanted a combat job again—the thought terrified him, the noise and flash and the smell of his body burning. "He's using them to strip your men, everybody's men, in the shortest possible time," he continued in a voice out of a universe distant from his mind. "The games are honest—that's my job—but the men play when they're stoned, and they play with a Doll on their arm begging them to go on until they've got nothing left. How many of those boys—" he gestured to where the truck, now long past, had been "—are going to last three days?"

"We give 'em advances when they're tapped out," said van Zuyle with a different kind of frown. "Enough to last their half days—*if* they're getting their jobs done here. Works out pretty good.

"As a matter of fact," he went on, "the whole business works out pretty good. I never saw a soldier's dive without shills and B-girls. Don't guess you ever did either, Commandant. Maybe they're better at it, the Dolls, but all that means is that I get my labor force back quicker—and Hammer gets his tanks back in line with that much fewer problems."

"The Dolls—" Jolober began.

"The Dolls are clean," shouted van Zuyle in a voice like edged steel. "They give full value for what you pay 'em. And I've never had a Doll knife one of my guys—which is a curst sight better'n anyplace I been staffed with human whores!"

"No," said Jolober, his strength a bulwark against the Slammer's anger. "But you've had your men knife or strangle Dolls, haven't you? All the units here've had incidents of that sort. Do you think it's chance?"

Van Zuyle blinked. "I think it's a cost of doing business," he said, speaking mildly because the question had surprised him.

"No," Jolober retorted. "It's a major profit center for Red Ike. The Dolls don't just drop soldiers when they've stripped them. They humiliate the men, taunt them . . . and when one of these kids breaks and chokes the life out of the bitch who's goading him, Red Ike pockets the damage assessment. And it comes out of money Placida would otherwise have paid Hammer's Slammers."

The Slammers officer began to laugh. It was Jolober's turn to blink in surprise.

"Sure," van Zuyle said, "androids like that cost a lot more'n gateposts or a few meters of fencing, you bet."

"He's the only source," said Jolober tautly. "Nobody knows where the Dolls come from—or where Ike does."

"Then nobody can argue the price isn't fair, can they?" van Zuyle gibed. "And you know what, Commandant? Take a look at this tank right here."

He pointed to one of the vehicles beside them. It was a command tank, probably the one in which Hoffritz's predecessor had ridden before it was hit by powerguns heavy enough to pierce its armor.

The first round, centered on the hull's broadside, had put the unit out of action and killed everyone aboard. The jet of energy had ignited everything flammable within the fighting compartment in an explosion which blew the hatches open. The enemy had hit the iridium carcase at least three times more, cratering the turret and holing the engine compartment.

"We couldn't replace this for the cost of twenty Dolls," van Zuyle continued. "And we're going to have to, you know, because she's a total loss. All I can do is strip her for salvage . . . and clean up as best I can for the crew, so we can say we had something to bury."

His too-pale, too-angry eyes glared at Jolober. "Don't talk to me about the cost of Dolls, Commandant. They're cheap at the price. I'll drive you back to the gate."

"You may not care about the dollar cost," said Jolober in a voice that thundered over the jeep's drive fans. "But what about the men you're sending back into line thinking they've killed somebody they loved—or that they *should*'ve killed her?"

"Commandant, that's one I can't quantify," the Slammers officer said. The fans' keening lowered as the blades bit the air at a steeper angle and began to thrust the vehicle out of the bivouac area. "First time a trooper kills a human here, that I *can* quantify: we lose him. If there's a bigger problem and the Bonding Authority decides to call it mutiny, then we lost a lot more than that.

"And I tell you, buddy," van Zuyle added with a one-armed gesture toward the wrecked vehicles now behind them. "We've lost too fucking much already on this contract."

The jeep howled past the guard at the bivouac entrance. Wind noise formed a deliberate damper on Jolober's attempts to continue the discussion. "Will you forward my request to speak to Colonel Hammer?" he shouted. "I can't get through to him myself."

The tank had left the gate area. Men in khaki, watched by Jolober's staff in white uniforms, had almost completed their task of restringing the perimeter fence. Van Zuyle throttled back, permitting the jeep to glide to a graceful halt three meters short of the workmen.

"The colonel's busy, Commandant," he said flatly. "And from now on, I hope you'll remember that *I* am too."

Jolober lifted his chair from the back seat. "I'm going to win this, Captain," he said. "I'm going to do my job whether or not I get any support."

The smile he gave van Zuyle rekindled the respect in the tanker's pale eyes.

There were elements of four other mercenary units bivouacked outside Paradise Port at the moment. Jolober could have visited them in turn—to be received with more or less civility, and certainly no more support than the Slammers officer had offered.

A demand for change by the mercenaries in Placidan service had to be just that: a demand by *all* the mercenaries. Hammer's Slammers were the highest-paid troops here, and by that standard—any other criterion would start a brawl—the premier unit. If the Slammers refused Jolober, none of the others would back him.

The trouble with reform is that in the short run, it causes more problems than continuing along the bad old ways. Troops in a combat zone, who know that each next instant may be their last, are more to be forgiven for short-term thinking than, say, politicians; but the pattern is part of the human condition.

Besides, nobody but Horace Jolober seemed to think there was anything to reform.

Jolober moved in a waking dream while his mind shuttled through causes and options. His data were interspersed with memories of Vicki smiling up at him from the bed and of his own severed leg toppling in blue-green silhouette. He shook his head violently to clear the images and found himself on the street outside the Port offices.

His stump throttled back the fans reflexively; but when Jolober's conscious mind made its decision, he turned away from the office building and headed for the garish façade of the China Doll across the way.

Rainbow pastels lifted slowly over the front of the building, the gradation so subtle that close up it was impossible to tell where one band ended and the next began. At random intervals of from thirty seconds to a minute, the gentle hues were replaced by glaring, supersaturated colors separated by dazzling blue-white lines.

None of the brothels in Paradise Port were sedately decorated, but the China Doll stood out against the competition.

As Jolober approached, a soldier was leaving and three more—one a woman—were in the queue to enter. A conveyor carried those wishing to exit, separated from one another by solid panels. The panels withdrew sideways into the wall as each client reached the street—but there was always another panel in place behind to prevent anyone from bolting into the building without being searched at the proper entrance.

All of the buildings in Paradise Port were designed the same way, with security as unobtrusive as it could be while remaining uncompromised. The entryways were three-meter funnels narrowing in a series of gaudy corbelled arches. Attendants—humans everywhere but in the China Doll—waited at the narrow end. They smiled as the customers passed—but anyone whom the detection devices in the archway said was armed was stopped right there.

The first two soldiers ahead of Jolober went through without incident. The third was a short man wearing lieutenant's pips and the uniform of Division Legere. His broad shoulders and chest narrowed to his waist as abruptly as those of a bulldog, and it was with a bulldog's fierce intransigence that he braced himself against the two attendants who confronted him.

"I am Lieutenant Alexis Condorcet!" he announced as though he were saying "major general." "What do you mean by hindering me?"

The attendants in the China Doll were Droids, figures with smoothly masculine features and the same blushing complexion which set Red Ike and the Dolls apart from the humans with whom they mingled.

They were not male—Jolober had seen the total sexlessness of an android whose tights had ripped as he quelled a brawl. Their bodies and voices were indistinguishable from one to another, and there could be no doubt that they were androids, artificial constructions whose existence proved that the Dolls could be artificial, too.

Though in his heart, Horace Jolober had never been willing to believe the Dolls were not truly alive. Not since Red Ike had introduced him to Vicki.

"Could you check the right-hand pocket of your blouse, Lieutenant Condorcet?" one of the Droids said.

"I'm not carrying a weapon!" Condorcet snapped. His hand hesitated, but it dived into the indicated pocket when an attendant started to reach toward it.

Jolober was ready to react, either by grabbing Condorcet's wrist from behind or by knocking him down with the chair. He didn't have time for any emotion, not even fear.

It was the same set of instincts that had thrown him to his feet for the last time, to wave off the attacking tanks.

Condorcet's hand came out with a roll of coins between two fingers. In a voice that slipped between injured and minatory he said, "Can't a man bring money into the Doll, then? Will you have me take my business elsewhere, then?"

"Your money's very welcome, sir," said the attendant who was reaching forward. His thumb and three fingers shifted in a sleight of hand; they reappeared holding a gold-striped China Doll chip worth easily twice the value of the rolled coins. "But let us hold these till you return. We'll be glad to give them back then without exchange."

The motion which left Condorcet holding the chip and transferred the roll to the attendant was also magically smooth.

The close-coupled soldier tensed for a moment as if he'd make an issue of it; but the Droids were as strong as they were polished, and there was no percentage in being humiliated.

"We'll see about that," said Condorcet loudly. He strutted past the attendants who parted for him like water before the blunt prow of a barge.

"Good afternoon, Port Commandant Jolober," said one of the Droids as they both bowed. "A pleasure to serve you again."

"A pleasure to feel wanted," said Jolober with an ironic nod of his own. He glided into the main hall of the China Doll.

The room's high ceiling was suffused with clear light which mimicked daytime outside. The hall buzzed with excited sounds even when the floor carried only a handful of customers. Jolober hadn't decided whether the space was designed to give multiple echo effects or if instead Red Ike augmented the hum with concealed sonic transponders.

Whatever it was, the technique made the blood of even the port commandant quicken when he stepped into the China Doll.

There were a score of gaming stations in the main hall, but they provided an almost infinite variety of ways to lose money. A roulette station could be collapsed into a skat table in less than a minute if a squad of drunken Frieslanders demanded it. The displaced roulette players could be accommodated at the next station over, where until then a Droid had been dealing desultory hands of fan-tan.

Whatever the game was, it was fair. Every hand, every throw, every pot was recorded and processed in the office of the port commandant. None of the facility owners doubted that a skewed result would be noticed at once by the computers, or that a result skewed in favor of the house would mean that Horace Jolober would weld their doors shut and ship all their staff off-planet.

Besides, they knew as Jolober did that honest games would get them most of the available money anyhow, so long as the Dolls were there to caress the winners to greater risks.

At the end of Paradise Port farthest from the gate were two establishments which specialized in the leftovers. They were staffed by human males, and their atmosphere was as brightly efficient as men could make it.

But no one whose psyche allowed a choice picked a human companion over a Doll.

The main hall was busy with drab uniforms, Droids neatly garbed in blue and white, and the stunningly gorgeous outfits of the Dolls. There was a regular movement of Dolls and uniforms toward the door on a room-width landing three steps up at the back of the hall. Generally the rooms beyond were occupied by couples, but much larger gatherings were possible if a soldier had money and the perceived need.

The curved doors of the elevator beside the front entrance opened even as Jolober turned to look at them. Red Ike stepped out with a smile and a Doll on either arm.

"Always a pleasure to see you, Commandant," Red Ike said in a tone as sincere as the Dolls were human. "Shana," he added to the red-haired Doll. "Susan—" he nodded toward the blond. "Meet Commandant Jolober, the man who keeps us all safe."

The redhead giggled and slipped from Ike's arm to Jolober's. The slim blond gave him a smile that would have been demure except for the fabric of her tank-top. It acted as a polarizing filter, so that when she swayed her bare torso flashed toward the port commandant.

"But come on upstairs, Commandant," Red Ike continued, stepping backwards into the elevator and motioning Jolober to follow him. "Unless your business is here—or in back?" He cocked an almost-human eyebrow toward the door in the rear while his face waited with a look of amused tolerance.

"We can go upstairs," said Jolober grimly. "It won't take long." His air cushion slid him forward. Spilling air tickled Shana's feet as she pranced along beside him; she giggled again.

There must be men who found that sort of girlish idiocy erotic or Red Ike wouldn't keep the Doll in his stock.

The elevator shaft was opaque and looked it from outside the car. The car's interior was a visiscreen fed by receptors on the shaft's exterior. On one side of the slowly rising car, Jolober could watch the games in the main hall as clearly as if he were hanging in the air. On the other, they lifted above the street with a perfect view of its traffic and the port offices—even though a concrete wall and the shaft's iridium armor blocked the view in fact.

The elevator switch was a small plate which hung in the "air" that was really the side of the car. Red Ike had toggled it up. Down would have taken the car—probably much faster—to the tunnel beneath the street, the escape route which Jolober had suspected even before the smiling alien had used it this afternoon.

But there was a second unobtrusive control beside the first. The blond Doll leaned past Jolober with a smile and touched it.

The view of the street disappeared. Those in the car had a crystalline view of the activities in back of the China Doll as if no walls or ceilings separated the bedrooms. Jolober met—or thought he met—the eyes of Tad Hoffritz, straining upward beneath a black-haired Doll.

"*Via!*" Jolober swore and slapped the toggle hard enough to feel the solidity of the elevator car.

"Susan, Susan," Red Ike chided with a grin. "She will have her little joke, you see, Commandant."

The blond made a moue, then winked at Jolober.

Above the main hall was Red Ike's office, furnished in minimalist luxury. Jolober found nothing attractive in the sight of chair seats and a broad onyx desk top hanging in the air, but the decor did show off the view. Like the elevator, the office walls and ceiling were covered by pass-through visiscreens.

The russet wasteland, blotched but not relieved by patterns of lichen, looked even more dismal from twenty meters up than it did from Jolober's living quarters.

Though the view appeared to be a panorama, there was no sign of where the owner himself lived. The back of the office was an interior wall, and the vista over the worms and pillows of lava was transmitted through not only the wall but the complex of rooms that was Red Ike's home.

On the roof beside the elevator tower was an aircar sheltered behind the concrete coping. Like the owners of all the other facilities comprising Paradise Port, Red Ike wanted the option of getting out *fast*, even if the elevator to his tunnel bolthole was blocked.

Horace Jolober had fantasies in which he watched the stocky humanoid scramble into his vehicle and accelerate away, vanishing forever as a fleck against the milky sky.

"I've been meaning to call on you for some time, Commandant," Red Ike said as he walked with quick little steps to his desk. "I thought perhaps you might like a replacement for Vicki. As you know, any little way in which I can make your task easier . . .?"

Shana giggled. Susan smiled slowly and, turning at a precisely-calculated angle, bared breasts that were much fuller than they appeared beneath her loose garment.

Jolober felt momentary desire, then fierce anger in

reaction. His hands clenched on the chair handles, restraining his violent urge to hurl both Dolls into the invisible walls.

Red Ike sat behind the desk top. The thin shell of his chair rocked on invisible gimbals, tilting him to a comfortable angle that was not quite disrespectful of his visitor.

"Commandant," he said with none of the earlier hinted mockery, "you and I really ought to cooperate, you know. We need each other, and Placida needs us both."

"And the soldiers we're here for?" Jolober asked softly. "Do they need you, Ike?"

The Dolls had become as still as painted statues.

"You're an honorable man, Commandant," said the alien. "It disturbs you that the men don't find what they need in Paradise Port."

The chair eased more nearly upright. The intensity of Red Ike's stare reminded Jolober that he'd never seen the alien blink.

"But men like that—all of them now, and most of them for as long as they live . . . all they really need, Commandant, is a chance to die. I don't offer them that, it isn't my place. But I sell them everything they pay for, because I too am honorable."

"You don't know what honor is!" Jolober shouted, horrified at the thought—the nagging possibility—that what Red Ike said was true.

"I know what it is to keep my word, Commandant Jolober," the alien said as he rose from behind his desk with quiet dignity. "I promise you that if you cooperate with me, Paradise Port will continue to run to the full satisfaction of your employers.

"And I also promise," Red Ike went on unblinkingly, "that if you continue your mad vendetta, it will be the worse for you."

"Leave here," Jolober said. His mind achieved not calm, but a dynamic balance in which he understood everything—so long as he focused only on the result, not the reasons. "Leave Placida, leave human space, Ike. You push too hard. So far you've been lucky—it's only me pushing back, and I play by the official rules."

He leaned forward in his saddle, no longer angry. The desktop between them was a flawless black mirror. "But the mercs out there, they play by their own rules, and they're not going to like it when they figure out the game you're running on them. Get out while you can."

"Ladies," Red Ike said. "Please escort the commandant to the main hall. He no longer has any business here."

Jolober spent the next six hours on the street, visiting each of the establishments of Paradise Port. He drank little and spoke less, exchanging salutes when soldiers offered them and, with the same formality, the greetings of owners.

He didn't say much to Vicki later that night, when he returned by the alley staircase which led directly to his living quarters.

But he held her very close.

The sky was dark when Jolober snapped awake, though his bedroom window was painted by all the enticing colors of the façades across the street. He was fully alert and already into the short-legged trousers laid on the mobile chair beside the bed when Vicki stirred and asked, "Horace? What's the matter?"

"I don't—" Jolober began, and then the alarms sounded: the radio implanted in his mastoid, and the siren on the roof of the China Doll.

"Go ahead," he said to Central, thrusting his arms into the uniform tunic.

Vicki thumbed up the room lights but Jolober didn't need that, not to find the sleeves of a white garment with this much sky-glow. He'd stripped a jammed tribarrel once in pitch darkness, knowing that he and a dozen of his men were dead if he screwed up—and absolutely confident of the stream of cyan fire that ripped moments later from his gun muzzles.

"Somebody shot his way into the China Doll," said the voice. "He's holed up in the back."

The bone-conduction speaker hid the identity of the man on the other end of the radio link, but it wasn't the switchboard's artificial intelligence. Somebody on the street was cutting through directly, probably Stecher.

"Droids?" Jolober asked as he mounted his chair and powered up, breaking the charging circuit in which the vehicle rested overnight.

"Chief," said the mastoid, "we got a man down. Looks bad, and we can't get medics to him because the gun's covering the hallway. D'ye want me to—"

"*Wait!*" Jolober said as he bulled through the side door under power. Unlocking the main entrance— the entrance to the office of the port commandant— would take seconds that he knew he didn't have. "Hold what you got, I'm on the way."

The voice speaking through Jolober's jawbone was clearly audible despite wind noise and the scream of his chair as he leaped down the alley staircase in a single curving arc. "Ah, Chief? We're likely to have a, a crowd control problem if this don't get handled real quick."

"I'm on the way," Jolober repeated. He shot onto the street, still on direct thrust because ground effect wouldn't move him as fast as he needed to go.

The entrance of the China doll was cordoned off, if four port patrolmen could be called a cordon. There were over a hundred soldiers in the street and more every moment that the siren—couldn't somebody cut it? Jolober didn't have time—continued to blare.

That wasn't what Stecher had meant by a "crowd control problem." The difficulty was in the way soldiers in the Division Legere's mottled uniforms were shouting—not so much as onlookers as a lynch mob.

Jolober dropped his chair onto its skirts—he needed the greater stability of ground effect. "Lemme through!" he snarled to the mass of uniformed backs which parted in a chorus of yelps when Jolober goosed his throttle. The skirt of his plenum chamber caught the soldiers just above the bootheels and toppled them to either side as the chair powered through.

One trooper spun with a raised fist and a curse in French. Jolober caught the man's wrist and flung him down almost absently. The men at the door relaxed visibly when their commandant appeared at their side.

Behind him, Jolober could hear off-duty patrolmen scrambling into the street from their barracks under the port offices. That would help, but—

"You, Major!" Jolober shouted, pointing at a Division Legere officer in the front of the crowd. The man was almost of a size with the commandant; fury had darkened his face several shades beyond swarthiness. "I'm deputizing you to keep order here until I've taken care of the problem inside."

He spun his chair again and drove through the doorway. The major was shouting to his back, "But the bastard's shot my—"

Two Droids were more or less where Jolober had expected them, one crumpled in the doorway and the other stretched full length a meter inside. The Droids were tough as well as strong. The second one had managed to grasp the man who shot him and be pulled a pace or two before another burst into the back of the Droid's skull had ended matters.

Stecher hadn't said the shooter had a submachine gun. That made the situation a little worse than it might have been; but it was so bad already that the increment was negligible.

Droids waited impassively at all the gaming stations, ready to do their jobs as soon as customers returned. They hadn't fled the way human croupiers would have—but neither did their programming say anything about dealing with armed intruders.

The Dolls had disappeared. It was the first time Jolober had been in the main hall when it was empty of their charming, enticing babble.

Stecher and two troopers in Slammers khaki, and a pair of technicians with a portable medicomp, stood on opposite sides of the archway leading into the back of the China Doll. A second patrolman was huddled behind the three room-wide steps leading up from the main hall.

Man down, Jolober thought, his guts ice.

The patrolman heard the chair and glanced back. "*Duck!*" he screamed as Sergeant Stecher cried, "*Watch—*"

Jolober throttled up, bouncing to the left as a three-shot burst snapped from the archway. It missed him by little enough that his hair rose in response to the ionized track.

There *was* a man down, in the corridor leading back from the archway. There was another man firing from a room at the corridor's opposite end, and he'd just proved his willingness to add the port commandant to the night's bag.

Jolober's chair leaped the steps to the broad landing where Stecher crouched, but it was his massive arms that braked his momentum against the wall. His tunic flapped and he noticed for the first time that he hadn't sealed it before he left his quarters. "Report," he said bluntly to his sergeant while running his thumb up the uniform's seam to close it.

"Their officer's in there," Stecher said, bobbing his chin to indicate the two Slammers kneeling beside him. The male trooper was holding the female and trying to comfort her as she blubbered.

To Jolober's surprise, he recognized both of them— the commo tech and the driver of the tank which'd nearly run him down that afternoon.

"He nutted, shot his way in to find a Doll," Stecher said quickly. His eyes flicked from the commandant to the archway, but he didn't shift far enough to look down the corridor. Congealed notches in the arch's plastic sheath indicated that he'd been lucky once already.

"Found her, found the guy she was with and put a burst into him as he tried to get away." Stecher thumbed toward the body invisible behind the shielding wall. "Guy from the Legere, an El-Tee named Condorcet."

"The bitch made him do it!" said the tank driver in a scream strangled by her own laced fingers.

"She's sedated," said the commo tech who held her.

In the perfect tones of Central's artificial intelligence, Jolober's implant said, "Major de Vigny of the Division Legere requests to see you. He is offering threats."

Letting de Vigny through would either take the pressure off the team outside or be the crack that made the dam fail. From the way Central put it, the dam wasn't going to hold much longer anyhow.

"Tell the cordon to pass him. But tell him keep his head down or he's that much more t'clean up t'morrow," Jolober replied with his mike keyed, making the best decision he could when none of 'em looked good.

"Tried knock-out gas but he's got filters," said Stecher. "Fast, too." He tapped the scarred jamb. "All the skin absorbtives're lethal, and I don't guess we'd get cleared t' use 'em anyhow?"

"Not while I'm in the chain of command," Jolober agreed grimly.

"She was with this pongo from the Legere," the driver was saying through her laced fingers. "Tad, he wanted her so much, so fucking *much*, like she was human or something . . ."

"The, ah, you know. Beth, the one he was plan-

ning to see," said the commo tech rapidly as he
stroked the back of the driver—Corporal Days—
Daisy. . . . "He tried to, you know, buy 'er from the
frog, but he wouldn't play. She got 'em, Beth did, to
put all their leave allowance on a coin flip. She'd take
all the money and go with the winner."

"The bitch," Daisy wailed. "The bitch the bitch
the bitch . . ."

The Legere didn't promote amateurs to battalion
command. The powerful major Jolober had seen outside rolled through the doorway, sized up the situation, and sprinted to the landing out of the shooter's
line of sight.

Line of fire.

"Hoffritz, can you hear me?" Jolober called. "I'm
the port commandant, remember?"

A single bolt from the submachine gun spattered
plastic from the jamb and filled the air with fresher
stenches.

The man sprawling in the corridor moaned.

"I've ordered up an assault team," said Major de
Vigny with flat assurance as he stood up beside Jolober.
"It was unexpected, but they should be here in a few
minutes."

Everyone else in the room was crouching. There
wasn't any need so long as you weren't in front of the
corridor, but it was the instinctive response to knowing somebody was trying to shoot you.

"Cancel the order," said Jolober, locking eyes with
the other officer.

"You aren't in charge when one of my men—"
began the major, his face flushing almost black.

"The gate closes when the alarm goes off!" Jolober
said in a voice that could have been heard over a
tank's fans. "And I've ordered the air defense batteries," he lied, "to fire on anybody trying to crash
through now. If you want to lead a mutiny against
your employers, Major, now's the time to do it."

The two big men glared at one another without

blinking. Then de Vigny said, "Blue Six to Blue Three," keying his epaulet mike with the code words. "Hold Team Alpha until further orders. Repeat, hold Alpha. Out."

"Hold Alpha," repeated the speaker woven into the epaulet's fabric.

"If Condorcet dies," de Vigny added calmly to the port commandant, "I will kill you myself, sir."

"Do you have cratering charges warehoused here?" Jolober asked with no emotion save the slight lilt of interrogation.

"What?" said de Vigny. "Yes, yes."

Jolober crooked his left ring finger so that Central would hear and relay his next words. "Tell the gate to pass two men from the Legere with a jeep and a cratering charge. Give them a patrol guide, and download the prints of the China Doll into his commo link so they can place the charge on the wall outside the room at the T of the back corridor."

De Vigny nodded crisply to indicate that he too understood the order. He began relaying it into his epaulet while Stecher drew and reholstered his needle stunner and Corporal Days mumbled.

"Has she tried?" Jolober asked, waving to the driver and praying that he wouldn't have to . . .

"He shot at 'er," the commo tech said, nodding sadly. "That's when she really lost it and the medics had to calm her down."

No surprises there. Certainly no good ones.

"Captain Hoffritz, it's the port commandant again," Jolober called.

A bolt spat down the axis of the corridor.

"That's right, you bastard, *shoot!*" Jolober roared. "You blew my legs off on Primavera. Now finish the job and *prove* you're a fuck-up who's only good for killing his friends. Come on, I'll make it easy. I'll come out and let you take your time!"

"Chief—" said Stecher.

Jolober slid away from the shelter of the wall.

The corridor was the stem of a T, ten meters long. Halfway between Jolober and the cross corridor at the other end, capping the T, lay the wounded man. Lieutenant Condorcet was a tough little man to still be alive with the back of his tunic smoldering around the holes punched in him by three powergun bolts. The roll of coins he'd carried to add weight to his fist wouldn't have helped; but then, nothing much helped when the other guy had the only gun in the equation.

Like now.

The door of the room facing the corridor and Horace Jolober was ajar. Beyond the opening was darkness and a bubble of dull red: the iridium muzzle of Hoffritz's submachine gun, glowing with the heat of the destruction it had spit at others.

De Vigny cursed; Stecher was pleading or even calling an order. All Jolober could hear was the roar of the tank bearing down on him, so loud that the slapping bolts streaming toward him from its cupola were inaudible.

Jolober's chair slid him down the hall. His arms were twitching in physical memory of the time they'd waved a scrap of white cloth to halt the oncoming armor.

The door facing him opened. Tad Hoffritz's face was as hard and yellow as fresh bone. He leaned over the sight of his submachine gun. Jolober slowed, because if he kept on at a walking pace he would collide with Condorcet, and if he curved around the wounded man it might look as if he were dodging what couldn't be dodged.

He didn't want to look like a fool and a coward when he died.

Hoffritz threw down the weapon.

Jolober bounced to him, wrapping the Slammers officer in both arms like a son. Stecher was shouting, "Medics!" but the team with the medicomp had been in motion as soon as the powergun hit the floor.

Behind all the babble was Major de Vigny's voice, remembering to stop the crew with the charge that might otherwise be set—and fired—even though the need was over.

"I *loved* her," Hoffritz said to Jolober's big shoulder, begging someone to understand what he didn't understand himself. "I, I'd been drinking and I came back . . ."

With a submachine gun that shouldn't have made it into Paradise Port . . . but the detection loops hadn't been replaced in the hours since the tanks ripped them away; and anyhow, Hoffritz was an officer, a company commander.

He was also a young man having a bad time with what he thought was a woman. Older, calmer fellows than Hoffritz had killed because of that.

Jolober carried Hoffritz with him into the room where he'd been holed up. "Lights," the commandant ordered, and the room brightened.

Condorcet wasn't dead, not yet; but Beth, the Doll behind the trouble, surely was.

The couch was large and round. Though drumhead-thin, its structure could be varied to any degree of firmness the paying half of the couple desired. Beth lay in the center of it in a tangle of long black hair. Her tongue protruded from a blood-darkened face, and the prints of the grip that had strangled her were livid on her throat.

"She told me she loved *him*," Hoffritz mumbled. The commandant's embrace supported him, but it also kept Hoffritz from doing something silly, like trying to run.

"After what I'd done," the boy was saying, "she tells me she doesn't love me after all. She says I'm no good to her in bed, that I never gave her any pleasure at all . . ."

"Just trying to maximize the claim for damages, son," Jolober said grimly. "It didn't mean anything real, just more dollars in Red Ike's pocket."

But Red Ike hadn't counted on Hoffritz shooting another merc. Too bad for Condorcet, too bad for the kid who shot him—

And just what Jolober needed to finish Red Ike on Placida.

"Let's go," Jolober said, guiding Hoffritz out of the room stinking of death and the emotions that led to death. "We'll get you to a medic."

And a cell.

Condorcet had been removed from the corridor, leaving behind only a slime of vomit. Thank the Lord he'd fallen face down.

Stecher and his partner took the unresisting Hoffritz and wrapped him in motion restraints. The prisoner could walk and move normally, so long as he did it slowly. At a sudden movement, the gossamer webs would clamp him as tightly as a fly in a spiderweb.

The main hall was crowded, but the incipient violence facing the cordon outside had melted away. Judging from Major de Vigny's brusque, bellowed orders, the victim was in the hands of his medics and being shifted to the medicomp in Division Legere's bivouac area.

That was probably the best choice. Paradise Port had excellent medical facilities, but medics in combat units got to know their jobs and their diagnostic/ healing computers better than anybody in the rear echelons.

"Commandant Jolober," said van Zuyle, the Slammers' bivouac commander, "I'm worried about my man here. Can I—"

"He's not your man any more, Captain," Jolober said with the weary chill of an avalanche starting to topple. "He's mine and the Placidan courts'—until I tell you different. We'll get him sedated and keep him from hurting himself, no problem."

Van Zuyle's face wore the expression of a man whipping himself to find a deity who doesn't respond. "Sir," he said, "I'm sorry if I—"

"You did the job they paid you t'do," Jolober said, shrugging away from the other man. He hadn't felt so weary since he'd awakened in the Legion's main hospital on Primavera: alive and utterly unwilling to believe that he could be after what happened.

"Outa the man's way," snarled one of the patrolmen, trying to wave a path through the crowd with her white-sleeved arms. "Let the commandant by!"

She yelped a curse at the big man who brushed through her gestures. "A moment, little one," he said—de Vigny, the Legere major.

"You kept the lid on good," Jolober said while part of his dazed mind wondered whose voice he was hearing. "Tomorrow I'll want to talk to you about what happened and how to keep from a repeat."

Anger darkened de Vigny's face. "I heard what happened," he said. "Condorcet was not the only human victim, it would seem."

"We'll talk," Jolober said. His chair was driving him toward the door, pushing aside anyone who didn't get out of the way. He didn't see them any more than he saw the air.

The street was a carnival of uniformed soldiers who suddenly had something to focus on that wasn't a memory of death—or a way to forget. There were dark undercurrents to the chatter, but the crowd was no longer a mob.

Jolober's uniform drew eyes, but the port commandant was too aloof and forbidding to be asked for details of what had really happened in the China Doll. In the center of the street, though—

"Good evening, Commandant," said Red Ike, strolling back toward the establishment he owned. "Without your courage, tonight's incident would have been even more unfortunate."

Human faces changed in the play of light washing them from the brothel fronts. Red Ike's did not. Colors overlay his features, but the lines did not modify as one shadow or highlight replaced another.

"It couldn't be more unfortunate for you, Ike," Jolober said to the bland alien while uniforms milled around them. "They'll pay you money, the mercs will. But they won't have you killing their men."

"I understand that the injured party is expected to pull through," Red Ike said emotionlessly. Jolober had the feeling that the alien's eyes were focused in his soul.

"I'm glad Condorcet'll live," Jolober said, too tired for triumph or subtlety. "But you're dead on Placida, Ike. It's just a matter of how long it takes me to wrap it up."

He broke past Red Ike, gliding toward the port offices and the light glowing from his room on the upper floor.

Red Ike didn't turn around, but Jolober thought he could feel the alien watching him nonetheless.

Even so, all Jolober cared about now was bed and a chance to reassure Vicki that everything was all right.

The alley between the office building and the Blue Parrot next door wasn't directly illuminated, but enough light spilled from the street to show Jolober the stairs.

He didn't see the two men waiting there until a third had closed the mouth of the alley behind him. Indonesian music began to blare from the China Doll.

Music on the exterior's a violation, thought the part of Jolober's mind that ran Paradise Port, but reflexes from his years as a combat officer noted the man behind him held a metal bar and that knives gleamed in the hands of the two by the stairs.

It made a hell of a fast trip back from the nightmare memories that had ruled Jolober's brain since he awakened.

Jolober's left stump urged the throttle as his torso shifted toward the alley mouth. The electronics reacted instantly but the mechanical links took a moment. Fans spun up, plenum chamber collapsed into a nozzle—

The attackers moved in on Jolober like the three wedges of a drill chuck. His chair launched him into the one with the club, a meter off the ground and rising with a hundred and eighty kilos of mass behind the impact.

At the last instant the attacker tried to duck away instead of swinging at Jolober, but he misjudged the speed of his intended victim. The center of the chair's frame, between the skirt and the saddle, batted the attacker's head toward the wall, dragging the fellow's body with it.

Jolober had a clear path to the street. The pair of knifemen thought he was headed that way and sprinted in a desperate attempt to catch a victim who moved faster than unaided humans could run.

They were in midstride, thinking of failure rather than defense, when Jolober pogoed at the alley mouth and came back at them like a cannonball.

But bigger and heavier.

One attacker stabbed at Jolober's chest and skidded the point off the battery compartment instead when the chair hopped. The frame slammed knife and man into the concrete wall from which they ricochetted to the ground, separate and equally motionless.

The third man ran away.

"Get 'em, boys!" Jolober bellowed as if he were launching his battalion instead of just himself in pursuit. The running man glanced over his shoulder and collided with the metal staircase. The noise was loud and unpleasant, even in comparison to the oriental music blaring from the China Doll.

Jolober bounced, cut his fan speed, and flared his output nozzle into a plenum chamber again. The chair twitched, then settled into ground effect.

Jolober's mind told him that he was seeing with a

clarity and richness of color he couldn't have equalled by daylight, but he knew that if he really focused on an object it would blur into shadow. It was just his brain's way of letting him know that he was still alive.

Alive like he hadn't been in years.

Crooking his ring finger, Jolober said, "I need a pick-up on three men in the alley between us and the Blue Parrot."

"Three men in the alley between HQ and the Blue Parrot," the artificial intelligence paraphrased.

"They'll need a medic." One might need burial. "And I want them sweated under a psycomp—who sent 'em after me, the works."

Light flooded the alley as a team of patrolmen arrived. The point man extended a surface-luminescent area light powered from a backpack. The shadows thrown by the meter-diameter convexity were soft, but the illumination was the blaze of noon compared of that of moments before.

"Chief!" bellowed Stecher. "You all right? Chief!" He wasn't part of the team Central vectored to the alley, but word of mouth had brought him to the scene of the incident.

Jolober throttled up, clamped his skirts, and boosted himself to the fourth step where everyone could see him. The man who'd run into the stairs moaned as the sidedraft spat grit from the treads into his face.

"No problem," Jolober said. No problem they wouldn't be able to cure in a week or two. "I doubt these three know any more than that they got a call from outside Port to, ah, handle me . . . but get what they have, maybe we can cross-reference with some outgoing traffic."

From the China Doll; or just maybe from the Blue Parrot, where Ike fled when the shooting started. But probably not. Three thugs, non-descripts from off-planet who could've been working for any establishment in Paradise Port *except* the China Doll.

"Sir—" came Stecher's voice.

"It'll keep, Sergeant," Jolober interrupted. "Just now I've got a heavy date with a bed."

Vicki greeted him with a smile so bright that both of them could pretend there were no tears beneath it. The air was steamy with the bath she'd drawn for him.

He used to prefer showers, back when he'd had feet on which to stand. He could remember dancing on Quitly's Planet as the afternoon monsoon battered the gun carriages his platoon was guarding and washed the soap from his body.

But he didn't have Vicki then, either.

"Yeah," he said, hugging the Doll. "Good idea, a bath."

Instead of heading for the bathroom, he slid his chair to the cabinet within arm's reach of the bed and cut his fans. Bending over, he unlatched the battery compartment—the knifepoint hadn't even penetrated the casing—and removed the powerpack.

"I can—" Vicki offered hesitantly.

"S'okay, dearest," Jolober replied as he slid a fresh pack from the cabinet into place. His stump touched the throttle, spinning the fans to prove that he had good contact, then lifted the original pack into the cabinet and its charging harness.

"Just gave 'em a workout tonight and don't want t' be down on power tomorrow," he explained as he straightened. Vicki could have handled the weight of the batteries, he realized, though his mind kept telling him it was ludicrous to imagine the little woman shifting thirty-kilo packages with ease.

But she wasn't a woman.

"I worry when it's so dangerous," she said as she walked with him to the bathroom, their arms around one another's waist.

"Look, for Paradise Port, it was dangerous," Jolober said in a light appearance of candor as he handed

Vicki his garments. "Compared to downtown in any capital city I've seen, it was pretty mild."

He lowered himself into the water, using the bars laid over the tub like a horizontal ladder. Vicki began to knead the great muscles of his shoulders, and Lord! but it felt good to relax after so long. . . .

"I'd miss you," she said.

"Not unless I went away," Jolober answered, leaning forward so that her fingers could work down his spine while the water lapped at them. "Which isn't going to happen any time soon."

He paused. The water's warmth unlocked more than his body. "Look," he said quietly, his chin touching the surface of the bath and his eyes still closed. "Red Ike's had it. He knows it, I know it. But I'm in a position to make things either easy or hard, and he knows that too. We'll come to terms, he and I. And you're the—"

"Urgent from the gate," said Jolober's mastoid implant.

He crooked his finger, raising his head. "Put him through," he said.

Her through. "Sir," said Feldman's attenuated voice, "a courier's just landed with two men. They say they've got an oral message from Colonel Hammer, and they wanted me to alert you that they're coming. Over."

"I'll open the front door," Jolober said, lifting himself abruptly from the water, careful not to mis-key the implant while his hands performed other tasks.

He wouldn't rouse the human staff. No need—and if the message came by courier, it wasn't intended for other ears.

"Ah, sir," Feldman added unexpectedly. "One of them insists on keeping his sidearms. Over."

"Then he can insist on staying outside my perimeter!" Jolober snarled. Vicki had laid a towel on the saddle before he mounted and was now using another to silently dry his body. "You can detach two guards to escort 'em if they need their hands held, but *nobody* brings powerguns into Paradise Port."

"Roger, I'll tell them," Feldman agreed doubtfully. "Over and out."

"I have a fresh uniform out," said Vicki, stepping back so that Jolober could follow her into the bedroom, where the air was drier.

"That's three, today," Jolober said, grinning. "Well, I've done a lot more than I've managed any three other days.

"Via," he added more seriously. "It's more headway than I've made since they appointed me commandant."

Vicki smiled, but her eyes were so tired that Jolober's body trembled in response. His flesh remembered how much he had already been through today and yearned for the sleep to which the hot bath had disposed it.

Jolober lifted himself on his hands so that Vicki could raise and cinch his trousers. He could do it himself, but he was in a hurry, and . . . besides, just as she'd said, Vicki was a part of him in a real way.

"Cheer up, love," he said as he closed his tunic. "It isn't done yet, but it's sure getting that way."

"Goodby, Horace," the Doll said as she kissed him.

"Keep the bed warm," Jolober called as he slid toward the door and the inner staircase. His head was tumbling with memories and images. For a change, they were all pleasant ones.

The port offices were easily identified at night because they *weren't* garishly illuminated like every other building in Paradise Port. Jolober had a small staff, and he didn't choose to waste it at desks. Outside of ordinary business hours, Central's artificial intelligence handled everything—by putting non-emergency requests on hold till morning, and by vectoring a uniformed patrol to the real business.

Anybody who insisted on personal service could get it by hammering at the Patrol entrance on the west side, opposite Jolober's private staircase. A patrolman would find the noisemaker a personal holding cell for the remainder of the night.

The front entrance was built like a vault door, not so much to prevent intrusion as to keep drunks from destroying the panel for reasons they'd be unable to remember sober. Jolober palmed the release for the separate bolting systems and had just begun to swing the door open in invitation when the two men in khaki uniforms, neither of them tall, strode up to the building.

"Blood and Martyrs!" Jolober said as he continued to back, not entirely because the door required it.

"You run a tight base here, Commandant," said Colonel Alois Hammer as he stepped into the waiting room. "Do you know my aide, Major Steuben?"

"By reputation only," said Jolober, nodding to Joachim Steuben with the formal correctness which that reputation enjoined. "Ah—with a little more information, I might have relaxed the prohibition on weapons."

Steuben closed the door behind them, moving the heavy panel with a control which belied the boyish delicacy of his face and frame. "If the colonel's satisfied with his security," Joachim said mildly, "then of course I am too."

The eyes above his smile would willingly have watched Jolober drawn and quartered.

"You've had some problems with troops of mine today," said Hammer, seating himself on one of the chairs and rising again, almost as quickly as if he had continued to walk. His eyes touched Jolober and moved on in short hops that covered everything in the room like an animal checking a new environment.

"Only reported problems occurred," said Jolober, keeping the promise he'd made earlier in the day. He lighted the hologram projection tank on the counter to let it warm up. "There was an incident a few hours ago, yes."

The promise didn't matter to Tad Hoffritz, not after the shootings; but it mattered more than life to Horace Jolober that he keep the bargains he'd made.

"According to Captain van Zuyle's report," Hammer said as his eyes flickered over furniture and recesses dim under the partial lighting, "you're of the opinion the boy was set up."

"What you do with a gun," said Joachim Steuben softly from the door against which he leaned, "is your own responsibility."

"As Joachim says," Hammer went on with a nod and no facial expression, "that doesn't affect how we'll deal with Captain Hoffritz when he's released from local custody. But it does affect how we act to prevent recurrences, doesn't it?"

"Load file Ike One into the downstairs holo," said Jolober to Central.

He looked at Hammer, paused till their eyes met. "Sure, he was set up, just like half a dozen others in the past three months—only they were money assessments, no real problem.

"And the data prove," Jolober continued coolly, claiming what his data suggested but could *not* prove, "that it's going to get a lot worse than what happened tonight if Red Ike and his Dolls aren't shipped out fast."

The holotank sprang to life in a three-dimensional cross-hatching of orange lines. As abruptly, the lines shrank into words and columns of figures. "Red Ike and his Dolls—they were all his openly, then—first show up on Sparrowhome a little over five years standard ago, according to Bonding Authority records. Then—"

Jolober pointed toward the figures. Colonel Hammer put his smaller, equally firm, hand over the commandant's and said, "Wait. Just give me your assessment."

"Dolls have been imported as recreational support in seven conflicts," said Jolober as calmly as if his mind had not just shifted gears. He'd been a good combat commander for the same reason, for dealing with the situation that occurred rather than the one he'd planned for. "There's been rear-echelon trouble each time, and the riot on Ketelby caused the Bonding Authority to order the disbandment of a battalion of Guardforce O'Higgins."

"There was trouble over a woman," said Steuben unemotionally, reeling out the data he gathered because he *was* Hammer's adjutant as well as his bodyguard. "A fight between a ranger and an artilleryman led to a riot in which half the nearest town was burned."

"Not a woman," corrected Jolober. "A Doll."

He tapped the surface of the holotank. "It's all here, downloaded from Bonding Authority archives. You just have to see what's happening so you know the questions to ask."

"You can get me a line to the capital?" Hammer asked as if he were discussing the weather. "I was in a hurry, and I didn't bring along my usual commo."

Jolober lifted the visiplate folded into the surface of the counter beside the tank and rotated it toward Hammer.

"I've always preferred non-humans for recreation areas," Hammer said idly as his finger played over the plate's keypad. "Oh, the troops complain, but I've never seen *that* hurt combat efficiency. Whereas real women gave all sorts of problems."

"And real men," said Joachim Steuben, with a deadpan expression that could have meant anything.

The visiplate beeped. "Main Switch," said a voice, tart but not sleepy. "Go ahead."

"You have my authorization code," Hammer said to the human operator on the other end of the connection. From Jolober's flat angle to the plate, he couldn't make out the operator's features—only that he sat in a brightly-illuminated white cubicle. "Patch me through to the chairman of the Facilities Inspection Committee."

"Senator Dieter?" said the operator, professionally able to keep the question short of being amazement.

"If he's the chairman," Hammer said. The words had the angry undertone of dynamite fuse burning.

"Yessir, she is," replied the operator with studied neutrality. "One moment please."

"I've been dealing with her chief aide," said Jolober in a hasty whisper. "Guy named Higgey. His pager's loaded—"

"Got you a long ways, didn't it, Commandant?" Hammer said with a gun-turret click of his head toward Jolober.

"Your pardon, sir," said Jolober, bracing reflexively to attention. He wasn't Hammer's subordinate, but they both served the same ideal—getting the job done. The ball was in Hammer's court just now, and he'd ask for support if he thought he needed it.

From across the waiting room, Joachim Steuben smiled at Jolober. *That* one had the same ideal, perhaps; but his terms of reference were something else again.

"The senator isn't at any of her registered work stations," the operator reported coolly.

"Son," said Hammer, leaning toward the visiplate, "you have a unique opportunity to lose the war for Placida. All you have to do is *not* get me through to the chairman."

"Yes, Colonel Hammer," the operator replied with an aplomb that made it clear why he held the job he did. "I've processed your authorization, and I'm running it through again on War Emergency Ord—"

The last syllable was clipped. The bright rectangle of screen dimmed gray. Jolober slid his chair in a short arc so that he could see the visiplate clearly past Hammer's shoulder.

"What is it?" demanded the woman in the dim

light beyond. She was stocky, middle-aged, and rather attractive because of the force of personality she radiated even sleepless in a dressing gown.

"This is Colonel Alois Hammer," Hammer said. "Are you recording?"

"On *this* circuit?" the senator replied with a frosty smile. "Of course I am. So are at least three other agencies, whether I will or no."

Hammer blinked, startled to find himself on the wrong end of a silly question for a change.

"Senator," he went on without the hectoring edge that had been present since his arrival. "A contractor engaged by your government to provide services at Paradise Port has been causing problems. One of the Legere's down, in critical, and I'm short a company commander over the same incident."

"You've reported to the port commandant?" Senator Dieter said, her eyes unblinking as they passed over Jolober.

"The commandant reported to me because your staff stonewalled him," Hammer said flatly while Jolober felt his skin grow cold, even the tips of the toes he no longer had. "I want the contractor, a non-human called Red Ike, off-planet in seventy-two hours with all his chattels. That specifically includes his Dolls. We'll work—"

"That's too soon," said Dieter, her fingers tugging a lock of hair over one ear while her mind worked. "Even if—"

"Forty-*eight* hours, Senator," Hammer interrupted. "This is a violation of your bond. And I promise you, I'll have the support of all the other commanders of units contracted to Placidan service. Forty-eight hours, or we'll withdraw from combat and you won't have a front line."

"You *can't*—" Dieter began. Then all muscles froze, tongue and fingers among them, as her mind considered the implications of what the colonel had just told her.

"I have no concern over being able to win my case at the Bonding Authority hearing on Earth," Hammer continued softly. "But I'm quite certain that the present Placidan government won't be there to contest it."

Dieter smiled without humor. "Seventy-two hours," she said as if repeating the figure.

"I've shifted the Regiment across continents in less time, Senator," Hammer said.

"Yes," said Dieter calmly. "Well, there are political consequences to any action, and I'd rather explain myself to my constituents than to an army of occupation. I'll take care of it."

She broke the circuit.

"I wouldn't mind getting to know that lady," said Hammer, mostly to himself, as he folded the visiplate back into the counter.

"That takes care of your concerns, then?" he added sharply, looking up at Jolober.

"Yes, sir, it does," said Jolober, who had the feeling he had drifted into a plane where dreams could be happy.

"Ah, about Captain Hoffritz . . ." Hammer said. His eyes slipped, but he snapped them back to meet Jolober's despite the embarrassment of being about to ask a favor.

"He's not combat-fit right now, Colonel," Jolober said, warming as authority flooded back to fill his mind. "He'll do as well in our care for the next few days as he would in yours. After that, and assuming that no one wants to press charges—"

"Understood," said Hammer, nodding. "I'll deal with the victim and General Claire."

"—then some accommodation can probably be arranged with the courts."

"It's been a pleasure dealing with a professional of your caliber, Commandant," Hammer said as he shook Jolober's hand. He spoke without emphasis, but nobody meeting his cool blue eyes could have imagined that Hammer would have bothered to lie about it.

"It's started to rain," observed Major Steuben as he muscled the door open.

"It's permitted to," Hammer said. "We've been wet be—"

"A jeep to the front of the building," Jolober ordered with his ring finger crooked. He straightened and said, "Ah, Colonel? Unless you'd like to be picked up by one of your own vehicles?"

"Nobody knows I'm here," said Hammer from the doorway. "I don't want van Zuyle to think I'm second-guessing him—I'm not, I'm just handling the part that's mine to handle."

He paused before adding with an ironic smile, "In any case, we're four hours from exploiting the salient Hoffritz's company formed when they took the junction at Kettering."

A jeep with two patrolmen, stunners ready, scraped to a halt outside. The team was primed for a situation like the one in the alley less than an hour before.

"Taxi service only, boys," Jolober called to the patrolmen. "Carry these gentlemen to their courier ship, please."

The jeep was spinning away in the drizzle before Jolober had closed and locked the door again. It didn't occur to him that it mattered whether or not the troops bivouacked around Paradise Port knew immediately what Hammer had just arranged.

And it didn't occur to him, as he bounced his chair up the stairs calling, "Vicki! We've won!" that he should feel any emotion except joy.

"Vicki!" he repeated as he opened the bedroom door. They'd have to leave Placida unless he could get Vicki released from the blanket order on Dolls—but he hadn't expected to keep his job anyway, not after he went over the head of the whole Placidan government.

"Vi—"

She'd left a light on, one of the point sources in the ceiling. It was a shock, but not nearly as bad a shock as Jolober would have gotten if he'd slid onto the bed in the dark.

"Who?" his tongue asked while his mind couldn't think of anything to say, could only move his chair to the bedside and palm the hydraulics to lower him into a sitting position.

Her right hand and forearm were undamaged. She flexed her fingers and the keen plastic blade shot from her fist, then collapsed again into a baton. She let it roll onto the bedclothes.

"He couldn't force me to kill you," Vicki said. "He was very surprised, very. . . ."

Jolober thought she might be smiling, but he couldn't be sure since she no longer had lips. The plastic edges of the knife Vicki took as she dressed him were not sharp enough for finesse, but she had not attempted surgical delicacy.

Vicki had destroyed herself from toes to her once-perfect face. All she had left was one eye with which to watch Jolober, and the parts of her body which she couldn't reach unaided. She had six ribs to a side, broader and flatter than those of a human's skeleton. After she laid open the ribs, she had dissected the skin and flesh of the left side further.

Jolober had always assumed—when he let himself think about it—that her breasts were sponge implants. He'd been wrong. On the bedspread lay a wad of yellowish fat streaked with blood vessels. He didn't have a background that would tell him whether or not it was human normal, but it certainly was biological.

It was a tribute to Vicki's toughness that she had remained alive as long as she had.

Instinct turned Jolober's head to the side so that he vomited away from the bed. He clasped Vicki's right hand with both of his, keeping his eyes closed so that he could imagine that everything was as it had been minutes before when he was triumphantly happy. His left wrist brushed the knife that should have remained an inert baton in any hands but his. He snatched up the weapon, feeling the blade flow out—

As it had when Vicki held it, turned it on herself.

"We are one, my Horace," she whispered, her hand squeezing his.

It was the last time she spoke, but Jolober couldn't be sure of that because his mind had shifted out of the present into a cosmos limited to the sense of touch: body-warm plastic in his left hand, and flesh cooling slowly in his right.

He sat in his separate cosmos for almost an hour, until the emergency call on his mastoid implant threw him back into an existence where his life had purpose.

"All units!" dried a voice on the panic push. "The—"

The blast of static which drowned the voice lasted only a fraction of a second before the implant's logic circuits shut the unit down to keep the white noise from driving Jolober mad. The implant would be disabled as long as the jamming continued—but jamming of this intensity would block even the most sophisticated equipment in the Slammers' tanks.

Which were probably carrying out the jamming.

Jolober's hand slipped the knife away without thinking—with fiery determination not to think—as his stump kicked the chair into life and he glided toward the alley stairs. He was still dressed, still mounted in his saddle, and that was as much as he was willing to know about his immediate surroundings.

The stairs rang. The thrust of his fans was a fitful gust on the metal treads each time he bounced on his way to the ground.

The voice could have been Feldman at the gate; she was the most likely source anyway. At the moment, Jolober had an emergency.

In a matter of minutes, it could be a disaster instead.

It was raining, a nasty drizzle which distorted the invitations capering on the building fronts. The street was empty except for a pair of patrol jeeps, bubbles in the night beneath canopies that would stop most of the droplets.

Even this weather shouldn't have kept soldiers from scurrying from one establishment to another, hoping to change their luck when they changed location. Overhanging façades ought to have been crowded with morose troopers, waiting for a lull—or someone drunk or angry enough to lead an exodus toward another empty destination.

The emptiness would have worried Jolober if he didn't have much better reasons for concern. The vehicles sliding down the street from the gate were unlighted, but there was no mistaking the roar of a tank.

Someone in the China Doll heard and understood the sound also, because the armored door squealed down across the archway even as Jolober's chair lifted him in that direction at high thrust.

He braked in a spray. The water-slicked pavement didn't affect his control, since the chair depended on thrust rather than friction—but being able to stop didn't give him any ideas about how he should proceed.

One of the patrol jeeps swung in front of the tank with a courage and panache which made Jolober proud of his men. The patrolman on the passenger side had ripped the canopy away to stand, waving a yellow light-wand with furious determination.

The tank did not slow. It shifted direction just enough to strike the jeep a glancing blow instead of center-punching it. That didn't spare the vehicle; its light frame crumpled like tissue before it resisted enough to spin across the pavement at twice the velocity of the slowly-advancing tank. The slight ad-

justment in angle did save the patrolmen, who were
thrown clear instead of being ground between concrete and the steel skirts.

The tank's scarred turret made it identifiable in
the light of the building fronts. Jolober crooked his
finger and shouted, "Commandant to Corporal Days.
For the *Lord's* sake, trooper, don't get your unit
disbanded for mutiny! Colonel Hammer's already gotten Red Ike ordered off-planet!"

There was no burp from his mastoid as Central
retransmitted the message a microsecond behind the
original. Only then did Jolober recall that the Slammers had jammed his communications.

Not the Slammers alone. The two vehicles behind
the tank were squat armored personnel carriers, each
capable of hauling an infantry section with all its
equipment. Nobody had bothered to paint out the
fender markings of the Division Legere.

Rain stung Jolober's eyes as he hopped the last
five meters to the sealed façade of the China Doll.
Anything could be covered, could be settled, except
murder—and killing Red Ike would be a murder of
which the Bonding Authority would have to take
cognizance.

"Let me in!" Jolober shouted to the door. The
armor was so thick that it didn't ring when he pounded
it. "Let me—"

Normally the sound of a mortar firing was audible
for a kilometer, a hollow *shoomp!* like a firecracker
going off in an oil drum. Jolober hadn't heard the
launch from beyond the perimeter because of the
nearby roar of drive fans.

When the round went off on the roof of the China
Doll, the charge streamed tendrils of white fire down
as far as the pavement, where they pocked the concrete. The snake-pit coruscance of blue sparks lighting the roof a moment later was the battery pack of
Red Ike's aircar shorting through the new paths the
mortar shell had burned in the car's circuitry.

The mercs were playing for keeps. They hadn't come to destroy the China Doll and leave its owner to rebuild somewhere else.

The lead tank swung in the street with the cautious delicacy of an elephant wearing a hoopskirt. Its driving lights blazed on, silhouetting the port commandant against the steel door. Jolober held out his palm in prohibition, knowing that if he could delay events even a minute, Red Ike would escape through his tunnel.

Everything else within the China Doll was a chattel which could be compensated with money.

There was a red flash and a roar from the stern of the tank, then an explosion muffled by a meter of concrete and volcanic rock. Buildings shuddered like sails in a squall; the front of the port offices cracked as its fabric was placed under a flexing strain that concrete was never meant to resist.

The rocket-assisted penetrators carried by the Slammers' tanks were intended to shatter bunkers of any thickness imaginable in the field. Red Ike's bolthole was now a long cavity filled with chunks and dust of the material intended to protect it.

The tanks had very good detection equipment, and combat troops live to become veterans by observing their surroundings. Quite clearly, the tunnel had not escaped notice when Tad Hoffritz led his company down the street to hoo-rah Paradise Port.

"Wait!" Jolober shouted, because there's always a chance until there's no chance at all.

"Get out of the way, Commandant!" boomed the tank's public address system, loudly enough to seem an echo of the penetrator's earth-shock.

"Colonel Hammer has—" Jolober shouted.

"We'd as soon not hurt you," the speakers roared as the turret squealed ten degrees on its gimbals. The main gun's bore was a 20-cm tube aligned perfectly with Jolober's eyes.

They couldn't hear him; they wouldn't listen if

they could; and anyway, the troopers involved in this weren't interested in contract law. They wanted justice, and to them that didn't mean a ticket off-planet for Red Ike.

The tribarrel in the tank's cupola fired a single shot. The bolt of directed energy struck the descending arch just in front of Jolober and gouged the plastic away in fire and black smoke. Bits of the covering continued to burn, and the underlying concrete added an odor of hot lime to the plastic and the ozone of the bolt's track through the air.

Jolober's miniature vehicle thrust him away in a flat arc, out of the door alcove and sideways in the street as a powergun fired from a port concealed in the China Doll's façade. The tank's main gun demolished the front wall with a single round.

The street echoed with the thunderclap of cold air filling the track seared through it by the energy bolt. The pistol shot an instant earlier could almost have been a proleptic reflection, confused in memory with the sun-bright cyan glare of the tank cannon—and, by being confused, forgotten.

Horace Jolober understood the situation too well to mistake its events. The shot meant Red Ike was still in the China Doll, trapped there and desperate enough to issue his Droids lethal weapons that must have been difficult even for *him* to smuggle into Paradise Port.

Desperate and foolish, because the pistol bolt had only flicked dust from the tank's iridium turret. Jolober had warned Red Ike that combat troops played by a different rulebook. The message just hadn't been received until it was too late. . . .

Jolober swung into the three-meter alley beside the China Doll. There was neither an opening here nor ornamentation, just the blank concrete wall of a fortress.

Which wouldn't hold for thirty seconds if the combat team out front chose to assault it.

The tank had fired at the building front, not the door. The main gun could have blasted a hole in the armor, but that wouldn't have been a large enough entrance for the infantry now deploying behind the armored flanks of the APCs.

The concrete wall shattered like a bomb when it tried to absorb the point-blank energy of the 20-cm gun. The cavity the shot left was big enough to pass a jeep with a careful driver. Infantrymen in battle armor, hunched over their weapons, dived into the China Doll. The interior lit with cyan flashes as they shot everything that moved.

The exterior lighting had gone out, but flames clawed their way up the thermoplastic façade. The fire threw a red light onto the street in which shadows of smoke capered like demons. Drips traced blazing lines through the air as they fell to spatter troops waiting their turn for a chance to kill.

The assault didn't require a full infantry platoon, but few operations have failed because the attackers had too many troops.

Jolober had seen the equivalent too often to doubt how it was going to go this time. He didn't have long; very possibly he didn't have long enough.

Standing parallel to the sheer sidewall, Jolober ran his fans up full power, then clamped the plenum chamber into a tight nozzle and lifted. His left hand paddled against the wall three times. That gave him balance and the suggestion of added thrust to help his screaming fans carry out a task for which they hadn't been designed.

When his palm touched the coping, Jolober used the contact to center him, and rotated onto the flat roof of the China Doll.

Sparks spat peevishly from the corpse of the aircar. The vehicle's frame was a twisted wire sculpture from which most of the sheathing material had burned away, but occasionally the breeze brought oxygen to a scrap that was still combustible.

The penthouse that held Ike's office and living quarters was a squat box beyond the aircar. The mortar shell had detonated just as the alien started to run for his vehicle. He'd gotten back inside as the incendiary compound sprayed the roof, but bouncing fragments left black trails across the plush blue floor of the office.

The door was a section of wall broad enough to have passed the aircar. Red Ike hadn't bothered to close it when he fled to his elevator and the tunnel exit. Jolober, skimming again on ground effect, slid into the office shouting, "Ike! This—"

Red Ike burst from the elevator cage as the door rotated open. He had a pistol and eyes as wide as a madman's as he swung the weapon toward the hulking figure in his office.

Jolober reacted as the adrenaline pumping through his body had primed him to do. The arm with which he swatted at the pistol was long enough that his fingers touched the barrel, strong enough that the touch hurled the gun across the room despite Red Ike's deathgrip on the butt.

Red Ike screamed.

An explosion in the elevator shaft wedged the elevator doors as they began to close and burped orange flame against the far wall.

Jolober didn't know how the assault team proposed to get to the roof, but neither did he intend to wait around to learn. He wrapped both arms around the stocky alien and shouted, "Shut up and hold *still* if you want to get out of here alive!"

Red Ike froze, either because he understood the warning—or because at last he recognized Horace Jolober and panicked to realize that the port commandant had already disarmed him.

Jolober lifted the alien and turned his chair. It glided toward the door at gathering speed, logy with the double burden.

There was another blast from the office. The assault team had cleared the elevator shaft with a cratering charge whose directed blast sprayed the room with the bits and vapors that remained of the cage. Grenades would be next, then grappling hooks and more grenades just before—

Jolober kicked his throttle as he rounded the aircar. The fans snarled and the ride, still on ground effect, became greasy as the skirts lifted undesirably.

The office rocked in a series of dense white flashes. The room lights went out and a large piece of shrapnel, the fuze housing of a grenade, powdered a fist-sized mass of the concrete coping beside Jolober.

His chair's throttle had a gate. With the fans already at normal maximum, he sphinctered his skirts into a nozzle and kicked again at the throttle. He could smell the chair's circuits frying under the overload as it lifted Jolober and Red Ike to the coping—

But it did lift them, and after a meter's run along the narrow track to build speed, it launched them across the black, empty air of the alley.

Red Ike wailed. The only sound Horace Jolober made was in his mind. He saw not a roof but the looming bow of a tank, and his fears shouted the word they hadn't been able to get out on Primavera either: *"No!"*

They cleared the coping of the other roof with a click, not a crash, and bounced as Jolober spilled air and cut thrust back to normal levels.

An explosion behind them lit the night red and blew chunks of Red Ike's office a hundred meters in the air.

Instead of trying to winkle out their quarry with gunfire, the assault team had lobbed a bunker-buster up the elevator shaft. The blast walloped Jolober even though distance and the pair of meter-high concrete copings protected his hunching form from dangerous fragments.

Nothing in the penthouse of the China Doll could have survived. It wasn't neat, but it saved lives where they counted—in the attacking force—and veteran soldiers have never put a high premium on finesse.

"You saved me," Red Ike said.

Jolober's ears were numb from the final explosion, but he could watch Red Ike's lips move in the flames lifting even higher from the front of the China Doll.

"I had to," Jolober said, marvelling at how fully human the alien seemed. "Those men, they're line soldiers. They think that because there were so many of them involved, nobody can be punished."

Hatches rang shut on the armored personnel carriers. A non-com snarled an order to stragglers that could be heard even over the drive fans.

Red Ike started toward the undamaged aircar parked beside them on this roof. Jolober's left hand still held the alien's wrist. Ike paused as if to pretend his movement had never taken place. His face was emotionless.

"Numbers made it a mutiny," Jolober continued. Part of him wondered whether Red Ike could hear the words he was speaking in a soft voice, but he was unwilling to shout.

It would have been disrespectful.

Fierce wind rocked the flames as the armored vehicles, tank in the lead as before, lifted and began to howl their way out of Paradise Port.

"I'll take care of you," Red Ike said. "You'll have Vicki back in three weeks, I promise. Tailored to *you*, just like the other. You won't be able to tell the difference."

"There's no me to take care of any more," said Horace Jolober with no more emotion than a man tossing his uniform into a laundry hamper.

"You see," he added as he reached behind him, "if they'd killed you tonight, the Bonding Authority would have disbanded both units *whatever* the Placidans wanted. But me? Anything I do is my responsibility."

Red Ike began to scream in a voice that became progressively less human as the sound continued.

Horace Jolober was strong enough that he wouldn't have needed the knife despite the way his victim struggled.

But it seemed like a fitting monument for Vicki.

THE BORDERS
OF INFINITY
Lois McMaster Bujold

Lois Bujold specializes in slinging her characters into seemingly hopeless situations to extract themselves by sheer force of wit. Her most beloved hero is Commodore Miles Naismith Vorkosigan, leader of the feared and respected Dendarii Mercenaries. In "The Borders of Infinity," Miles's mission is to rescue a certain important inmate from the Cetagandan prison camp on Marilac. The circumstances he finds there call for a major change of plans, and even the Commodore is daunted by the circumstances: after all, he has no backup, no weapons, and no clothes.

—E.M.

How could I have died and gone to hell without noticing the transition?

The opalescent force dome capped a surreal and alien landscape, frozen for a moment by Miles's disorientation and dismay. The dome defined a perfect circle, half a kilometer in diameter. Miles stood just inside its edge, where the glowing concave surface dove into the hard-packed dirt and disappeared. His imagination followed the arc buried beneath his feet to the far side, where it erupted again to complete the sphere. It was like being trapped inside an eggshell. An unbreakable eggshell.

Within was a scene from an ancient limbo. Dispirited men and women sat, or stood, or mostly lay down, singly or in scattered irregular groups, across the breadth of the arena. Miles's eye searched anxiously for some remnant of order or military grouping, but the inhabitants seemed splashed randomly as a liquid across the ground.

Perhaps he had been killed just now, just entering this prison camp. Perhaps his captors had betrayed him to his death, like those ancient Earth soldiers who had lured their victims sheeplike into poisoned showers, diverting and soothing their suspicions with stone soap, until their final enlightenment burst upon them in a choking cloud. Perhaps the annihilation of his body had been so swift, his neurons had not had time to carry the information to his brain. Why else did so many antique myths agree that hell was a circular place?

Dagoola IV Top Security Prison Camp #3. This was it? This naked . . . dinner plate? Miles had vaguely visioned barracks, marching guards, daily head counts, secret tunnels, escape committees.

It was the dome that made it all so simple, Miles realized. What need for barracks to shelter prisoners from the elements? The dome did it. What need for guards? The dome was generated from without. Nothing inside could breach it. No need for guards, or head counts. Tunnels were a futility, escape committees an absurdity. The dome did it all.

The only structures were what appeared to be big grey plastic mushrooms evenly placed about every hundred meters around the perimeter of the dome. What little activity there was seemed clustered around them. Latrines, Miles recognized.

Miles and his three fellow prisoners had entered through a temporary portal, which had closed behind them before the brief bulge of force dome containing their entry vanished in front of them. The nearest inhabitant of the dome, a man, lay a few meters away upon a sleeping mat identical to the one Miles now clutched. He turned his head slightly to stare at the little party of newcomers, smiled sourly, and rolled over on his side with his back to them. Nobody else nearby even bothered to look up.

"Holy shit," muttered one of Miles's companions. He and his two buddies drew together unconsciously. The three had been from the same unit once, they'd said. Miles had met them bare minutes ago, in their final stages of processing, where they had all been issued their total supply of worldly goods for life in Dagoola #3.

A single pair of loose grey trousers. A matching short-sleeved grey tunic. A rectangular sleeping mat, rolled up. A plastic cup. That was all. That, and the new numbers encoded upon their skins. It bothered Miles intensely that their captors had chosen to locate the numbers in the middle of their backs, where they couldn't see them. He resisted a futile urge to twist and crane his neck anyway, though his hand snaked up under his shirt to scratch a purely psychosomatic itch. You couldn't feel the encode either.

Some motion appeared in the tableau. A group of four or five men approaching. The welcoming committee at last? Miles was desperate for information. Where among all these countless grey men and women—no, not countless, Miles told himself firmly. They were all accounted for here.

The battered remnants of the 3rd and 4th Armored All-Terrain Rangers. The ingenious and tenacious civilian defenders of Garson Transfer Station. Winoweh's 2nd Battalion had been captured almost intact. And the 14th Commandos, survivors of the high-tech fortress at Fallow Core. Particularly the survivors of Fallow Core. Ten thousand, two hundred fourteen exactly. The planet Marilac's finest. Ten thousand, two hundred fifteen, counting himself. Ought he to count himself?

The welcoming committee drew up in a ragged bunch a few meters away. They looked tough and tall and muscular and not noticeably friendly. Dull, sullen eyes, full of a deadly boredom that even their present calculation did not lighten.

The two groups, the five and the three, sized each other up. The three turned, and started walking stiffly and prudently away. Miles realized belatedly that he, not a part of either group, was thus left alone.

Alone and immensely conspicuous. Self-consciousness, body-consciousness, normally held at bay by the simple fact that he didn't have time to waste on it, returned to him with a rush. If he stood on tiptoe, he might just measure five feet tall. Twisted spine, oversized head, bones rendered brittle and breakable by the same congenital accident that had stolen his height. His legs were even in length now, after the last operation, but surely not long enough to outrun these five. And where did one run to, in this place? He crossed off flight as an option.

Fight? Get serious.

This isn't going to work, he realized sadly, even as he started walking toward them. But it was more dignified than being chased down with the same result.

He tried to make his smile austere rather than foolish. No telling whether he succeeded. "Hi, there. Can you tell me where to find Colonel Guy Tremont's 14th Commando Division?"

One of the five snorted sardonically. Two moved behind Miles.

Well, a snort was almost speech. Expression, anyway. A start, a toehold. Miles focused on that one. "What's your name and rank and company, soldier?"

"No ranks in here, mutant. No companies. No soldiers. No nothing."

Miles glanced around. Surrounded, of course. Naturally. "You got some friends, anyway."

The talker almost smiled. "You don't."

Miles wondered if perhaps he had been premature in crossing off flight as an option. "I wouldn't count on that if I were—*unh!*" The kick to his kidneys, from behind, cut him off—he damn near bit his tongue—he fell, dropping bedroll and cup and landing in a tangle. A barefoot kick, no combat boots this time, thank God—by the rules of Newtonian physics, his attacker's foot ought to hurt just as much as his back. Fine. Jolly. Maybe they'd bruise their knuckles, punching him out. . . .

One of the gang gathered up Miles's late wealth, cup and bedroll. "Want his clothes? They're too little for me."

"Naw."

"Yeah," said the talker. "Take 'em anyway. Maybe bribe one of the women."

The tunic was jerked off over Miles's head, the pants over his feet. Miles was too busy protecting his head from random kicks to fight much for his clothes, trying obliquely to take as many hits as possible on his belly or ribcage, not arms or legs or jaw. A cracked rib was surely the most injury he could afford right now, here, at the beginning. A broken jaw would be the worst.

His assailants desisted only a little before they discovered by experimentation the secret weakness of his bones.

"*That's* how it is in here, mutant," said the talker, slightly winded.

"I was born naked," Miles panted from the dirt. "Didn't stop me."

"Cocky little shit," said the talker.

"Slow learner," remarked another.

The second beating was worse than the first. Two cracked ribs at least—his jaw barely escaped being smashed, at the cost of something painfully wrong in his left wrist, flung up as a shield. This time Miles resisted the impulse to offer any verbal parting shots.

He lay in the dirt and wished he could pass out.

He lay a long time, cradled in pain. He was not sure how long. The illumination from the force dome was even and shadowless, unchanging. Timeless, like eternity. Hell was eternal, was it not? This place had too damn many congruencies with hell, that was certain.

And here came another demon. . . . Miles blinked the approaching figure into focus. A man, as bruised and naked as Miles himself, gaunt-ribbed, starveling, knelt in the dirt a few meters away. His face was bony, aged by stress—he might have been 40, or 50—or 25.

His eyes were unnaturally prominent, due to the shrinking of his flesh. Their whites seemed to gleam feverishly against the dirt darkening his skin. Dirt, not beard stubble—every prisoner in here, male and female, had their hair cut short and the hair follicles stunned to prevent re-growth. Perpetually clean-shaved and crew-cut. Miles had undergone the same process bare hours ago. But whoever had processed this fellow must have been in a hurry. The hair stunner had missed a line on his cheek and a few dozen hairs grew there like a stripe on a badly-mown lawn. Even curled as they were, Miles could see they were several centimeters long, draggling down past the man's jaw. If only he knew how fast hair grew, he could calculate how long this fellow had been here. *Too long, whatever the numbers*, Miles thought with an inward sigh.

The man had the broken-off bottom half of a plastic cup, which he pushed cautiously toward Miles. His breath whistled raggedly past his yellowish teeth, from exertion or excitement or disease—probably not disease, they were all well immunized here. Escape, even through death, was not that easy. Miles rolled over and propped himself stiffly on his elbow, regarding his visitor through the thinning haze of his aches and pains.

The man scrabbled back slightly, smiled nervously. He nodded toward the cup. "Water. Better drink. The cup's cracked, and it all leaks out if you wait too long."

"Thanks," croaked Miles. A week ago, or in a previous lifetime, depending on how you counted time, Miles had dawdled over a selection of wines, dissatisfied with this or that nuance of flavor. His lips cracked as he grinned in memory. He drank. It was perfectly ordinary water, lukewarm, faintly redolent of chlorine and sulfur. *A refined body, but the bouquet is a bit presumptuous.* . . .

The man squatted in studied politeness until Miles finished drinking, then leaned forward on his knuckles in restrained urgency. "Are you the One?"

Miles blinked. "Am I the what?"

"The One. The *other* one, I should say. The scripture says there has to be two."

"Uh," Miles hesitated cautiously, "what exactly does the scripture say?"

The man's right hand wrapped over his knobbly left wrist, around which was tied a rag screwed into a sort of rope. He closed his eyes; his lips moved a moment, and then he recited aloud, ". . . but the pilgrims went up that hill with ease, because they had these two men to lead them by the arms; also they had left their garments behind them, for though they went in with them, they came out without them." His eyes popped back open to stare hopefully at Miles.

So, now we begin to see why this guy seems to be all by himself. . . . "Are you, perchance, the other One?" Miles shot at a venture.

The man nodded shyly.

"I see. Um . . ." How was it that he always attracted the nut cases? He licked the last drops of water from his lips. The fellow might have some screws loose, but he was certainly an improvement over the last lot, always presuming he didn't have another personality or two of the homicidal loonie variety tucked away in his head. No, in that case he'd be introducing himself as the Chosen Two, and not be looking for outside assistance. "Um . . . what's your name?"

"Suegar."

"Suegar. Right, all right. My name is Miles, by the way."

"Huh." Suegar grimaced in a sort of pleased irony. "Your name means 'soldier,' did you know?"

"Uh, yeah, so I've been told."

"But you're not a soldier . . . ?"

No subtle expensive trick of clothing line or uniform style here to hide from himself, if no one else, the peculiarities of his body. Miles flushed. "They were taking anything, toward the end. They made me a recruiting clerk. I never did get to fire my gun. Listen, Suegar—how did you come to know you were the One, or at any rate one of the Ones? Is it something you've always known?"

"It came on me gradually," confessed Suegar, shifting to sit cross-legged. "I'm the only one in here with the words, y'see." He caressed his rag rope again. "I've hunted all up and down the camp, but they only mock me. It was a kind of process of elimination, y'see, when they all gave up but me."

"Ah." Miles too sat up, only gasping a little in pain. Those ribs were going to be murder for the next few days. He nodded toward the rope bracelet. "Is that where you keep your scripture? Can I see it?" And how the hell had Suegar ever gotten a plastic flimsy, or loose piece of paper or whatever, in here?

Suegar clutched his arms protectively to his chest and shook his head. "They've been trying to take them from me for months, y'see. I can't be too careful. Until you prove you're the One. The devil can quote scripture, y'know."

Yes, that was rather what I had in mind. . . . Who knew what opportunities Suegar's "scripture" might contain? Well, maybe later. For now, keep dancing. "Are there any other signs?" asked Miles. "You see, I don't know that I'm your One, but on the other hand I don't know I'm not, either. I just got here, after all."

Suegar shook his head again. "It's only five or six sentences, y'see. You have to interpolate a lot."

I'll bet. Miles did not voice the comment aloud. "However did you come by it? Or get it in here?"

"It was at Port Lisma, y'see, just before we were captured," said Suegar. "House-to-house fighting. One of my boot heels had come a bit loose, and it clicked when I walked. Funny, with all that barrage coming down around our ears, how a little thing like that can get under your skin. There was this bookcase with a glass front, real antique books made of paper—I smashed it open with my gun butt and tore out part of a page from one, and folded it up to stick in my boot heel, to make a sort of shim, y'see, and stop the clicking. Didn't look at the book. Didn't even know it was scripture till later. At least, I think it's scripture. It sounds like scripture, anyway. It must be scripture."

Suegar twisted his beard hairs nervously around his finger. "When we were waiting to be processed, I'd pulled it out of my boot, just idle-like, y'know. I had it in my hand—the processing guard saw it, but he just didn't take it away from me. Probably thought it was just a harmless piece of paper. Didn't know it was scripture. I still had it in my hand when we were dumped in here. D'you know, it's the only piece of writing in this whole camp?" he added rather proudly. "It must be scripture."

"Well . . . you take good care of it, then," advised Miles kindly. "If you've preserved it this long, it was obviously meant to be your job."

"Yeah . . ." Suegar blinked. Tears? "I'm the only one in here with a job, aren't I? So I must be one of the Ones."

"Sounds good to me," said Miles agreeably. "Say, ah," he glanced around the vast featureless dome, "how do you find your way around in here, anyway?" The place was decidedly undersupplied with landmarks. It reminded Miles of nothing so much as a penguin rookery. Yet penguins seemed able to find their rocky nests. He was going to have to start thinking like a penguin—or get a penguin to direct him—he studied his guide bird, who had gone absent and was doodling in the dirt. Circles, naturally.

"Where's the mess hall?" Miles asked more loudly. "Where did you get that water?"

"Water taps are on the outside of the latrines," said Suegar, "but they only work part of the time. No mess hall. We just get rat bars. Sometimes."

"Sometimes?" said Miles angrily. He could count Suegar's ribs. "Dammit, the Cetagandans are claiming loudly to be treating their POW's by Interstellar Judiciary Commission rules. So many square meters of space per person, 3,000 calories a day, at least 50 grams of protein, two liters of drinking water—you should be getting at least two IJC standard ration bars a day. Are they starving you?"

"After a while," Suegar sighed, "you don't really care if you get yours or not." The animation that his interest in Miles as a new and hopeful object in his world had lent Suegar seemed to be falling away. His breathing had slowed, his posture slumped. He seemed about to lie down in the dirt. Miles wondered if Suegar's sleeping mat had suffered the same fate at his own. Quite some time ago, probably.

"Look, Suegar—I think I may have a relative in this camp somewhere. A cousin of my mother's. D'you think you could help me find him?"

"It might be good for you, to have a relative," Suegar agreed. "It's not good to be by yourself, here."

"Yeah, I found that out. But how can you find anyone? It doesn't look too organized."

"Oh, there's—there's groups and groups. Everyone pretty much stays in the same place after a while."

"He was in the 14th Commandos. Where are they?"

"None of the *old* groups are left, much."

"He was Colonel Tremont. Colonel Guy Tremont."

"Oh, an officer." Suegar's forehead wrinkled in

worry. "That makes it harder. You weren't an officer, were you? Better not let on, if you were—"

"I was a clerk," repeated Miles.

"—because there's groups here who don't like officers. A clerk. You're probably OK, then."

"Were you an officer, Suegar?" asked Miles curiously.

Suegar frowned at him, twisted his beard hairs. "Marilac Army's gone. If there's no army, it can't have officers, can it?"

Miles wondered briefly if he might get farther faster by just walking away from Suegar and trying to strike up a conversation with the next random prisoner he came across. Groups and groups. And, presumably, groups, like the five burly surly brothers. He decided to stick with Suegar for a while longer. For one thing, he wouldn't feel quite so naked if he wasn't naked by himself.

"Can you take me to anybody who used to be in the 14th?" Miles urged Suegar anew. "Anybody, who might know Tremont by sight."

"You don't know him?"

"We'd never met in person. I've seen vids of him. But I'm afraid his appearance may be . . . changed, by now."

Suegar touched his own face pensively. "Yeah, probably."

Miles clambered painfully to his feet. The temperature in the dome was just a little cool, without clothes. A voiceless draft raised the hairs on his arms. If he could just get one garment back, would he prefer his pants, to cover his genitals, or his shirt, to disguise his crooked back? Screw it. No time. He held out a hand to help Suegar up. "Come on."

Suegar glanced up at him. "You can always tell a newcomer. You're still in a hurry. In here, you slow down. Your brain slows down. . . ."

"Your scripture got anything to say on that?" inquired Miles impatiently.

" '. . . they therefore went up here with much agility and speed, through the foundation of the city . . .' " Twin verticals appeared between Suegar's eyebrows, as he frowned speculatively at Miles.

Thank you, thought Miles, *I'll take it.* He pulled Suegar up. "Come on, then."

Neither agility nor speed, but at least progress. Suegar led him on a shambling walk across a quarter of the camp, through some groups, in wide arcs around others. Miles saw the surly brothers again at a distance, sitting on their collection of mats. Miles upped his estimation of the size of the tribe from five to about fifteen. Some men sat in twos or threes or sixes, a few sat alone, as far as possible from any others, which still wasn't very far.

The largest group by far consisted entirely of women. Miles studied them with electric interest as soon as his eye picked up the size of their unmarked boundary. There were several hundred of them at least. None were matless, although some shared. Their perimeter was actually patrolled, by groups of half a dozen or so strolling slowly about. They apparently defended two latrines for their exclusive use.

"Tell me about the girls, Suegar," Miles urged his companion, with a nod toward their group.

"Forget the girls." Suegar's grin actually had a sardonic edge. "They do not put out."

"What, not at all? None of them? I mean, here we all are, with nothing to do but entertain each other. I'd think at least some of them would be interested." Miles's reason raced ahead of Suegar's answer, mired in unpleasantness. How unpleasant did it get in here?

For answer, Suegar pointed upward to the dome. "You know we're all monitored in here. They can see everything, pick up every word if they want. That is, if there's still anybody out there. They may have all gone away, and just forgotten to turn the dome off. I have dreams about that, sometimes. I dream that I'm here, in this dome, forever. Then I wake up, and

I'm here, in this dome. . . . Sometimes I'm not sure if I'm awake or asleep. Except that the food is still coming, and once in a while—not so often, any more— somebody new, like you. The food could be auto- mated, though, I suppose. You could be a dream. . . ."

"They're still out there," said Miles grimly.

Suegar sighed. "You know, in a way, I'm almost glad."

Monitored, yes. Miles knew all about the monitor- ing. He put down an urge to wave and call *Hi, Mom!* Monitoring must be a stultifying job for the goons out there. He wished they might be bored to death. "But what's that got to do with the girls, Suegar?"

"Well, at first everybody was pretty inhibited by that—" he pointed skywards again. "Then after a while we discovered that they didn't interfere with anything we did. At all. There were some rapes. . . . Since then things have been—deteriorating."

"Hm. Then I suppose the idea of starting a riot, and breaching the dome when they bring troops inside to restore order, is a no-go?"

"That was tried once, a long time ago. Don't know how long." Suegar twisted his hairs. "They don't have to come inside to stop a riot. They can reduce the dome's diameter—they reduced it to about a hundred meters, that time. Nothing to stop them reducing it down to one meter, with all of us still inside, if they choose. It stopped the riot, anyway. Or they can reduce the gas permeability of the dome to zilch and just let us breathe ourselves into a coma. That's happened twice."

"I see," said Miles. It made his neck crawl.

A bare hundred or so meters away, the side of the dome began to bulge inward like an aneurysm. Miles touched Suegar's arm. "What's happening there? More new prisoners being delivered?"

Suegar glanced around. "Uh, oh. We're not in a real good position, here." He hovered a moment, as if uncertain whether to go forward or back.

A wave of movement rippled through the camp from the bulge outward, of people getting to their feet. Faces turned magnetically toward the side of the dome. Little knots of men came together; a few sprinters began running. Some people didn't get up at all. Miles glanced back towards the women's group. About half of them were forming rapidly into a sort of phalanx.

"We're so close—what the hell, maybe we've got a chance," said Suegar. "Come on!" He started toward the bulge at his most rapid pace, a jog. Miles perforce jogged too, trying to jar his ribs as little as possible. But he was quickly winded, and his rapid breathing added an excruciating torque to his torso.

"What are we doing?" Miles started to pant to Suegar, before the dome's extruding bulge dissolved with a fading twinkle, and he saw what they were doing, saw it all.

Before the force dome's shimmering barrier now sat a dark brown pile, roughly a meter high, two meters deep, three meters wide. IJC standard ration bars, Miles recognized. Rat bars, apocryphally named after their supposed principal ingredient. Fifteen hundred calories each. Twenty-five grams of protein, 50% of the human MDR for vitamins A, B, C, and the rest of the alphabet—tasted like a shingle sprinkled with sugar and would sustain life and health forever or for as long as you could stand to keep eating them.

Shall we have a contest, children, to guess how many rat bars are in that pile? Miles thought. *No contest. I don't even have to measure the height and divide by three centimeters. It has to be 10,215 exactly. How ingenious.*

The Cetagandan Psy Ops corps must contain some remarkable minds. If they ever fell into his hands, Miles wondered, should he recruit them—or exterminate them? This brief fantasy was overwhelmed by the need to keep to his feet in the present reality, as

10,000 or so people, minus the wholly despairing and those too weak to move, all tried to descend on the same six square meters of the camp at once.

The first sprinters reached the pile, grabbed up armloads of rat bars, and started to sprint off. Some made it to the protection of friends, divided their spoils, and started to move away from the center of the growing human maelstrom. Others failed to dodge clots of operators like the burly surly brothers, and were violently relieved of their prizes. The second wave of sprinters, who didn't get away in time, were pinned up against the side of the dome by the incoming bodies.

Miles and Suegar, unfortunately, were in this second category. Miles's view was reduced to a sweating, heaving, stinking, swearing mass of elbows and chests and backs.

"Eat, eat!" Suegar urged around stuffed cheeks as he and Miles were separated by the pack. But the bar Miles had grabbed was twisted out of his hands before he had gathered his wits enough to follow Suegar's advice. Anyway, his hunger was nothing to his terror of being crushed, or worse, falling underfoot. His own feet pummeled over something soft, but he was unable to push back with enough strength to give the person—man, woman, who knew?—a chance to get up again.

In time the press lessened, and Miles found the edge of the crowd and broke free again. He staggered a little way off and fell to the dirt to sit, shaken and shaking, pale and cold. His breath rasped unevenly in his throat. It took him a long time to get hold of himself again.

Sheer chance, that this had hit his rawest nerve, his darkest fears, threatened his most dangerous weakness. *I could die here*, he realized, *without ever seeing the enemy's face*. But there seemed to be no new bones broken, except possibly in his left foot. He was not too sure about his left foot. The elephant who had trod on it was surely getting more than his fair share of rat bars.

All right, Miles thought at last. *That's enough time spent on R&R. On your feet, soldier.* It was time to go find Colonel Tremont.

Guy Tremont. The real hero of the siege of Fallow Core. The defiant one, the one who'd held, and held, and held, after General Xian fled, after Baneri was killed.

Xian had sworn to return, but then Xian had run into that meat grinder at Vassily Station. HQ had promised re-supply, but then HQ and its vital shuttleport had been taken by the Cetagandans.

But by this time Tremont and his troops had lost communication. So they held, waiting, and hoping. Eventually resources were reduced to hope and rocks. Rocks were versatile, they could either be boiled for soup or thrown at the enemy. At last Fallow Core was taken. Not surrendered. Taken.

Guy Tremont. Miles wanted very much to meet Guy Tremont.

On his feet and looking around, Miles spotted a distant shambling scarecrow being pelted off from a group with clods of dirt. Suegar paused out of range of their missiles, still pointing to the rag on his wrist and talking. The three or four men he was haranguing turned their backs to him by way of a broad hint.

Miles sighed and started trudging toward him. "Hey, Suegar!" he called and waved when he got closer.

"Oh, there you are." Suegar turned and brightened, and joined him. "I lost you." Suegar rubbed dirt out of his eyebrows. "Nobody wants to listen, y'know?"

"Yeah, well, most of them have heard you at least once by now, right?"

"Pro'bly twenty times. I keep thinking I might

have missed one, y'see. Maybe the very One, the other One."

"Well, I'd be glad to listen to you, but I've really got to find Colonel Tremont first. You said you knew somebody . . . ?"

"Oh, right. This way." Suegar led off again.

"Thanks. Say, is every chow call like that last one?"

"Pretty much."

"What's to keep some—group—from just taking over that arc of the dome?"

"It's never issued at the same place twice. They move it all around the perimeter. There was a lot of strategy debated at one time, as to whether it was better to be at the center, so's you're never more than half a diameter away, or near the edge, so's to be up front at least part of the time. Some guys had even worked out the mathemetics of it, probabilities and all that."

"Which do you favor?"

"Oh, I don't have a spot, I move around and take my chances." His right hand touched his rag. "It's not the most important thing, anyway. Still, it was good to eat—today. Whatever day this is."

"Today is November 2, '97, Earth Common Era."

"Oh? Is that all?" Suegar pulled his beard strands out straight and rolled his eyes, attempting to look across his face at them. "Thought I'd been here longer than that. Why, it hasn't even been three years. Huh." He added apologetically, "In here it's always today."

"Mm," said Miles. "So the rat bars are always delivered in a pile like that, eh?"

"Yeah."

"Damned ingenious."

"Yeah," Suegar sighed. Rage, barely breathed, was camouflaged in that sigh, in the twitch of Suegar's hands. *So, my madman is not so simple. . . .*

"Here we are," Suegar added. They paused before

a group defined by half a dozen sleeping mats in a rough circle. One man looked up and glowered.

"Go away, Suegar. I ain't in the mood for a sermon."

"That the colonel?" whispered Miles.

"Naw, his name's Oliver. I knew him—a long time ago. He was at Fallow Core, though," Suegar whispered back. "He can take you to him."

Suegar bundled Miles forward. "This is Miles. He's new. Wants to talk to you." Suegar himself backed away. Helpfully, Miles realized. Suegar was aware of his unpopularity, it seemed.

Miles studied the next link in his chain. Oliver had managed to retain his grey pajamas, sleeping mat, and cup intact, which reminded Miles again of his own nakedness. On the other hand, Oliver did not seem to be in possession of any ill-gotten duplicates. Oliver might be as burly as the surly brothers, but was not otherwise related. That was good. Not that Miles in his present state need have any more worries about thievery.

Oliver stared at Miles without favor, then seemed to relent. "What d'you want?" he growled.

Miles opened his hands. "I'm looking for Colonel Guy Tremont."

"Ain't no colonels in here, boy."

"He was a cousin of my mother's. Nobody in the family—nobody in the outside world—has heard anything from or about him since Fallow Core fell. I—I'm not from any of the other units or pieces of units that are in here. Colonel Tremont is the only person I know anything about at all." Miles clasped his hands together and tried to look waif-like. Real doubt shook him, drew down his brows. "Is he still alive, even?"

Oliver frowned. "Relative, eh?" He scratched the side of his nose with a thick finger. "I suppose you got a right. But it won't do you any good, boy, if that's what you're thinking."

"I . . ." Miles shook his head. "At this point, I just want to *know*."

"Come on, then." Oliver levered himself to his feet with a grunt and lumbered off without looking over his shoulder.

Miles limped in his wake. "Are you taking me to him?"

Oliver made no answer until they'd finished their journey, only a few dozen meters, among and between sleeping mats. One man swore, one spat; most ignored them.

One mat lay at the edge of a group, almost far enough away to look alone. A figure lay curled up on his side with his back to them. Oliver stood silent, big fists on hips, and regarded it.

"Is that the colonel?" Miles whispered urgently.

"No, boy." Oliver sucked on his lower lip. "Only his remains."

Miles, alarmed, knelt down. Oliver was speaking poetically, Miles realized with relief. The man breathed. "Colonel Tremont? Sir?"

Miles's heart sank again, as he saw that breathing was about all that Tremont did. He lay inert, his eyes open but fixed on nothing. They did not even flick toward Miles and dismiss him with contempt. He was thin, thinner than Suegar even. Miles traced the angle of his jaw, the shape of his ear, from the holovids he'd studied. The remains of a face, like the ruined fortress of Fallow Core. It took nearly an archeologist's insight to recognize the connections between past and present.

He was dressed, his cup sat upright by his head, but the dirt around his mat was churned to acrid, stinking mud. From urine, Miles realized. Tremont's elbows were marked with lesions, the beginning of decubiti, bedsores. A damp patch on the grey fabric of his trousers over his bony hips hinted at more advanced and horrible sores beneath.

Yet somebody must be tending him, Miles thought, *or he wouldn't be looking even this good.*

Oliver knelt beside Miles, bare toes squishing in the mud, and pulled a hunk of rat bar from beneath the elastic waistband of his trousers. He crumbled a bit between his thick fingers and pushed it between Tremont's lips. "Eat," he whispered. The lips almost moved; the crumbs dribbled to the mat. Oliver tried again, seemed to become conscious of Miles's eyes upon him, and stuffed the rest of the rat bar back into his pants with an unintelligible grumble.

"Was—was he injured when Fallow Core was overrun?" asked Miles. "Head injury?"

Oliver shook his head. "Fallow Core wasn't stormed, boy."

"But it fell on October 6th, it was reported, and—"

"It fell on October 5th. Fallow Core was betrayed." Oliver turned and walked away before his stiffened face could betray any emotion.

Miles knelt in the mud and let his breath trickle out slowly.

So. And so.

Was this the end of his quest, then?

He wanted to pace and think, but walking still hurt too much. He hobbled a little way off, trying not to accidentally infringe upon the territory of any sizeable group, and sat, then lay in the dirt with his hands behind his head, staring up at the pearly glow of the dome sealed like a lid over them all.

He considered his options, one, two, three. He considered them carefully. It didn't take long.

I thought you didn't believe in good guys and bad guys? He had cauterized his emotions, he'd thought, coming in here, for his own protection, but he could feel his carefully cultivated impartiality slipping. He was beginning to hate that dome in a really intimate, personal way. Aesthetically elegant, form united with function as perfectly as an eggshell, a marvel of physics—perverted into an instrument of torture.

Subtle torture . . . Miles reviewed the Interstellar Judiciary Commission's rules for the treatment of POW's, to which Cetaganda was a signatory. So many square meters of space per person, yes, they were certainly supplied with that. No prisoner to be solitarily confined for a period exceeding 24 hours—right, no solitude in here except by withdrawal into madness. No dark periods longer than 12 hours, that was easy, no dark periods at all, the perpetual glare of noon instead. No beatings—indeed, the guards could say with truth that they never laid a hand on their prisoners. They just watched, while the prisoners beat each other up instead. Rapes, even more strictly forbidden, doubtless handled the same way.

Miles had seen what they could do with their issue of two IJC standard ration bars per person per day. The rat bar riot was a particularly neat touch, he thought. No one could fail to participate (he rubbed his growling stomach). The enemy might have seeded the initial breakdown by sending in a short pile. But maybe not—the first person who snatched two instead of one left another foodless. Maybe next time that one took three, to make up for it, and so it quickly snowballed. Breaking down any hope of order, pitting group against group, person against person in a scrambling dogfight, a twice-a-day reminder of their powerlessness and degradation. None could afford for long to hold themselves aloof unless they wished to embrace slow starvation.

No forced labor—hah, check. That would require the imposition of order. Access to medical personnel— right, the various units' own medics must be mixed in out there somewhere. He re-ran the wording of that paragraph through his memory again—by God, it *did* say "personnel," didn't it? No medicine, just medical personnel. Empty-handed, naked doctors and medtechs. His lips drew back in a mirthless grin.

Accurate lists of prisoners taken had been duly dispatched, as required. But no other communication . . .

Communication. This lack of word from the outside world might drive even him crazy shortly. It was as bad as prayer, talking to a God who never talked back. No wonder they all seemed touched with a sort of solipsistic schizophrenia here. Their doubts infected him. *Was* anybody still out there? Could his voice be heard and understood?

Ah, blind faith. The leap of faith. His right hand clenched, as if crushing an eggshell. "This," he enunciated clearly, "calls for a major change of plans."

He drove himself to his feet to go find Suegar again.

Miles found him not far off, hunkered in the dirt doodling. Suegar looked up with a brief smile. "Did Oliver take you to—to your cousin?"

"Yes, but I came too late. He's dying."

"Yeah . . . I was afraid that might be the case. Sorry."

"Me too." Miles was momentarily distracted from his purpose by a practical curiosity. "Suegar, what do they do with dead bodies here?"

"There's a rubbish pile of sorts, over against one side of the dome. The dome sort of extrudes and laps it up every once in a while, same way as food and new prisoners are introduced. Usually by the time a body swells and starts to stink, somebody'll drag it over there. I take 'em sometimes."

"No chance of anybody sneaking out in the rubbish pile, I suppose?"

"They microwave-incinerate it all before the portal's opened."

"Ah." Miles took a deep breath, and launched himself. "Suegar, it's come to me. I *am* the other One."

Suegar nodded serenely, unsurprised. "I'd had it figured."

Miles paused, nonplussed. Was that all the response . . . ? He had expected something more energetic, either pro or con. "It came to me in a vision," he declared dramatically, following his script anyway.

"Oh, yeah?" Suegar's attention sharpened gratifyingly. "I've never gotten a vision," he added with envy. "Had to figure it all out, y'know, from context. What's it like? A trance?"

Shit, and here I thought this guy talked with elves and angels. . . . Miles backed down slightly. "No, it's like a thought, only more compelling. It storms your will—burns like lust, only not so easy to satisfy. Not like a trance, because it drives you outward, not inward." He hesitated, unsettled, having spoken more truth than he'd intended.

Suegar looked vastly encouraged. "Oh, good. I was afraid for a second you might be one of those guys who start talking to people nobody else can see."

Miles glanced upward involuntarily, returned his gaze straightly to Suegar.

"—so that's a vision. Why, I've felt like that." His eyes seemed to focus and intensify.

"Didn't you recognize it in yourself?" asked Miles blandly.

"Not by name . . . it's not a comfortable thing, to be chosen so. I tried to evade it for a long time, but God finds ways of dealing with draft dodgers."

"You're too modest, Suegar. You've believed in your scripture, but not in yourself. Don't you know that when you're given a task, you're given the power to accomplish it as well?"

Suegar sighed in joyous satisfaction. "I knew it was a job for two. It's just like the scripture said."

"Uh, right. So now we are two. But we must be more. I guess we'd better start with your friends."

"That won't take much time," said Suegar wryly. "You got a step two in mind, I hope?"

"Then we'll start with your enemies. Or your nod-

ding acquaintances. We'll start with the first bleeding body that crosses our path. It doesn't matter
where we start, because I mean to have them all, in
the end. All, to the last and least." A particularly apt
quote shot across his memory, and he declaimed
vigorously, " 'Those who have ears, let them hear.'
All." Miles sent a real prayer up from his heart with
that one.

"All right," Miles pulled Suegar to his feet, "let's
go preach to the unconverted."

Suegar laughed suddenly. "I had a top kick once
who used to say, 'Let's go kick some ass,' in just that
tone of voice."

"That, too," Miles grimaced. "You understand, uni-
versal membership in this congregation won't come
all voluntary. But you leave the recruiting to me,
hear?"

Suegar stroked his beard hairs, regarded Miles
from beneath raised brows. "A clerk, eh?"

"Right."

"Yes, sir."

They started with Oliver.

Miles gestured. "May we step into your office?"

Oliver rubbed his nose with the back of his hand
and sniffed. "Let me give you a piece of advice, boy.
You ain't gonna make it in here as a stand-up comic.
Every joke that can possibly be made has been run
into the ground. Even the sick ones."

"Very well." Miles sat cross-legged, near Oliver's
mat but not too near. Suegar hunkered down behind
Miles's shoulder, not so welded to the ground, as if
ready to skip backwards if necessary. "I'll lay it out
straight, then. I don't like the way things are run
around here."

Oliver's mouth twisted sardonically; he did not
comment aloud. He didn't need to.

"I'm going to change them," Miles added.

"Shit," said Oliver, and rolled back over.

"Starting here and now."

After a moment's silence Oliver added, "Go away or I'll pound you."

Suegar started to get up; Miles irritably motioned him back down.

"He was a commando," Suegar whispered worriedly. "He can break you in half."

"Nine-tenths of the people in this camp can break me in half, including the girls," Miles whispered back. "It's not a significant consideration."

Miles leaned forward, grasped Oliver's chin, and twisted his face back toward him. Suegar sucked his breath through his teeth with a whistle at this dangerous tactic.

"Now, there's this about cynicism, Sergeant. It's the universe's most supine moral position. Real comfortable. If nothing can be done, then you're not some kind of shit for not doing it, and you can lie there and stink to yourself in perfect peace."

Oliver batted Miles's hand down, but did not turn away again. Rage flared in his eyes. "Suegar tell you I was a sergeant?" he hissed.

"No, it's written on your forehead in letters of fire. Listen up, Oliver—"

Oliver rolled over and up as far as supporting his upper body with his knuckles on his sleeping mat. Suegar flinched, but did not flee.

"You listen up, mutant," Oliver snarled. "We've done it all already. We've done drill, and games, and clean living, exercise, and cold showers, except there ain't no cold showers. We've done group sings and floor shows. We've done it by the numbers, by the book, by candlelight. We've done it by force, and made real war on each other. After that we did sin and sex and sadism till we were ready to puke. We've done it all at least ten times. You think you're the first reformer to come through here?"

"No, Oliver," Miles leaned into his face, his eyes

boring into Oliver's burning eyes unscorched. His voice fell to a whisper. "I think I'm the last."

Oliver was silent a moment, then barked a laugh. "By God, Suegar has found his soul-mate at last. Two loonies together, just like his scripture says."

Miles paused thoughtfully, sat up as straight as his spine would allow. "Read me your scripture again, Suegar. The full text." He closed his eyes for total concentration, also to discourage interruptions from Oliver.

Suegar rustled around and cleared his throat nervously. " 'For those that shall be the heirs of salvation,' " he began. " 'Thus they went along toward the gate. Now you must note that the city stood upon a mighty hill, but the pilgrims went up that hill with ease, because they had these two men to lead them by the arms; also they had left their mortal garments behind them in the river, for though they went in with them, they came out without them. They therefore went up here with much agility and speed, through the foundation upon which the city was framed higher than the clouds. They therefore went up through the regions of the air . . .' " He added apologetically, "It breaks off there. That's where I tore the page. Not sure what that signifies."

"Probably means that after that you're supposed to improvise for yourself," Miles suggested, opening his eyes again. So, that was the raw material he was building on. He had to admit the last line in particular gave him a turn, a chill like a bellyfull of cold worms. So be it. Forward.

"There you are, Oliver. That's what I'm offering. The only hope worth breathing for. Salvation itself."

"Very uplifting," sneered Oliver.

" 'Uplifted' is just what I intend you all to be. You've got to understand, Oliver, I'm a fundamentalist. I take my scriptures *very* literally."

Oliver opened his mouth, then closed it with a snap. Miles had his utter attention.

Communication at last, Miles breathed inwardly. *We have connected.*

"It would take a miracle," said Oliver at last, "to uplift this whole place."

"Mine is not a theology of the elect. I intend to preach to the masses. Even," he was definitely getting into the swing of this, "the sinners. Heaven is for everyone.

"But miracles, by their very nature, must break in from outside. We don't carry them in our pockets—"

"You don't, that's for sure," muttered Oliver with a glance at Miles's undress.

"—we can only pray, and prepare ourselves for a better world. But miracles come only to the prepared. Are you prepared, Oliver?" Miles leaned forward, his voice vibrating with energy.

"Sh . . ." Oliver's voice trailed off. He glanced for confirmation, oddly enough, at Suegar. "Is this guy for real?"

"He thinks he's faking it," said Suegar blandly, "but he's not. He's the One, all right and tight."

The cold worms writhed again. Dealing with Suegar, Miles decided, was like fencing in a hall of mirrors. Your target, though real, was never quite where it looked like it should be.

Oliver inhaled. Hope and fear, belief and doubt, intermingled in his face. "How shall we be saved, Rev'rend?"

"Ah—call me Brother Miles, I think. Yes. Tell me—how many converts can you deliver on your own naked, unsupported authority?"

Oliver looked extremely thoughtful. "Just let them see that light, and they'll follow it anywhere."

"Well . . . well . . . salvation is for all, to be sure, but there may be certain temporary practical advantages to maintaining a priesthood. I mean, blessed also are they who do not see, and yet believe."

"It's true," agreed Oliver, "that if your religion

failed to deliver a miracle, that a human sacrifice would certainly follow."

"Ah . . . quite," Miles gulped. "You are a man of acute insight."

"That's not an insight," said Oliver. "That's a personal guarantee."

"Yes, well . . . to return to my question. How many followers can you raise? I'm talking bodies here, not souls."

Oliver frowned, cautious still. "Maybe twenty."

"Can any of them bring in others? Branch out, hook in more?"

"Maybe."

"Make them your corporals, then. I think we had better disregard any previous ranks here. Call it, ah, the Army of the Reborn. No. The Reformation Army. That scans better. We shall be re-formed. The body has disintegrated like the caterpillar in its chrysalis, into nasty green gook, but we shall re-form into the butterfly and fly away."

Oliver sniffed again. "Just what reforms you planning?"

"Just one, I think. The food."

Oliver gave him a disbelieving stare. "You sure this isn't just a scam to get yourself a free meal?"

"True, I *am* getting hungry . . ." Miles backed off from the joke as Oliver remained icily unimpressed. "But so are a lot of other people. By tomorrow, we can have them all eating out of our hands."

"When would you want these twenty guys?"

"By the next chow call." Good, he'd startled the man.

"That soon?"

"You understand, Oliver, the belief that you have all the time in the world is an illusion this place fosters on purpose. Resist it."

"You're sure in a hurry."

"So, you got a dental appointment? I think not. Besides, I'm only half your mass. I gotta move twice as fast just to keep up the momentum. Twenty, plus. By next chow call."

"What the hell do you think you're gonna be able to do with twenty guys?"

"We're going to take the food pile."

Oliver's lips tightened in disgust. "Not with twenty guys, you're not. No go. Besides, it's been done. I told you we'd made real war in here. It'd be a quick massacre."

"—and then, after we've taken it—we re-distribute it. Fair and square, one rat bar per customer, all controlled and quartermasterly. To sinners and all. By the next chow call everybody who's ever been shorted will be coming over to us. And then we'll be in a position to deal with the hard cases."

"You're nuts. You can't do it. Not with twenty guys."

"Did I say we were only going to have twenty guys? Suegar, did I say that?"

Suegar, listening in rapt fascination, shook his head.

"Well, I ain't sticking my neck out to get pounded unless you can produce some visible means of support," said Oliver. "This could get us killed."

"Can do," Miles promised recklessly. One had to start lifting somewhere; his imaginary bootstraps would do well enough. "I will deliver 500 troops to the sacred cause by chow call."

"You do that, and I'll walk the perimeter of this camp naked on my hands," retorted Oliver.

Miles grinned. "I may hold you to that, Sergeant. Twenty plus. By chow call." Miles stood. "Come on, Suegar."

Oliver waved them off irritably. They retreated in good order. When Miles looked back over his shoulder, Oliver had arisen, and was walking toward a group of occupied mats tangential to his own, waving down an apparent acquaintance.

"So where do we get 500 troops before next chow

call?" Suegar asked. "I better warn you, Oliver was the best thing I had. The next is bound to be tougher."

"What," said Miles, "is your faith wavering so soon?"

"I believe," said Suegar, "I just don't see. Maybe that makes me blessed, I dunno."

"I'm surprised. I thought it was pretty obvious. There." Miles pointed across the camp toward the unmarked border of the women's group.

"Oh." Suegar stopped short. "Oh, oh. I don't think so, Miles."

"Yes. Let's go."

"You won't get in there without a change-of-sex operation."

"What, as God-driven as you are, haven't you tried to preach your scripture to them?"

"I tried. Got pounded. Tried elsewhere after that."

Miles paused, and pursed his lips, studying Suegar. "It wasn't defeat, or you wouldn't have hung on long enough to meet me. Was it—ah, shame, that drained your usual resolve? You got something to work off in that quarter?"

Suegar shook his head. "Not personally. Except maybe, sins of omission. I just didn't have the heart to harass 'em any more."

"This whole place is suffering from sins of omission." A relief, that Suegar wasn't some sort of self-confessed rapist. Miles's eyes swept the scene, teasing out the pattern from the limited cues of position, grouping, activity. "Yes . . . predator pressure produces herd behavior. Social—fragmentation here being what it is, the pressure must be pretty high, to hold a group of that size together. But I hadn't noticed any incidents since I got here. . . ."

"It comes and goes," said Suegar. "Phases of the moon or something."

Phases of the moon, right. Miles sent up a prayer of thanks in his heart to whatever gods might be—to Whom it may concern—that the Cetagandans appeared to have implanted some standard time-release anti-ovulant in all their female prisoners, along with their other immunizations. Bless the forgotten individual who'd put *that* clause in the IJC rules, forcing the Cetagandans into more subtle forms of legal torture. And yet, would the presence of pregnancies, infants, and children among the prisoners have been another destabilizing stress—or a stabilizing force deeper and stronger than all the previous loyalties the Cetagandans seemed to have so successfully broken down? From a purely logistical viewpoint, Miles was elated that the question was theoretical.

"Well . . ." Miles took a deep breath, and pulled an imaginary hat down over his eyes at an aggressive angle. "I'm new here, and so temporarily unembarrassed. Let he who is without sin cast the first lure. Besides, I have an advantage for this sort of negotiation. I'm clearly not a threat." He marched forward.

"I'll wait for you here," called Suegar helpfully, and hunkered down where he was.

Miles timed his forward march to intersect a patrol of six women strolling down their perimeter. He arranged himself in front of them and swept off his imaginary hat to hold strategically over his crotch. "Good afternoon, ladies. Allow me to apologize for m'beh—"

His opening line was interrupted by a mouthful of dirt abruptly acquired as his legs were swept backward and his shoulders forward by the four women who had parted around him, dumping him neatly on his face. He had not even managed to spit it out when he found himself plucked up and whirled dizzily through the air, still face-down, by hands grasping his arms and legs. A muttered count of three, and he was soaring in a short forlorn arc, to land in a heap not far from Suegar. The patrollers walked on without another word.

"See what I mean?" said Suegar.

Miles turned his head to look at him. "You had

that trajectory calculated to the centimeter, didn't you?" he said smearily.

"Just about," agreed Suegar. "I figured they could heave you quite a bit farther than usual, on account of your size."

Miles scrambled back up to a sitting position, still trying to get his wind. Damn the ribs, which had grown almost bearable, but which now wrung his chest with electric agony at every breath. In a few minutes he got up and brushed himself off. As an afterthought, he picked up his invisible hat, too. Dizzied, he had to brace his hands on his knees a moment.

"All right," he muttered, "back we go."

"Miles—"

"It's gotta be done, Suegar. No other choice. Anyway, I can't quit, once I've started. I've been told I'm pathologically persistent. I *can't* quit."

Suegar opened his mouth to object, then swallowed his protest. "Right," he said. He settled down cross-legged, his right hand unconsciously caressing his rag rope library. "I'll wait till you call me in." He seemed to fall into a reverie, or meditation—or maybe a doze.

Miles's second foray ended precisely like the first, except that his trajectory was perhaps a little wider and a little higher. The third attempt went the same way, but his flight was much shorter.

"Good," he muttered to himself. "Must be tiring 'em out."

This time he skipped in parallel to the patrol, out of reach but well within hearing. "Look," he panted, "you don't have to do this piecemeal. Let me make it easy for you. I have this teratogenic bone disorder— I'm not a mutant, you understand, my genes are normal, it's just their expression got distorted, from my mother being exposed to a certain poison while she was pregnant—it was a one-shot thing, won't affect any children *I* might have—I always felt it was easier to get dates when that was clearly understood, *not* a mutant—anyway, my bones are brittle, in fact any one of you could probably break every one in my body. You may wonder why I'm telling you all this—in fact, I usually prefer not to advertise it—you have to stop and listen to me. I'm not a threat—do I look like a threat?—a challenge, maybe, not a threat—are you going to make me run all around this camp after you? slow down, for God's sake—" He would be out of wind, and therefore verbal ammunition, very shortly at this rate. He hopped around in front of them and planted himself, arms outstretched.

"—so if you *are* planning to break every bone in my body, please do it now and get it over with, because I'm going to keep coming back here until you do."

At a brief hand signal from their leader the patrol stopped, facing him.

"Take him at his word," suggested a tall redhead. Her short brush of electric copper hair fascinated Miles to distraction; he pictured missing masses of it having fallen to the floor at the clippers of the ruthless Cetagandan prison processors. "I'll break the left arm if you'll break the right, Conr," she continued.

"If that's what it takes to get you to stop and listen to me for five minutes, so be it," Miles responded, not retreating. The redhead stepped forward and braced herself, locking his left elbow in an arm bar, putting on the pressure.

"Five minutes, right?" Miles added desperately as the pressure mounted. Her stare scorched his profile. He licked his lips, closed his eyes, held his breath, and waited. The pressure reached critical—he rose on his toes . . .

She released him abruptly, so that he staggered. "Men," she commented disgustedly. "Always gotta make everything a peeing contest."

"Biology is Destiny," gasped Miles, popping his eyes back open.

"—or are you some kind of pervert—do you get off on being beaten up by women?"

God, I hope not. He remained unbetrayed by unauthorized salutes from his nether parts, just barely. If he was going to be around that redhead much he was definitely going to have to get his pants back somehow. "If I said yes, would you refrain, just to punish me?" he offered.

"Shit, no."

"It was just a thought—"

"Cut the crap, Beatrice," said the patrol leader. At a jerk of her head the redhead stepped back into formation. "All right, runt, you've got your five minutes. Maybe."

"Thank you, ma'am." Miles took a breath, and reordered himself as best he could with no uniform to adjust. "First, let me apologize for intruding upon your privacy in this undress. Practically the first persons I met upon entering this camp were a self-help group—they helped themselves to my clothes, among other things—"

"I saw that," confirmed Beatrice-the-redhead unexpectedly. "Pitt's bunch."

Miles pulled off his hat and swept her a bow with it. "Yes, thank you."

"You moon people behind you when you do that," she commented dispassionately.

"That's their look-out," responded Miles. "For myself, I want to talk to your leader, or leaders. I have a serious plan for improving the tone of this place with which I wish to invite your group to collaborate. Bluntly, you are the largest remaining pocket of civilization, not to mention military order, in here. I'd like to see you expand your borders."

"It takes everything we've got to keep our borders from being overrun, son," replied the leader. "No can do. So take yourself off."

"Jack yourself off, too," suggested Beatrice. "You ain't gettin' any in here.'"

Miles sighed, and turned his hat around in his hands by its wide brim. He spun it for a moment on one finger, and locked eyes with the redhead. "Note my hat. It was the one garment I managed to keep from the ravages of the burly surly brothers—Pitt's bunch, you say."

She snorted at the turn of phrase. "Those jerks . . . why just a hat? Why not pants? Why not a full-dress uniform while you're at it?" she added sarcastically.

"A hat is a more useful object for communicating. You can make broad gestures," he did so, "denote sincerity," he held it over his heart, "or indicate embarrassment," over his genitals, with a hang-dog crouch, "or rage—" he flung it to earth as if he might drive it into the ground, then picked it up and brushed it off carefully, "or determination—" he jammed it on his head and yanked the brim down over his eyes, "or make courtesies." He swept it off again in salute to her. "Do you see the hat?"

She was beginning to be amused. "Yes . . ."

"Do you see the feathers on the hat?"

"Yes . . ."

"Describe them."

"Oh—plumey things."

"How many?"

"Two. Bunched together."

"Do you see the color of the feathers?"

She drew back, suddenly self-conscious again, with a sidewise glance at her companions. "No."

"When you can see the color of the feathers," said Miles softly, "you'll also understand how you can expand your borders to infinity."

She was silent, her face closed and locked. But the patrol leader muttered, "Maybe this little runt better talk to Tris. Just this once."

The woman in charge had clearly been a front line trooper once, not a tech like the majority of the females. She had certainly not acquired the muscles that flowed like braided leather cords beneath her skin from crouching by the hour in front of a holovid display in some rear-echelon underground post. She had toted the real weapons that spat real death, and sometimes broke down; had rammed against the limits of what could really be done by flesh and bone and metal, and been marked by that deforming press. Illusion had been burned out of her like an infection, leaving a cauterized scar. Rage burned permanently in her eyes like a fire in a coal seam, underground and unquenchable. She might be 35, or 40.

God, I'm in love, thought Miles. *Brother Miles wants YOU for the Reformation Army* . . . then got hold of his thoughts. Here, now, was the make-or-break point for his scheme, and all the persiflage, verbal misdirection, charm, chutzpah, and bullshit he could muster weren't going to be enough, not even tied up with a big blue bow.

The wounded want power, nothing else; they think it will keep them from being hurt again. This one will not be interested in Suegar's strange message—at least, not yet. . . . Miles took a deep breath.

"Ma'am, I'm here to offer you command of this camp."

She stared at him as if he were something she'd found growing on the walls in a dark corner of the latrine. Her eyes raked over his nudity; Miles could feel the claw marks glowing from his chin to his toes.

"Which you store in your duffle bag, no doubt," she growled. "Command of this camp doesn't exist, mutant. So it's not yours to give. Deliver him to our perimeter in pieces, Beatrice."

He ducked the redhead. He would pursue correction of the mutant business later. "Command of this camp is mine to *create*," he asserted. "Note, please, that what I offer is power, not revenge. Revenge is too expensive a luxury. Commanders can't afford it."

Tris uncoiled from her sleeping mat to her full

height, then had to bend her knees to bring her face level to his, hissing, "Too bad, little turd. You almost interested me. Because I *want* revenge. On every man in this camp."

"Then the Cetagandans have succeeded; you've forgotten who your real enemy is."

"Say, rather, that I've discovered who my real enemy is. Do you want to know the things they've done to us—our own guys—"

"The Cetagandans want you to believe this," a wave of his hand embraced the camp, "is something you're doing to each other. So fighting each other, you become their puppets. They watch you all the time, you know, voyeurs of your humiliation."

Her glance flicked upward, infinitesimally; good. It was almost a disease among these people, that they would look in any direction at all in preference to up at the dome.

"Power is better than revenge," suggested Miles, not flinching before her snake-cold, set face, her hot coal eyes. "Power is a live thing, by which you reach out to grasp the future. Revenge is a dead thing, reaching out from the past to grasp you."

"—and you're a bullshit artist," she interrupted, "reaching out to grasp whatever's going down. I've got you pegged now. *This* is power." She flexed her arm under his nose, muscles coiling and loosing. "This is the only power that exists in here. You haven't got it, and you're looking for some to cover your ass. But you've come to the wrong store."

"No," Miles denied, and tapped his forehead. "*This* is power. And I own the store. This controls that," he slapped his bunched fist. "Men may move mountains, but ideas move men. Minds can be reached through bodies—what else is the point of all this," he waved at the camp, "but to reach your minds through your bodies. But that power flows both ways, and the outflow is the stronger tide.

"When you have allowed the Cetagandans to reduce your power to *that* alone," he squeezed her bicep for emphasis—it was like squeezing a rock covered in velvet, and she tensed, enraged at the liberty, "then you have allowed them to reduce you to your weakest part. And they win."

"They win anyway," she snapped, shrugging him off. He breathed relief that she hadn't chosen to break his arm. "Nothing that we do within this circle will result in any net change. We're still prisoners, whatever we do. They can cut off the food, or the damn air, or squeeze us to mush. And time's on their side. If we spill our guts restoring order—if that's what you're trying to work up to—all they have to do is wait for it to break down again. We're *beaten*. We're *taken*. There's nobody left *out there*. We're here forever. And you'd better start getting used to the idea."

"I've heard that song before," said Miles. "Use your head. If they meant to keep you forever, they could have incinerated you at the start, and saved the considerable expense of operating this camp. No. It's your minds they want. You are all here because you were Marilac's best and brightest, the hardest fighters, the strongest, baddest, most dangerous. The ones any potential resisters to the occupation would look to for leadership. It's the Cetagandans' plan to break you, and then return you to your world like little innoculated infections, counseling surrender to your people.

"When this is killed," he touched her forehead, oh so lightly, "then the Cetagandans have nothing more to fear from this," one finger on her bicep, "and you will all go free. To a world whose horizon will encircle you just like this dome, and just as inescapably. The war's not over. You are *here* because the Cetagandans are still waiting for the surrender of Fallow Core."

He thought for a moment she might murder him,

strangle him on the spot. She must certainly prefer ripping him apart to letting him see her weep.

She regained her protective bitter tension with a toss of her head, a gulp of air. "If that's true, then following you puts us farther from freedom, not closer."

Damn, a logician to boot. She didn't have to pound him, she could parse him to death if he didn't scramble. He scrambled. "There is a subtle difference between being a prisoner and being a slave. I don't mistake either for being free. Neither do you."

She fell silent, staring at him through slitted eyes, pulling unconsciously on her lower lip. "You're an odd one," she said at last. "Why do you say 'you' and not 'we'?"

Miles shrugged casually. Blast—he rapidly reviewed his pitch—she was right, he had. A little too close to the edge, there. He might yet make an opportunity of the mistake, though. "Do I look like the flower of Marilac's military might? I'm an outsider, trapped in a world I never made. A traveller—a pilgrim—just passing through. Ask Suegar."

She snorted. "That loonie."

She'd missed the catch. Rats, as Elli would say. He missed Elli. Try again later. "Don't discount Suegar. He has a message for you. I found it fascinating."

"I've heard it. I find it irritating. . . . So what do you want out of this? And don't tell me 'nothing,' 'cause I won't believe you. Frankly, I think you're after command of the camp yourself, and I'm not volunteering to be your stepping stone in some empire-building scheme."

She was thinking at speed now, and constructively, actually following out trains of thought besides that of having him removed to her border in bits. He was getting warmer. . . .

"I only wish to be your spiritual advisor. I do not want—indeed, can't use—command. Just an advisor."

It must have been something about the term "advisor" that clicked, some old association of hers. Her eyes flicked fully open suddenly. He was close enough to see her pupils dilate. She leaned forward, and her index finger traced the faint indentations on his face beside his nose caused by certain control leads in a space armor helmet. She straightened again, and her first two fingers in a V caressed the deeper marks permanently flanking her own nose. "What did you say you were, before?"

"A clerk. Recruiting office," Miles replied sturdily.

"I . . . see."

And if what she saw was the absurdity of someone claiming to be a rear-echelon clerk having worn combat armor often and long enough to have picked up its stigmata, he was in. Maybe.

She coiled herself back up on her sleeping mat, and gestured toward its other end. "Sit down, chaplain. And keep talking."

Suegar was genuinely asleep when Miles found him again, sitting up cross-legged and snoring. Miles tapped him on the shoulder.

"Wake up, Suegar, we're home."

He snorted to consciousness. "God, I miss coffee. Huh?" He blinked at Miles. "You're still in one piece?"

"It was a near thing. Look, this garments-in-the-river bit—now that we've found each other, do we have to go *on* being naked? Or is the prophecy sufficiently fulfilled?"

"Huh?"

"Can we get dressed now?" Miles repeated patiently.

"Why—I don't know. I suppose, if we were meant to have clothes, they'd be given to us—"

Miles prodded and pointed. "There. They're given to us."

Beatrice stood a few meters away in a hip-shot

pose of bored exasperation, a bundle of grey cloth under her arm. "You two loonies want this stuff or not? I'm going back."

"You got them to give you clothes?" Suegar whispered in amazement.

"Us, Suegar, us." Miles motioned to Beatrice. "I think it's all right."

She fired the bundle at him, sniffed, and stalked away.

"Thanks," Miles called. He shook out the fabric. Two sets of grey pajamas, one small, one large. Miles had only to turn up the bottoms of the pants legs one fold to keep them from catching under his heels. They were stained and stiff with old sweat and dirt, and had probably been peeled off a corpse, Miles reflected. Suegar crawled into his and stood fingering the grey fabric in wonder.

"They gave us clothes. *Gave* us," he muttered. "How'd you do that?"

"They gave us everything, Suegar. Come on, I've got to talk to Oliver again." Miles dragged Suegar off determinedly. "I wonder how much time we've actually got before the next chow call? Two in each 24-hour cycle, to be sure, but I wouldn't be surprised if it's irregular, to increase your temporal disorientation—after all, it's the only clock in here . . ."

Movement caught Miles's eye, a man running. It wasn't the occasional flurry of someone outrunning a hostile group; this one just ran, head down, flat out, bare feet thumping the dirt in frantic rhythm. He followed the perimeter generally, except for a detour around the border of the women's group. As he ran, he wept.

"What's this?" Miles asked Suegar, with a nod at the approaching figure.

Suegar shrugged. "It takes you like that some-times. When you can't stand sitting in here any more. I saw a guy run till he died, once. Around and around and around . . ."

"Well," Miles decided, "this one's running to us."

"He's gonna be running away from us in a second . . ."

"Then help me catch him."

Miles hit him low and Suegar high. Suegar sat on his chest. Miles sat on his right arm, halving his effective resistance. He must have been a very young soldier when he was captured—maybe he had lied about his age at induction—for even now he had a boy's face, ravaged by tears and his personal eternity inside this hollow pearl. He inhaled in sobbing gasps and exhaled in garbled obscenities. After a time he quieted.

Miles leaned into his face and grinned wolfishly. "You a party animal, boy?"

"Yeah . . ." his white-rimmed eyes rolled, right and left, but no rescue approached.

"How 'bout your friends? They party animals too?"

"The best," the boy asserted, perhaps secretly shaken by the suspicion that he'd fallen into the hands of someone even crazier than himself. "You better clear off me, mutant, or they'll take you apart."

"I want to invite you and your friends to a *major* party," Miles chanted. "We gonna have a party tonight that's an his-tor-i-cal event. You know where to find Sergeant Oliver, late of the 14th Commandos?"

"Yeah . . ." the boy admitted cautiously.

"Well, you go get your friends and report to him. You better reserve your seat aboard his ve-hic-le now, 'cause if you're not on it, you gonna be *under* it. The Reformation Army is moving out. You copy?"

"Copy," he gasped, as Suegar pressed his fist into the boy's solar plexus for emphasis.

"Tell him Brother Miles sent you," Miles called as the boy staggered off, glancing nervously over his shoulder. "You can't hide in here. If you don't show, I'll send the Cosmic Commandos to find you."

Suegar shook out his cramped limbs, his new used clothes. "Think he'll come?"

Miles grinned. "Fight or flight. That one'll be all right." He stretched himself, recaptured his original orientation. "Oliver."

In the end they had not 20, but 200. Oliver had picked up 46. The running boy brought in 18. The signs of order and activity in the area brought in the curious—a drifter at the edge of the group had only to ask, "What's going on?" to be inducted and promoted to corporal on the spot. Interest among the spectators was aroused to a fever when Oliver's troops marched up to the women's border—and were admitted within. They picked up another 75 volunteers instantly.

"Do you know what's going on?" Miles asked one such, as he fed them through a short gauntlet of inspection and told them off to one of the 14 command groups he had devised.

"No," the man admitted. He waved an arm eagerly toward the center of the women's group. "But I wanta go where *they're* going . . ."

Miles cut the admissions off at 200 total in deference to Tris's growing nervousness at this infiltration of her borders, and promptly turned the courtesy into a card in his own hand in their still-continuing strategy debate. Tris wanted to divide her group in the usual way, half for the attack, half to maintain home base and keep the borders from collapsing. Miles was insisting on an all-out effort.

"If we win, you won't need guards anymore."

"What if we lose?"

Miles lowered his voice. "We don't dare lose. This is the only time we'll have surprise on our side. Yes, we can fall back—re-group—try again—I for one am prepared—no, compelled—to keep trying till it kills me. But after this, what we're trying to do will be fully apparent to any counter-group, and they'll have time to plan counter-strategies of their own. I have a particular aversion to stalemates. I prefer winning wars to prolonging them."

She sighed, momentarily drained, tired, old. "I've been at war a long time, y'know? After a while even losing a war can start to look preferable to prolonging it."

He could feel his own resolve slip, sucked into the vortex of that same black doubt. He pointed upwards, dropped his voice to a rasping whisper. "But not, surely, to *those* bastards."

She glanced upwards. Her shoulders straightened. "No. Not to those . . ." She took a deep breath. "All right, chaplain. You'll get your all-out effort. Just once . . ."

Oliver returned from a circuit of the command groups and squatted beside them. "They've got their orders. How many's Tris contributing to each group?"

"Commandant Tris," Miles quickly corrected for her as her brows beetled. "It's gonna be an all-out shot. You'll get every walking body in here."

Oliver made a quick calculation in the dirt with his finger for a stylus. "That'll put about 50 in each group—ought to be enough . . . matter of fact, what say we set up 20 groups? It'll speed distribution when we get the lines set up. Could make the difference between bringing this off, and not."

"No," Miles cut in quickly as Tris began to nod agreement. "It has to be 14. Fourteen battle groups make 14 lines for 14 piles. Fourteen is—is a theologically significant number," he added as they stared doubtfully at him.

"Why?" asked Tris.

"For the 14 apostles," Miles intoned, tenting his hands piously.

Tris shrugged. Suegar scratched his head, started to speak—Miles speared him with a baleful glance, and he stilled.

Oliver eyed him narrowly. "Huh." But he did not argue further.

Then came the waiting. Miles stopped worrying about his uppermost fear—that their captors would introduce the next food pile early, before his plans were in place—and started worrying about his second greatest fear, that the food pile would come so late he'd lose control of his troops and they would start to wander off, bored and discouraged. Getting them all assembled had made Miles feel like a man pulling on a goat with a rope made of water. Never had the insubstantial nature of the Idea seemed more self-apparent.

Oliver tapped him on the shoulder and pointed. "Here we go . . ."

A side of the dome about a third of the way around the edge from them began to bulge inward.

The timing was perfect. His troops were at the peak of readiness. Too perfect . . . the Cetagandans had been watching all this, surely they wouldn't miss an opportunity to make life more difficult for their prisoners. If the food pile wasn't early, it had to be late. Or . . .

Miles bounded to his feet, screaming, "Wait! Wait! Wait for my order!"

His sprint groups wavered, drawn toward the anticipated goal. But Oliver had chosen his group commanders well—they held, and held their groups, and looked to Oliver. They *had* been soldiers once. Oliver looked to Tris, flanked by her lieutenant Beatrice, and Tris looked to Miles, angrily.

"What is it now? We're gonna lose our advantage . . ." she began, as the general stampede throughout the camp started toward the bulge.

"If I'm wrong," Miles moaned, "I'm going to kill myself—wait, dammit! On my order. I can't see— Suegar, give me a boost—" He clambered up on the thin man's shoulders and stared toward the bulge.

The force wall had only half twinkled out when the first distant cries of disappointment met his straining ears. Miles's head swivelled frantically. How many wheels within wheels—if the Cetagandans knew, and he knew they knew, and they knew he knew they knew, and . . . He cut off his internal gibber as a second bulge began, on the opposite side of the camp from the first.

Miles's arm flung out, pointing toward it like a man rolling dice. "There! There! Go, go, go!"

Tris caught on then, whistling and shooting him a look of startled respect, before whirling and dashing off to double-time the main body of their troops after the sprint groups. Miles slithered off Suegar and started limping after.

He glanced back over his shoulder, as the rolling grey mass of humanity crashed up against the opposite side of the dome and reversed itself. He felt suddenly like a man trying to outrun a tidal wave. He indulged himself with one brief anticipatory whimper, and limped faster.

One more chance to be mortally wrong—no. His sprint groups had reached the pile, and the pile was really there. Already they were starting to break it down. The support troops surrounded them with a wall of bodies as they began to spread out along the perimeter of the dome. The Cetagandans had outfoxed themselves. This time.

Miles was reduced from the commander's eagle overview to the grunt's worm's-eye as the tidal wave overtook him. Someone shoved him from behind, and his face hit the dirt. He thought he recognized the back of the surly Pitt, vaulting over him, but he wasn't certain—surely Pitt would have stepped on, not over him. Suegar yanked him up by the left arm, and Miles bit back a scream of pain. There was enough howling already.

Miles recognized the running boy, squaring off with another tough. Miles shoved past him with a shouted reminder—"You're supposed to be yelling *Get in line!*, NOT *Get fucked!* . . . The signal always gets degraded in combat," he muttered to himself. "Always . . ."

Beatrice materialized beside him. Miles clung to her instantly. Beatrice had personal space, her own private perimeter, maintained even as Miles watched by a casual elbow to somebody's jaw with a quite sickening crack. It he tried that, Miles reflected enviously, not only would he smash his own elbow, but his opponent's nipple would probably be quite undamaged. Speaking of nipples, he found himself face to—well, not face—confronting the redhead. He resisted the urge to cuddle into the soft grey fabric covering home base with a contented sigh on the grounds that it would certainly get both his arms broken. He uncrossed his eyes and looked up into her face.

"C'mon," she said, and dragged him off through the mob. Was the noise level dropping? The human wall of his own troops parted just enough to let them squeeze through.

They were near the exit point of the chow line. It was working, by God it was working. The 14 command groups, still bunched rather too closely along the dome wall—but that could be improved next run—were admitting the hungry supplicants one at a time. The expediters kept the lines moving at top speed, and channeled the already-supplied along the perimeter behind the human shield wall in a steady stream, to flow back out into the larger camp at the edge of the mob. Oliver had put his toughest-looking bravos to work in pairs, patrolling the outflow and making sure no one's rat bar was taken by force.

It was a long time since anyone here had had a chance to be a hero. Not a few of the newly-appointed policemen were approaching their work with great enthusiasm—maybe some personal grudges being worked off there—Miles recognized one of the burly

surlys prone beneath a pair of patrollers, apparently
getting his face beaten in. Miles, remembering what
he was about, tried not to find music in the meaty
thunks of fists on flesh.

Miles and Beatrice and Suegar bucked the stream
of rat bar-clutching prisoners back toward the distribution piles. With a slightly regretful sigh, Miles
sought out Oliver and dispatched him to the exit to
restore order among his order-keepers.

Tris had the distribution piles and their immediate
lines under tight control. Miles congratulated himself on having the women hand out the food. He had
definitely tuned into a deep emotional resonance
there. Not a few of the prisoners even muttered a
sheepish "thank you" as their rat bars were shoved
into their hands, and so did the ones in line behind
them, when their turns came.

Nyah! Miles thought upward to the bland and
silent dome. *You don't have the monopoly on psy-
chological warfare any more, you bastards. We're
gonna reverse your peristalsis, and I hope you barf
your bowels out—*

An altercation at one of the food piles interrupted
his meditations. Miles's lip curled with annoyance as
he saw Pitt in the middle of it. He limped hastily
toward it.

Pitt, it appeared, had repaid his rat bar not with a
"thank you" but with a leer, a jeer, and a filthy
remark. At least three of the women within hearing
were trying to rip him apart, without success; he was
big and beefy and had no inhibitions about fighting
back. One of the females, not much taller than Miles
himself, was knocked back in a heap and didn't get
up again. In the meantime, the line was jammed,
and the smooth civilized flow of would-be diners
totally disrupted. Miles cursed under his breath.

"You, you, you, and—you," Miles tapped shoulders, "grab that guy. Get him out of here—back to
the dome wall—"

Miles's draftees were not terribly pleased with their assignment, but by this time Tris and Beatrice had run up and led the attack with rather more science. Pitt was seized and pulled away, behind the lines. Miles made sure the rat bar distribution pile was running again before turning his attention to the savage, foul-mouthed Pitt. Oliver and Suegar had joined him by this time.

"I'm gonna rip the bastard's balls off," Tris was saying. "I command—"

"A military command," Miles interrupted. "If this one is accused of disorderly conduct, you should court martial him."

"He is a rapist and a murderer," she replied icily. "Execution's too good for him. He's got to die *slowly*."

Miles pulled Suegar aside. "It's tempting, but I feel real uneasy about handing him over to her just now. And yet . . . real uneasy. Why is that?"

Suegar eyed him respectfully. "I think you're right. You see, there's—there's too many guilty."

Pitt, now in a foaming fury, spotted Miles. "You! You little cunt-licking wimp—you think *they* can protect you?" He jerked his head toward Tris and Beatrice. "They ain't got the muscle. We've run 'em over before and we'll run 'em over again. We wouldn'ta lost the damn war if we'd had real soldiers —like the Barrayarans. They didn't fill their army with cunts and cunt-lickers. And they ran the Cetagandans right off their planet—"

"Somehow," Miles growled, drawn in, "I doubt you're an expert on the Barrayarans' defense of their homeworld in the First Cetagandan War. Or you might have learned something—"

"Did Tris make you an honorary girl, mutant?" jeered Pitt in return. "It wouldn't take much—"

Why am I standing here bandying words with this low-life crazy? Miles asked himself as Pitt raved on. *No time. Let's finish it.*

Miles stepped back and folded his arms. "Has it

occurred to any of you yet that this man is clearly a Cetagandan agent?"

Even Pitt was shocked to silence.

"The evidence is plain," Miles went on forcefully, raising his voice so all bystanders could hear. "He is a ringleader in your disruption. By example and guile he has corrupted the honest soldiers around him, set them one against another. You were Marilac's best. The Cetagandans could not count on your fall. So they planted a seed of evil among you. Just to make sure. And it worked—wonderfully well. You never suspected—"

Oliver grabbed Miles's ear and muttered, "Brother Miles—I know this guy. He's no Cetagandan agent. He's just one of a whole lot of—"

"Oliver," Miles hissed back through clenched teeth, "*shut up.*" And continued in his clearest parade-ground bellow, "Of course he's a Cetagandan spy. A mole. And all this time you thought this was something you were doing to *yourselves.*"

And where the devil does not exist, Miles thought to himself, *it may become expedient to invent him.* His stomach churned, but he kept his face set in righteous rage. He glanced at the faces around him. Not a few were as white as his must be, though for a different reason. A low mutter rose among them, partly bewildered, partly ominous.

"Pull off his shirt," Miles ordered, "and lay him down on his face. Suegar, give me your cup."

Suegar's plastic cup had a jagged point along its broken edge. Miles sat on Pitt's buttocks, and using the point as a stylus scratched the words

CETA
SPY

across Pitt's back in large print. He dug deep and ruthlessly, and the blood welled. Pitt screamed and swore and bucked.

Miles scrambled to his feet, shaking and breathless from more than just the physical exertion.

"Now," he ordered, "give him his rat bar and escort him to the exit."

Tris's teeth opened in objection, clicked back down. Her eyes burned into Pitt's back as he was hustled off. Her gaze turned rather more doubtfully to Miles, as she stood on one side of him and Oliver on the other.

"Do you really think he was a Cetagandan?" she asked Miles lowly.

"No way," scoffed Oliver. "What the hell's the charade all about, Brother Miles?"

"I don't doubt Tris's accusation of his other crimes," said Miles tightly. "You must know. But he couldn't be punished for them without dividing the camp, and so undermining Tris's authority. This way, Tris and the women have their revenge without half the men being set against them. The commandant's hands are clean, yet justice is done on a criminal, and a hard case who would doubtless be stockade bait outside is removed from under our feet. Furthermore, any like-minded souls are handed a warning they can't ignore. It works on every level."

Oliver's face had grown expressionless. After a silent moment he remarked, "You fight dirty, Brother Miles."

"I can't afford to lose." Miles shot him a black look from beneath his own lowered brows. "Can you?"

Oliver's lips tightened. "No."

Tris made no comment at all.

Miles personally oversaw the delivery of rat bars to all those prisoners too sick or weak or beaten to have attempted the chow line.

Colonel Tremont lay too still upon his mat, curled up, staring blankly. Oliver knelt and closed the drying, fixed eyes. The colonel might have died anytime in the last few hours.

"I'm sorry," said Miles sincerely. "Sorry I came so late."

"Well . . ." said Oliver, "well . . ." He stood, chewing on his lip, shook his head, and said no more. Miles and Suegar, Tris and Beatrice, helped Oliver carry the body, mat, clothes, cup and all, to the rubbish pile. Oliver shoved the rat bar he had reserved under the dead man's arm. No one attempted to strip the corpse after they had turned away, although another one stiffening there had already been so robbed, lying naked and tumbled.

They stumbled across Pitt's body shortly thereafter. The cause of death was most probably strangulation, but the face was so battered that its empurpling was not a certain clue.

Tris, squatting beside it, looked up at Miles in slow re-estimation. "I think you may be right about power after all, little man."

"And revenge?"

"I thought I could never get my fill of it," she sighed, contemplating the thing beside her. "Yeah . . . that too."

"Thank you." Miles prodded the body with his toe. "Make no mistake, *that* is a loss for our side."

Miles made Suegar let somebody else drag it to the rubbish pile.

Miles held a council of war immediately after chow call. Tremont's pallbearers, whom Miles had begun to think of as his general staff, and the 14 group leaders gathered around him at a spot near the borders of the women's group. Miles paced back and forth before them, gesturing energetically.

"I commend the group leaders for an excellent job, and Sergeant Oliver for choosing them. By bringing this off, we have bought not only the allegiance of the greater part of the camp, but time as well. Each chow call after this should run a little easier, a little smoother, each become a real-life practice drill for the next.

"And make no mistake, this is a military exercise.

We're at war again. We've already suckered the Cetagandans into breaking their carefully calculated routine and making a counter-move. We acted. They reacted. Strange as it may all seem to you, *we* had the offensive advantage.

"Now we start planning our next strategies. I want your thinking on what the next Cetagandan challenge will be." *Actually, I want you thinking, period.* "So much for the sermon—Commandant Tris, take over." Miles forced himself to sit down cross-legged, yielding the floor to his chosen one whether she wanted it or not. He reminded himself that Tris had been a field officer, not a staff officer; she needed the practice more than he did.

"Of course, they can send in short piles again, like they did before," she began after clearing her throat. "It's been suggested that's how this mess got started in the first place." Her glance crossed Miles's, who nodded encouragingly. "This means we're going to have to start keeping head counts, and work out a strict rotation schedule in advance of people to divide their rations with the short-changed. Each group leader must choose a quartermaster and a couple of accountants to double-check his count."

"An equally disruptive move the Cetagandans may try," Miles couldn't help putting in, "is to send in an overstock, giving us the interesting problem of how to equitably divide the extras. I'd provide for that, too, if I were you." He smiled blandly up at Tris.

She raised an eyebrow at him, and continued. "They may also try dividing the chow pile, complicating our problem of capturing it so as to strictly control its re-distribution. Are there any other really dirty tricks any of you can anticipate?" She couldn't help glancing at Miles.

One of the group leaders raised his hand hesitantly. "'Ma'am—they're listening to all this. Aren't we doing their thinking for them?"

Miles rose to answer that one, loud and clear. "Of

course they're listening. We've doubtless got their quivering attention." He made a rude gesture domewards. "Let them. Every move they make is a message from outside, a shadow marking their shape, information about them. We'll take it."

"Suppose," said another group leader even more hesitantly, "they cut off our air again? Permanently?"

"Then," said Miles smoothly, "they lose their hard-won position one-up on the IJC, which they've gone to enormous trouble to gain. It's a propaganda coup they've been making much of lately, particularly since our side, in the stress of the way things are going back home, hasn't been able to maintain its own troops in style, let alone any captured Cetagandans. The Cetagandans, whose published view is that they're sharing their Imperial government with us out of cultural generosity, are claiming this as a demonstration of their superior civilization and good manners—"

Some jeers and catcalls marked the prisoners' view of this assertion, and Miles smiled and went on. "The death rate reported for this camp is so extraordinary, it's caught the IJC's attention. The Cetagandans have managed to account for it so far, through three separate IJC inspections, but 100% would be a bit extreme even for them to justify." A shiver of agreement, compressed rage, ran through his rapt listeners.

Miles sat again. Oliver leaned over to him to whisper, "How the hell did you come by all that information?"

Miles smirked. "Did it sound convincing? Good."

Oliver sat back, looking unnerved. "You don't have any inhibitions at all, do you?"

"Not in combat."

Tris and her group leaders spent the next two hours laying out chow call scenario flow charts, and their tactical responses at each branching. They broke up to let the group leaders pass it on to their chosen subordinates, and Oliver to his crew of supplementary Enforcers.

Tris paused before Miles, who had succumbed to gravity sometime during the second hour and now lay in the dirt staring somewhat blankly at the dome, blinking in an effort to keep his blurring eyes open. He had not slept in the day and a half before entering this place. He was not sure how much time had passed since then.

"I thought of one more scenario," Tris remarked. "What do we do if they do nothing at all? Do nothing, change nothing."

Miles smiled sleepily. "It seems most probable. That attempted double-cross on the last chow call was a slip on their part, I think."

"But in the absence of an enemy, how long can we go on pretending we're an army?" she persisted. "You scraped us up off the bottom for this. When it runs down at last, what then?"

Miles curled up on his side, drowning in weird and shapeless thoughts, and enticed by the hint of an erotic dream about a tall aggressive redhead. His yawn cracked his face. "Then we pray for a miracle. Remind me to discuss miracles with you . . . later. . . ."

He half-woke once when somebody shoved a sleeping mat under him. He gave Beatrice a sleepy bedroom smile.

"Crazy mutant," she snarled at him, and rolled him roughly onto the pad. "Don't you go thinking this was my idea."

"Why Suegar," Miles muttered, "I think she *likes* me." He cuddled back into the entwining limbs of the dream-Beatrice in fleeting peace.

To Miles's secret dismay, his analysis proved right. The Cetagandans returned to their original rat bar routine, unresponsive again to their prisoners' internal permutations. Miles was not sure he liked that. True, it gave him ample opportunity to fine-tune his distribution scheme. But some harassment from the dome would have directed the prisoners' attention outward, given them a foe again, above all broken the paralyzing boredom of their lives. In the long run, Tris must prove right.

"I hate an enemy who doesn't make mistakes," Miles muttered irritably, and flung his efforts into events he could control.

He found a phlegmatic prisoner with a steady heartbeat to lie in the dirt and count his own pulse, and began timing distribution, and then working on reducing timing.

"It's a spiritual exercise," he announced when he had his 14 quartermasters start issuing the rat bars 200 at a time, with 30-minute breaks between groups.

"It's a change of pace," he explained in an aside to Tris. "If we can't induce the Cetagandans to provide some variety, we'll just have to do it ourselves." He also finally got an accurate head count of the surviving prisoners. Miles was everywhere, exhorting, prodding, pushing, restraining.

"If you really want it to go faster, make more bleeding piles," Oliver protested.

"Don't blaspheme," said Miles, and went to work inducing his groups to cart their rat bars away to distribution piles spaced evenly around the perimeter.

At the end of the 19th chow call since he had entered the camp, Miles judged his distribution system complete and theologically correct. Calling every two chow calls a "day," he had been there nine days.

"I'm all done," he realized with a groan, "and it's *too early*."

"Weeping because you have no more worlds to conquer?" inquired Tris with a sarcastic grin.

By the 32nd chow call, the system was still running smoothly, but Miles was getting frayed.

"Welcome to the long haul," said Beatrice dryly. "You better start pacing yourself, Brother Miles. If what Tris says is true, we're going to be in here even

longer because of you. I must remember to thank
you for that properly sometime." She treated him to
a threatening smirk, and Miles prudently remembered an errand on the opposite side of the camp.

She was right, Miles thought, depressed. Most
prisoners here counted their captivity not in days
and weeks, but months and years. He himself was
likely to be gibbering nuts in a space of time that
most of them would regard as a mere breath. He
wondered glumly what form his madness would take.
Manic, inspired by the glittering delusion that he
was—say—the Conquerer of Komarr? Or depres-
sive, like Tremont, curling up in himself until he was
no one at all, a sort of human black hole?

Miracles. There had been leaders throughout history who had been wrong in their timing for armag-
eddon, leading their shorn flocks up the mountain to
await an apotheosis that never came. Their later lives
were usually marked by obscurity and drinking problems. Nothing to drink in here. Miles wanted about
six doubles, right now.

Now. Now. Now.

Miles took to walking the dome perimeter after
each chow call, partly to make or at least pretend to
inspection, partly to burn off a little of his uncomfort-
ably accumulating nervous energy. It was getting
harder and harder to sleep. There had been a period
of quiet in the camp after the chow calls were successfully regulated, as if their ordering had been a
crystal dropped in a supersaturated solution. But in
the last few days the number of fistfights broken up
by the Enforcers had risen. The Enforcers themselves were getting quicker to violence, acquiring a
potentially unsavory swagger. Phases of the moon.
Who could outrace the moon?

"Slow down, Miles," complained Suegar, ambling
along beside him.

"Sorry." Miles restrained his stride and broke his

self-absorption to look around. The glowing dome rose on his left hand, seeming to pulse to an unsettling hum just out of the range of his hearing. Quiet spread out on his right, groups of people mostly sitting. Not that much visible change since his first day in here. Maybe a little less tension, maybe a little more concerted care being taken of the injured or ill. Phases of the moon. He shook off his unease and smiled cheerfully at Suegar.

"You getting any more positive responses to your sermons these days?" Miles asked.

"Well—nobody tries to beat me up anymore," said Suegar. "But then, I haven't been preaching so often, being busy with the chow calls and all. And then, there are the Enforcers now. It's hard to say."

"You going to keep trying?"

"Oh, yes." Suegar paused. "I've seen worse places than this, y'know. I was at a mining camp once, when I was scarcely more than a kid. A fire gem strike. For a change, instead of one big company or the government muscling in, it had gotten divided up into hundreds and hundreds of little claims, usually about two meters square. Guys dug out there by hand, with trowels and whisk brooms—big fire gems are delicate, y'know, they'll shatter at a careless blow—they dug under the broiling sun, day after day. A lot of these guys had less clothes than us now. A lot of 'em didn't eat as good, or as regular. Working their butts off. More accidents, more disease than here. There were fights, too, in plenty.

"But they lived for the future. Performed the most incredible feats of physical endurance for hope, all voluntary. They were obsessed. They were—well, you remind me a lot of them. They wouldn't quit for *nothing*. They turned a mountain into a chasm in a year, with hand trowels. It was nuts. I loved it.

"This place," Suegar glanced around, "just makes me scared shitless." His right hand touched his rag rope bracelet. "It'll suck up your future, swallow you

down—it's like death is just a formality, after that.
Zombie town, suicide city. The day I stop trying,
this place'll eat me."

"Mm," agreed Miles. They were nearing what Miles
thought of as the farthest point of their circuit, across
the camp from the women's group at whose now-
permeable borders Miles and Suegar kept their sleeping mats.

A couple of men walking the perimeter from the
opposite direction coalesced with another grey-
pajama'd pair. As if casually and spontaneously, three
more arose from their mats on Miles's right. He
could not be sure without turning his head, but
Miles thought he caught more peripheral motion
closing in behind him.

The approaching four stopped a few meters in
front of them. Miles and Suegar hesitated. Grey-clad
men, all variously larger than Miles—who wasn't?
—frowning, full of a fierce tension that arced to
Miles and scree'd down his nerves. Miles recognized
only one of them, an ex-surly brother he'd seen in
Pitt's company. Miles didn't bother taking his eyes
off Pitt's lieutenant to look around for Enforcers. For
one thing, he was pretty sure one of the men in the
company facing them *was* an Enforcer.

And the worst of it was, getting cornered—if you
could call it that in here—was his own fault, for
letting his movements fall into a predictable daily
routine. A stupid, basic, beginner's mistake, that;
inexcusable.

Pitt's lieutenant stepped forward, chewing on his
lip, staring at Miles with hollowed eyes. *He's psych-
ing himself up*, Miles realized. *If all he wanted was
to beat me to a pulp, he could do it in his sleep*. The
man slid a carefully-braided rag rope through his
fingers. A strangling cord . . . no, it wasn't going to
be another beating. This time, it was going to be
premeditated murder.

"You," said Pitt's lieutenant hoarsely. "I couldn't

figure you out at first. You're not one of us. You could never have been one of us. Mutant . . . You gave me the clue yourself. Pitt wasn't a Cetagandan spy. *You* are!" And lunged forward.

Miles dodged, overwhelmed by onslaught and insight. Damn, he'd known there must be a good reason scragging Pitt that way had felt so much like a mistake despite its efficiency. The false accusation was two-edged, as dangerous to its wielder as its victim—Pitt's lieutenant might even believe *his* accusation true—Miles had started a witch-hunt. Poetic justice, that he be its first victim, but where would it end? No wonder their captors hadn't interfered lately. Their silent Cetagandan watchers must be falling off their station chairs laughing right now— mistake piled on mistake, culminating here by dying stupidly like vermin at the hands of vermin in this verminous hole. . . .

Hands grabbed him; he contorted spasmodically, kicking out, but only half-broke their hold. Beside him Suegar whirled, kicked, struck, shouted with demonic energy. He had reach, but lacked mass. Miles lacked both reach and mass. Still Suegar managed to break an assailant's hold on Miles for a moment.

Suegar's left arm, flashing out for a backhand blow, was caught and locked. Miles winced in sympathetic anticipation of the familiar muffled crack of breaking bones, but instead the man stripped off the rag rope bracelet from Suegar's wrist.

"Hey, Suegar!" the man taunted, dancing backward. "Look what I got!"

Suegar's head swivelled, his attention wrenched from his determined defense of Miles. The man peeled the wrinkled, tattered piece of paper from its cloth covering and waved it in the air. Suegar cried out in dismay and started to plunge toward him, but found himself blocked by two other bodies. The man tore the paper in half twice, then paused, as if momentarily puzzled how to dispose of it—then, with a sudden grin, stuffed the pieces in his mouth and started chewing. Suegar screamed.

"Dammit," cried Miles furiously, "it was me you wanted! You didn't have to do that—" He jammed his fist with all his strength into the smirking face of the nearest attacker, whose attention had been temporarily distracted by Suegar's show.

He could feel his bones shatter all the way back through his wrist. He was so damn *tired* of the bones, tired of being hurt again and again. . . .

Suegar was screaming and sobbing and trying to gain on the paper chewer, who stood and chewed on through his grin. Suegar had lost all science in his attack, flailing like a windmill. Miles saw him go down, then had no attention left for anything but the anaconda coil of the strangling cord, settling over his own neck. He managed to get one hand between the cord and his throat, but it was the broken one. Cables of pain shuddered up his arm, seeming to burrow under his skin all the way to his shoulder. The pressure in his head mounted to bursting, closing down his vision. Dark purple and yellow moire-patterned clouds boiled up in his eyes like thunderheads. A flashing brush of red hair sizzled past his tunneling vision. . . .

He was on the ground then, with blood, wonderful blood, thudding back into his oxygen-starved brain. It hurt good, hot and pulsing. He lay for a moment not caring about anything else. It would be so good not to have to get up again. . . .

The damn dome, cold and white and featureless, mocked his returning vision. Miles jerked onto his knees, staring around wildly. Beatrice, some Enforcers, and some of Oliver's commando buddies were chasing Miles's would-be assassins across the camp. Miles had probably only passed out for a few seconds. Suegar lay on the ground a couple of meters off.

Miles crawled over to Suegar. The thin man lay curled up around his stomach, his face pale green and clammy, involuntary shivers coursing through his body. Not good. Shocky. Keep patient warm and administer synergine. No synergine. Miles peeled clumsily out of his tunic and laid it over Suegar. "Suegar? You all right? Beatrice chased the barbarians off . . ."

Suegar looked up and smiled briefly, but the smile was reabsorbed almost immediately by distancing pain.

Beatrice came back eventually, mussed and breathing heavily. "You loonies," she greeted them dispassionately. "You don't need a bodyguard, you need a bloody keeper." She flopped onto her knees beside Miles to stare at Suegar. Her lips thinned to a white slit. She glanced at Miles, her eyes darkening, the creases between her brows deepening.

I've changed my mind, Miles thought. *Don't start caring for me, Beatrice, don't start caring for anybody. You'll only get hurt. Over and over and over . . .*

"You better come back to my group," said Beatrice.

"I don't think Suegar can walk."

Beatrice rounded up some muscle, and the thin man was rolled onto a sleeping mat and carried, too much like Colonel Tremont's corpse for Miles's taste, back to their now-usual sleeping place.

"Find a doctor for him," Miles demanded.

Beatrice came back, strong-arming an angry, older woman.

"He's probably got a busted belly," snarled the doctor. "If I had a diagnostic viewer, I could tell you just what was busted. You got a diagnostic viewer? He needs synergine and plasma. You got any? I could cut him, and glue him back together, and speed his healing with electra-stim, if I had an operating theatre. Put him back on his feet in three days, no sweat. You got an operating theatre? I thought not.

"Stop looking at me like that. I used to think I was a healer. It took this place to teach me I was nothing but an interface between the technology and the patient. Now the technology is gone, and I'm just nothing."

"But what can we do?" asked Miles.

"Cover him up. In a few days he'll either get better or die, depending on what got busted. That's all." She paused, standing with folded arms and regarding Suegar with rancor, as if his injury was a personal affront. And so it was, for her: another load of grief and failure, grinding her hard-won healer's pride into the dirt. "I think he's going to die," she added.

"I think so too," said Miles.

"Then what did you want me for?" She stomped off.

Later she came back with a sleeping mat and a couple of extra rags, and helped put them around and over Suegar for added insulation, then stomped off again.

Tris reported to Miles. "We got those guys who tried to kill you rounded up. What do you want done with 'em?"

"Let them go," said Miles wearily. "They're not the enemy."

"The hell they're not!"

"They're not my enemies, anyway. It was just a case of mistaken identity. I'm just a hapless traveller, passing through."

"Wake up, little man. I don't happen to share Oliver's belief in your 'miracle.' You're not passing through here. This is the last stop."

Miles sighed. "I'm beginning to think you're right." He glanced at Suegar, breathing shallowly and too fast, beside whom he crouched in watch. "You're almost certainly right, by this time. Nevertheless— let them go."

"Why?" she wailed, outraged.

"Because I said to. Because I asked you to. Would you have me beg for them?"

"Aargh! No. All right!" She wheeled away, running her hands through her clipped hair and muttering under her breath.

A timeless time passed. Suegar lay on his side not speaking, though his eyes flicked open now and then to stare unseeing. Miles moistened his lips with water periodically. A chow call came and went without incident or Miles's participation; Beatrice passed by and dropped two rat bars beside them, stared at them with a carefully-hardened gaze of general disapproval, and stalked off.

Miles cradled his injured hand and sat cross-legged, mentally reviewing the catalogue of errors that had brought him to this pass. He contemplated his seeming genius for getting his friends killed. He had a sick premonition that Suegar's death was going to be almost as bad as Sergeant Bothari's, six years ago, and he had known Suegar only weeks, not years. Repeated pain, as he had reason to know, made one more afraid of injury, not less, a growing, gut-wrenching dread. Not again, never again . . .

He lay back and stared at the dome, the white, unblinking eye of a dead god. And had more friends than he knew already been killed by this megalomanic escapade? It would be just like the Cetagandans, to leave him in here all unknowing, and let the growing doubt and fear gradually drive him crazy.

Swiftly drive him crazy—the god's eye blinked.

Miles blinked in sympathetic nervous recoil, opened his eyes wide, stared at the dome as if his eyes could bore right through it. Had it blinked? Had the flicker been hallucinatory? Was he losing it?

It flickered again. Miles shot to his feet, inhaling, inhaling, inhaling.

The dome blinked out. For a brief instant, planetary night swept in, fog and drizzle and the kiss of a cold wet wind. This planet's unfiltered air smelled like rotten eggs. The unaccustomed dark was blinding.

"*CHOW CALL!*" Miles screamed at the top of his lungs.

Then limbo transmuted to chaos in the brilliant flash of a smart bomb going off beyond a cluster of buildings. Red light glared off the underside of an enormous billowing cloud of debris, blasting upward. A racketing string of similar hits encircled the camp, peeled back the night, deafened the unprotected. Miles, still screaming, could not hear his own voice. A returning fire from the ground clawed the clouds with lines of colored light.

Tris, her eyes stunned, rocketed past him. Miles grabbed her by the arm with his good hand and dug in his heels to brake her, yanking her down so he could scream in her ear.

"This is it! Get the 14 group leaders organized, make 'em get their first blocks of 200 lined up and waiting all around the perimeter. Find Oliver, we've *got* to get the Enforcers moving to get the rest waiting their turn under control. If this goes exactly as we drilled it, we'll all get off." *I hope.* "But if they mob the shuttles like they used to mob the rat bar pile, none of us will. You copy?"

"I never believed—I didn't think—*shuttles?*"

"You don't have to think. We've drilled this 50 times. Just follow the chow drill. The *drill!*"

"You *sneaky* little sonofabitch!" The acknowledging wave of her arm, as she dashed off, was very like a salute.

A string of flares erupted in the sky above the camp, as if a white strobe of lightning went on and on, casting a ghastly illumination on the scene below. The camp seethed like a termite mound kicked over. Men and women were running every which way in shouting confusion. Not exactly the orderly vision Miles had had in mind—why, for example, had his people chosen a night drop and not a day-time one?—he would grill his staff later on that point, after he got done kissing their feet—

"Beatrice!" Miles waved her down. "Start passing the word! We're doing the chow call drill. But instead of a rat bar, each person gets a shuttle seat. Make 'em understand that—don't let anybody go haring off into the night or they'll miss their flight. Then come back here and stay by Suegar. I don't want him getting lost or trampled on. *Guard*, you copy?"

"I'm not a damn dog. What shuttles?"

The sound Miles's ears had been straining for penetrated the din at last, a high-pitched, multi-faceted whine that grew louder and louder. They loomed down out of the boiling scarlet-tinged clouds like monstrous beetles, carapaced and winged, feet extending even as they watched. Fully armored combat drop shuttles, two, three, six . . . seven, eight . . . Miles lips moved as he counted. Thirteen, fourteen, by God. They *had* managed to get #B-7 out of the shop in time.

Miles pointed. "*My* shuttles."

Beatrice stood with her mouth open, staring upward. "My God. They're beautiful." He could almost see her mind start to ratchet forward. "But they're not *ours*. Not Cetagandan either. Who the hell . . . ?"

Miles bowed. "This is a paid political rescue."

"*Mercenaries?*"

"We're not something wriggly with too many legs that you found in your sleeping bag. The proper tone of voice is *Mercenaries!*—with a glad cry."

"But—but—but—"

"*Go*, dammit. Argue *later*."

She flung up her hands and ran.

Miles himself started tackling every person within reach, passing on the order of the day. He captured one of Oliver's taller commando buddies and demanded a boost on his shoulders. A quick look around showed 14 coagulating knots of people in the mob scattered around the perimeter in nearly the right positions. The shuttles hovered, engines howling, then thumped to the ground one by one all around the camp.

"It'll have to do," Miles muttered to himself. He slapped the commando's shoulder. "Down."

He forced himself to walk to the nearest shuttle, a run on the shuttles being just the scenario he had poured out blood and bone and pride these last— three, four?—weeks to avoid.

A quartet of fully-armed and half-armored troops were the first down the shuttle ramp, taking up guard positions. Good. They even had their weapons pointed in the right direction, toward the prisoners they were here to rescue. A larger patrol, fully armored, followed to gallop off double time, leapfrogging their own covering-fire range into the dark toward the Cetagandan installations surrounding the dome circle. Hard to judge which direction held the most danger—from the continuing fireworks, his fighter shuttles were providing plenty of external distraction for the Cetagandans.

At last came the man Miles most wanted to see, the shuttle's comm officer.

"Lieutenant, uh," he connected face and name, "Murka! Over here!"

Murka spotted him. He fumbled excitedly with his equipment and called into his audio pick-up, "Commodore Tung! Commodore Tung! He's *here*, I *got* him!"

Miles peeled the comm set ruthlessly from the lieutenant's head, who obligingly ducked down to permit the theft, and jammed it on his own head left-handed in time to hear Tung's voice reply tinnily, "Well, for God's sake don't lose him again, Murka. Sit on him if you have to."

"I want my staff," called Miles into the pick-up.

"Have you retreived Elli and Elena yet? How much time have we got for this?"

"Yes, sir, no, and about two hours—if we're lucky," Tung's voice snapped back. "Good to have you back aboard, Admiral Naismith."

"You're telling me . . . Get Elena and Elli. Priority One."

"Working. Tung out."

Miles turned to find that the rat bar group leader in this section had actually succeeded in marshalling his first group of 200, and was engaged in making the second 200 sit back down in a block to wait their turns. Excellent. The prisoners were being channeled up the ramp one at a time through a strange gauntlet. A mercenary slit the back of each grey tunic with a swift slice from a vibra-knife. A second mercenary slapped each prisoner across the back with a medical stunner. A third made a pass with a surgical hand-tractor, roughly ripping out the Cetagandan serial numbers encoded beneath the skin. He didn't bother to waste time on bandaging after. "Go to the front and sit five across, go to the front and sit five across, go to the front . . ." he chanted, droning in time to his hypnotically moving device.

Miles's sometime-adjutant Captain Thorne appeared, hurrying out of the glare and black shadows, flanked by one of the fleet's ship's surgeons and—praise be—a soldier carrying some of Miles's clothes, and boots. Miles dove for the boots, but was captured instead by the surgeon.

She ran a med stunner between his bare uneven shoulderblades, and zipped a hand-tractor across in its path.

"Ow!" Miles yelped. "Couldn't you wait one bleeding second for the stun to cut in?" The pain faded rapidly to numbness as Miles's left hand patted for the damage. "What's this all about?"

"Sorry, sir," said the surgeon insincerely. "Stop that, your fingers are dirty." She applied a plastic bandage. Rank hath its privileges. "Captain Bothari-Jesek and Commander Quinn learned something from their fellow Cetagandan prison monitors that we hadn't known before you went in. These encodes are permeated with drug beads, whose lipid membranes are kept aligned by a low-power magnetic field the Cetagandans were generating in the dome. An hour out of the dome, and the membranes start to break down, releasing a poison. About four hours later the subject dies—very unpleasantly. A little insurance against escapes, I guess."

Miles shuddered, and said faintly, "I see." He cleared his throat, and added more loudly, "Captain Thorne, mark a commendation—with *highest* honors—to Commander Elli Quinn and Captain Elena Bothari-Jesek. The, ah, our employer's intelligence service didn't even have that one. In fact, our employer's intelligence data lacked on a truly vast number of points. I shall have to speak to them—sharply—when I present the bill for this expanded operation. Before you put that away, doctor, numb my hand, please." Miles stuck out his right hand for the surgeon's inspection.

"Did it again, did you?" muttered the surgeon. "I'd think you'd learn . . ." A pass with the medical stunner, and Miles's swollen hand disappeared from his senses entirely, nothing left from the wrist down. Only his eyes assured him it was still attached to his arm.

"Yes, but will they pay for the expanded operation?" asked Captain Thorne anxiously. "This started out as a one-shot lightning strike to hook out one guy, just the sort of thing little outfits like us specialize in—now it's straining the whole Dendarii fleet. These damn prisoners outnumber *us* two to one. This wasn't in the original contract. What if our perennial mystery employer decides to stiff us?"

"They won't," said Miles. "My word. But—there's no doubt I'll have to deliver the bill in person."

"God help them, then," muttered the surgeon, and took herself off to continue pulling encodes from the waiting prisoners.

Commodore Ky Tung, a squat, middle-aged Eurasian in half-armor and a command channel headset, turned up at Miles's elbow as the first shuttles loaded with prisoners clapped their locks shut and screamed up into the black fog. They took off in first-come, first-served positions, no waiting. Knowing Tung's passion for tight formations, Miles judged time must be their most dangerous limiting factor.

"What are we loading these guys onto, upstairs?" Miles asked Tung.

"We gutted a couple of used freighters. We can cram about 5,000 in the holds of each. The ride out is going to be fast and nasty. They'll all have to lie down and breathe as little as possible."

"What are the Cetagandans scrambling to catch us?"

"Right now, barely more than some police shuttles. Most of their local space military contingent just happens to be on the other side of their sun just now, which is why we just happened to pick this moment to drop by . . . we had to wait for their practice maneuvers again, in case you were starting to wonder what was keeping us. In other words, the same scenario as our original plan to pull Colonel Tremont."

"Except expanded by a factor of 10,000. And we've got to get in—what, four lifts? instead of one," said Miles.

"Yeah, but get this," grinned Tung. "They sited these prison camps on this miserable outpost planet so's they wouldn't have to expend troops and equipment guarding them—counted on distance from Marilac, and the downgearing of the war there, to discourage rescue attempts. But in the period since you went in, half of their original guard complement has been pulled to other hot spots. Half!"

"They were relying on the dome." Miles eyed him. "And for the bad news?" he murmured.

Tung's smile soured. "This round, our total time window is only two hours."

"Ouch. Half their local space fleet is still too many. And they'll be back in two hours?"

"One hour, forty minutes, now." A sidewise flick of Tung's eyes betrayed the location of his ops clock, holovid-projected by his command headset into the air at a corner of his vision.

Miles did a calculation in his head, and lowered his voice. "Are we going to be able to lift the last load?"

"Depends on how fast we can lift the first three," said Tung. His ordinarily stoic face was more unreadable than ever, betraying neither hope nor fear.

Which depends in turn on how effectively I managed to drill them all . . . What was done was done; what was coming was not yet. Miles wrenched his attention to the immediate now.

"Have you found Elli and Elena yet?"

"I have three patrols out searching."

He hadn't found them yet. Miles's guts tightened. "I wouldn't have even attempted to expand this operation in midstream if I hadn't known they were monitoring me, and could translate all those oblique hints back into orders."

"Did they get 'em all right?" asked Tung. "We argued over some of their interpretations of your double-talk on the vids."

Miles glanced around. "They got 'em right . . . you got vids of all this?" A startled wave of Miles's hand took in the circle of the camp.

"Of you, anyway. Right off the Cetagandan monitors. They burst-transmitted them all daily. Very—er—entertaining, sir," Tung added blandly.

Some people would find entertainment in watching someone swallow slugs, Miles reflected. "Very dangerous . . . when was your last communication with them?"

"Yesterday." Tung's hand clamped on Miles's arm, restraining an involuntary leap. "You can't do better than my three patrols, sir, and I haven't any to spare to go looking for *you*."

"Yah, yah." Miles slapped his right fist into his left palm in frustration before remembering that was a bad idea. His two co-agents, his vital link between the dome and the Dendarii, missing. The Cetagandans shot spies with depressing consistency. After, usually, a series of interrogations that rendered death a welcome release. . . . He tried to reassure himself with logic. If they'd blown their covers as Cetagandan monitor techs, and been interrogated, Tung would have run into a meat grinder here. He hadn't, ergo, they hadn't. Of course, they might have been killed by friendly fire, just now. . . . Friends. He had too many friends to stay sane in this crazy business.

"You," Miles retrieved his clothes from the still-waiting soldier, "go over there," he pointed, "and find a redhaired lady named Beatrice and an injured man named Suegar. Bring them to me. Carry him carefully, he has internal injuries."

The soldier saluted and marched off. Ah, the pleasure again of being able to give a command without having to follow it up with a supporting theological argument. Miles sighed. Exhaustion waited to swallow him, lurking at the edge of his adrenalin-spurred bubble of hyperconsciousness. All the factors—shuttles, timing, the approaching enemy, distance to the getaway jump point, formed and reformed in all their possible permutations in his mind. Small variations in timing in particular multiplied into major troubles. But he'd known it would be like this back when he'd started. A miracle they'd got this far. No—he glanced at Tung, at Thorne—not a miracle, but the extraordinary initiative and devotion of his people. *Well done, oh, well done . . .*

Thorne helped him as he fumbled to dress himself one-handed. "Where the hell is my command headset?" Miles asked.

"We were told you were injured, sir, and in a state of exhaustion. You were scheduled for immediate evacuation."

"Damn presumptuous of somebody . . ." Miles bit back ire. No place in this schedule for running errands topside. Besides, if he had his headset, he'd be tempted to start giving orders, and he wasn't yet sufficiently briefed on the internal complexities of the operation from the Dendarii fleet's point of view. Miles swallowed his observer status without further comment. It did free him for rear guard.

Miles's batman reappeared, with Beatrice and four drafted prisoners, carrying Suegar on his mat to lay at Miles's feet.

"Get my surgeon," Miles said. His soldier obediently trotted off and found her. She knelt beside the semi-conscious Suegar and pulled the encode from his back. A knot of tension unwound in Miles's neck at the reassuring hiss of a hypospray of synergine.

"How bad?" Miles demanded.

"Not good," the surgeon admitted, checking her diagnostic viewer. "Burst spleen, oozing hemorrhage in the stomach—this one had better go direct to surgery on the command ship. Medtech—" she motioned to a Dendarii waiting with the guards for the return of the shuttle, and gave triage instructions. The medtech swathed Suegar in a thin foil heat wrap.

"I'll make sure he gets there," promised Miles. He shivered, envying the heat wrap a little as the drizzly acid fog beaded in his hair and coiled into his bones.

Tung's expression and attention were abruptly absorbed by a message from his comm set. Miles, who had yielded Lieutenant Murka's headset back to him so that he might continue his duties, shifted from foot to foot in agony for news. *Elena, Elli, if I've killed you* . . .

Tung spoke into his pick-up. "Good. Well done. Report to the A7 drop site." A jerk of his chin switched channels. "Sim, Nout, fall back with your patrols to your shuttle drop site perimeters. They've been found."

Miles found himself bent over with his hand supported on gelid knees, waiting for his head to clear, his heart lurching in huge slow gulps. "Elli and Elena? Are they all right?"

"They didn't call for a medtech . . . you sure you don't need one yourself? You're green."

"I'm all right." Miles's heart steadied, and he straightened up, to meet Beatrice's questing eyes. "Beatrice, would you please go get Tris and Oliver for me? I need to talk to them before the next shuttle relay goes up."

She shook her head helplessly and wheeled away. She did not salute. On the other hand, she didn't argue, either. Miles was insensibly cheered.

The booming racket around the dome circle had died down to the occasional whine of small-arms fire, human cry, or blurred amplified voice. Fires burned in the distance, red-orange glows in the muffling fog. Not a surgically clean operation . . . the Cetagandans were going to be extremely pissed when they'd counted their casualties, Miles judged. Time to be gone, and long gone. He tried to keep the poisoned encodes in mind, as anodyne to the vision of Cetagandan clerks and techs crushed in the rubble of their burning buildings, but the two nightmares seemed to amplify instead of cancelling each other out.

Here came Tris and Oliver, both looking a little wild-eyed. Beatrice took up station at Tris's right shoulder.

"Congratulations," Miles began, before they could speak. He had a lot of ground to cover and not much time left. "You have achieved an army." A wave of his arm swept the orderly array of prisoners—ex-prisoners—spread across the camp in their shuttle groups. They waited quietly, most seated on the ground. Or was it the Cetagandans who had in-grained such patience in them? Whatever.

"Temporarily," said Tris. "This is the lull, I be-lieve. If things hot up, if you lose one or more shuttles, if somebody panics and it spreads—"

"You can tell anybody who's inclined to panic they can ride up with me if it'll make them feel better. Ah—better also mention that I'm going up in the *last* load," said Miles.

Tung, dividing his attention between this confab and his headset, grimaced in exasperation at this news.

"That'll settle 'em," grinned Oliver.

"Give them something to think about, anyway," conceded Tris.

"Now I'm going to give you something to think about. The new Marilac resistance. You're it," said Miles. "My employer originally engaged me to res-cue Colonel Tremont, that he might raise a new army and carry on the fight. When I found him . . . as he was, dying, I had to decide whether to follow the letter of my contract, and deliver a catatonic or a corpse, or the spirit—and deliver an army. I chose this, and I chose you two. *You* must carry on Colonel Tremont's work."

"I was only a field lieutenant," began Tris in hor-ror, in chorus with Oliver's, "I'm a grunt, not a staff officer. Colonel Tremont was a genius—"

"You are his heirs now. *I* say so. Look around you. Do I make mistakes in choosing my subordinates?"

After a moment's silence Tris muttered, "Appar-ently not."

"Build yourselves a staff. Find your tactics genuises, your technical wizards, and put 'em to work for you. But the drive, and the decisions, and the direction, must be yours, forged in this pit. It is you two who will remember this place, and so remember what it is you are doing, and why, always."

Oliver spoke quietly. "And when do we muster out of this army, Brother Miles? My time was up during the siege of Fallow Core. If I'd been anywhere else, I could have gone home."

"Until the Cetagandan army of occupation rolled down your street."

"Even then. The odds aren't good."

"The odds were worse for Barrayar, in its day, and they ran the Cetagandans right off. It took 20 years, and more blood than either of you have seen in your lives combined, but they did it," asserted Miles.

Oliver seemed more struck by this historical precedent than Tris, who said skeptically, "Barrayar had those crazy Vor warriors. Nuts who rushed into battle, who *liked* to die. Marilac just doesn't have that sort of cultural tradition. We're civilized—or we were, once. . . ."

"Let me tell you about the Barrayaran Vor," cut in Miles. "The loonies who sought a glorious death in battle found it very early on. This rapidly cleared the chain of command of the accumulated fools. The survivors were those who learned to fight dirty, and live, and fight another day, and win, and win, and win, and for whom nothing, not comfort, or security, not family or friends or their immortal souls, was more important than winning. Dead men are losers by definition. Survival and victory. They weren't supermen, or immune to pain. They sweated in confusion and darkness. And with not one-half the physical resources Marilac possesses even now, they won. When you're Vor," Miles ran down a little, "there is no mustering out."

After a silence Tris said, "Even a volunteer patriotic army must eat. And we won't beat the Cetagandans by firing spitballs at them."

"There will be financial and military aid forthcoming through a covert channel other than myself. If there is a Resistance command to deliver it to."

Tris measured Oliver by eye. The fire in her burned closer to the surface than Miles had ever seen it, coursing down those corded muscles. The whine of the first returning shuttles pierced the fog. She spoke quite softly. "And here I thought I was the atheist, Sergeant, and you were the believer. Are you coming with me—or mustering out?"

Oliver's shoulders bowed. With the weight of history, Miles realized, not defeat, for the heat in his eyes matched Tris's. "Coming," he grunted.

Miles caught Tung's eyes. "How we doing?"

Tung shook his head, held up fingers. "About six minutes slow, unloading upstairs."

"Right." Miles turned back to Tris and Oliver. "I want you both to go up on this wave, in separate shuttles, one to each troopship. When you get there, start expediting the off-loading of your people. Lieutenant Murka will give you your shuttle assignment—" he motioned Murka over, and packed them off.

Beatrice lingered. "I'm inclined to panic," she informed Miles in a distant tone. Her bare toe smudged whorls in the dampening dirt.

"I don't need a bodyguard any more," Miles said. He grinned. "A keeper, maybe . . ."

A smile lighted her eyes that did not yet reach her mouth. Later, Miles promised himself. Later, he would make that mouth laugh.

The second wave of shuttles began to lift, even as the remnants of the returning first wave were still landing. Miles prayed everyone's sensors were operating properly, passing each other in this fog. Their timing could only get more ragged from now on. The fog itself was coagulating into a cold rain, silver needles pelting down.

The focus of the operation was narrowing rapidly now, more of machines and numbers and timing, less of loyalties and souls and fearsome obligations.

An emotionally pathological mind, devoid of love and fear, might even call it fun, Miles thought. He began jotting scores left-handed in the dirt, numbers up, down, in transit, remaining, but the dirt was turning to gluey black mud and did not retain the impressions.

"Shit," Tung hissed suddenly through clenched teeth. The air before his face blurred in a flurry of vid-projected incoming information, his eyes flicking through it with practiced rapidity. His right hand bunched and twitched, as if tempted to wrench off his headset and stamp it into the mud in frustration and disgust. "That tears it. We just lost two shuttles out of the second wave."

Which two? Miles's mind screamed. *Oliver, Tris . . .* He forced his first question to be, "How?" *I swear, if they crashed into each other, I'm going to go find a wall and beat my head on it till I go numb. . . .*

"Cetagandan fighter broke through our cordon. He was going for the troop freighters, but we nailed him in time. Almost in time."

"You got identifications on which two shuttles? And were they loaded or returning?"

Tung's lips moved in subvocalization. "A-4, fully loaded. B-7, returning empty. Loss total, no survivors. Fighter shuttle 5 from the *Triumph* is disabled by enemy fire; pilot recovery now in progress."

He hadn't lost his commanders. His hand-picked and carefully nurtured successors to Colonel Tremont were safe. He opened his eyes, squeezed shut in pain, to find Beatrice, to whom the shuttle IDs meant nothing, waiting anxiously for interpretation.

"Two hundred dead?" she whispered.

"Two hundred six," Miles corrected. The faces, names, voices of the six familiar Dendarii fluttered through his memory. The 200 ciphers must have had faces too. He blocked them out, as too crushing an overload.

"These things happen," Beatrice muttered numbly.

"You all right?"

"Of course I'm all right. These things happen. Inevitable. I am not a weepy wimp who folds under fire." She blinked rapidly, lifting her chin. "Give me . . . something to do. Anything."

Quickly, Miles added for her. *Right*. He pointed across the camp. "Go to Pel and Liant. Divide their remaining shuttle groups into blocks of 33, and add them to each of the remaining third-wave shuttle groups. We'll have to send the third wave up overloaded. Then report back to me. Go quick, the rest will be back in minutes."

"Yessir," she saluted. For her sake, not his; for order, structure, rationality, a lifeline. He returned the salute gravely.

"They were already overloaded," objected Tung as soon as she was out of earshot. "They're going to fly like bricks with 233 squeezed on board. And they'll take longer to load on here and unload topside."

"Yes. God." Miles gave up scratching figures in the useless mud. "Run the numbers through the computer for me, Ky. I don't trust myself to add two and two just now. How far behind will we be by the time the main body of the Cetagandans comes in range? Come close as you can, no fudge factors, please."

Tung mumbled into his headset, reeled off numbers, margins, timing. Miles tracked every detail with predatory intensity. Tung concluded bluntly. "At the end of the last wave, five shuttles are still going to be waiting to unload when the Cetagandan fire fries us."

A thousand men and women . . .

"May I respectfully suggest, sir, that the time has come to start cutting our losses?" added Tung.

"You may, Commodore."

"Option One, maximally efficient; only drop seven shuttles in the last wave. Leave the last five shuttle loads of prisoners on the ground. They'll be re-taken, but at least they'll be alive." Tung's voice grew persuasive on this last line.

"Only one problem, Ky. *I* don't want to stay here."

"You can still be on the last shuttle up, just like you said. By the way, sir, have I expressed myself yet, sir, on what a genuinely dumbshit piece of grandstanding that is?"

"Eloquently, with your eyebrows, a while ago. And while I'm inclined to agree with you, have you noticed yet how closely the remaining prisoners keep watching me? Have you ever watched a cat sneaking up on a horned hopper?"

Tung stirred uneasily, eyes taking in the phenomenon Miles described.

"I don't fancy gunning down the last thousand in order to get my shuttle into the air."

"Skewed as we are, they might not realize there were no more shuttles coming till after you were in the air."

"So we just leave them standing there, waiting for us?" *The sheep look up, but are not fed . . .*

"Right."

"You like that option, Ky?"

"Makes me want to puke, but—consider the 9,000 others. And the Dendarii fleet. The idea of dropping them all down the rat hole in a pre-doomed effort to pack up all these—miserable sinners of yours, makes me want to puke a lot more. Nine-tenths of a loaf is *much* better than none."

"Point taken. Let us go on to option two, please. The flight out of orbit is calculated on the speed of the slowest ship, which is . . . ?"

"The freighters."

"And the *Triumph* remains the swiftest?"

"Betcher ass." Tung had captained the *Triumph*, once.

"And the best armored."

"Yo. So?" Tung saw perfectly well where he was

being driven. His obtuseness was but a form of oblique balking.

"So. The first seven shuttles up on the last wave lock onto the troop freighters and boost on schedule. We call back five of the *Triumph*'s fighter pilots and dump and destroy their craft. One's damaged already, right? The last five of these drop shuttles clamp to the *Triumph* in their place, protected from the now-arriving fire of the Cetagandan ships by the *Triumph*'s full shielding. Pack the prisoners into the *Triumph*'s corridors, lock shuttle hatches, boost like hell."

"The added mass of a thousand people—"

"Would be less that that of a couple of the drop shuttles. Dump and blow them too, if you have to, to fit the mass/acceleration window."

"—would overload life support—"

"The emergency oxygen will take us to the wormhole jump point. After Jump the prisoners can be distributed among the other ships at our leisure."

Tung's voice grew anguished. "Those combat drop shuttles are *brand new*. And my fighters—*five* of them—do you realize how hard it will be to recoup the funds to replace 'em? It comes to—"

"I asked you to calculate the time, Ky, not the price tag," said Miles through his teeth. He added more quietly, "I'll tack them on to our bill for services rendered."

"You ever hear the term *cost overrun*, boy? You will. . . ." Tung switched his attention back to his headset, itself but an extension of the tactics room aboard the *Triumph*. Calculations were made, new orders entered and executed.

"It flies," sighed Tung. "Buys a damned expensive fifteen minutes. If nothing else goes wrong . . ." he trailed off in a frustrated mumble, as impatient as Miles himself with his inability to be three places at once.

"There comes my shuttle back," Tung noted aloud.

He glanced at Miles, plainly unwilling to leave his admiral to his own devices, as plainly itching to be out of the acid rain and dark and mud and closer to the nerve center of operations.

"Get gone," said Miles. "You can't ride up with me anyway, it's against procedure."

"Procedure, hah," said Tung blackly.

With the lift-off of the third wave, there were barely 2,000 prisoners left on the ground. Things were thinning out, winding down; the armored combat patrols were falling back now from their penetration of the surrounding Cetagandan installations, back toward their assigned shuttle landing sites. A dangerous turning of the tide, should some surviving Cetagandan officer recover enough organization to harry their retreat.

"See you aboard the *Triumph*," Tung emphasized. He paused to brace Lieutenant Murka, out of Miles's earshot. Miles grinned in sympathy for the overworked lieutenant, in no doubt about the orders Tung was now laying on him. If Murka didn't come back with Miles in tow, he'd probably be wisest not to come back at all.

Nothing left now but a little last waiting. Hurry up and wait. Waiting, Miles realized, was very bad for him. It allowed his self-generated adrenalin to wear off, allowed him to feel how tired and hurt he really was. The illuminating flares were dying to a red glow.

There was really very little time between the fading of the labored thunder of the last third wave shuttle to depart, and the screaming whine of the first fourth-wave shuttle plunging back. Alas that this had more to do with being skewed than being swift. The Marilacans still waited in their rat bar blocks, discipline still holding. Of course, nobody'd told them about the little problem in timing they faced. But the nervous Dendarii patrols, chivvying them up the ramps, kept things moving at a pace to Miles's taste. Rear guard was never a popular position to draw, even among the lunatic fringe who defaced their weapons with notches and giggled among themselves while speculating upon newer and more grotesque methods of blowing away their enemies.

Miles saw the semi-conscious Suegar carried up the ramp first. Suegar would actually reach the *Triumph*'s sickbay faster in his company, Miles calculated, on this direct flight, than had he been sent on an earlier shuttle to one of the troop freighters and had to await a safe moment to transfer.

The arena they were leaving had grown silent and dark, sodden and sad, ghostly. *I will break the doors of hell, and bring up the dead* . . . there was something not quite right about the half-remembered quote. No matter.

This shuttle's armored patrol, the last, drew back out of the fog and darkness, electronically whistled in like a pack of sheepdogs by their master Murka, who stood at the foot of the ramp as liaison between the ground patrol and the shuttle pilot, who was expressing her anxiety to be gone with little whining revs on the engines.

Then from the darkness—plasma fire, sizzling through the rain-sodden, saturated air. Some Cetagandan hero—officer, troop, tech, who knew?—had crawled up out of the rubble and found a weapon—and an enemy to fire it at. Splintered afterimages, red and green, danced in Miles's eyes. A Dendarii patroller rolled out of the dark, a glowing line across the back of his armor smoking and sparking until quenched in the black mud. His armor legs seized up, and he lay wriggling like a frantic fish in an effort to peel out of it. A second plasma burst, ill-aimed, spent itself turning a few kilometers of fog and rain to superheated steam on a straight line to some unknown infinity.

Just what they needed, to be pinned down by sniper fire *now*. . . . A pair of Dendarii rear guards started back into the fog. An excited prisoner—ye gods, it was Pitt's lieutenant again—grabbed up the armor-paralyzed soldier's weapon and made to join them.

"No! Come back later and fight on your own time, your jerk!" Miles sloshed toward Murka. "Fall back, load up, get in the air! Don't stop to fight! No time!"

Some of the last of the prisoners had fallen flat to the ground, burrowing like mudpuppies, a sound sensible reflex in any other context. Miles dashed among them, slapping rumps. "Get *aboard*, up the *ramp*, go, go, go!" Beatrice popped up out of the mud and mimicked him, shakily driving her fellows before her.

Miles skidded to a stop beside his fallen Dendarii and snapped the armor clamps open left-handed. The soldier kicked off his fatal carapace, rolled to his feet, and limped for the safety of the shuttle. Miles ran close behind him.

Murka and one patrolman waited at the foot of the ramp.

"Get ready to pull in the ramp and lift on my mark," Murka began to the shuttle pilot. "R—" his words were lost in an explosive pop as the plasma beam sliced across his neck. Miles could feel the searing heat from it pass centimeters above his head as he stood next to his lieutenant. Murka's body crumpled.

Miles dodged, paused to yank off Murka's comm headset. The head came too. Miles had to brace it with his numb hand to pull the headset free. The weight of the head, its density and roundness, hammered into his senses. The precise memory of it would surely be with him until his dying day. He let it fall by Murka's body.

He staggered up the ramp, a last armored Dendarii pulling on his arm. He could feel the ramp sag peculiarly under their feet, glanced down to see a half-melted seam across it where the plasma arc that had killed Murka had passed on.

He fell through the hatchway, clutching the headset and yelling into it, "Lift, lift! Mark, now! Go!"

"Who is this?" came the shuttle pilot's voice back.

"Naismith."

"Yes, *sir*."

The shuttle heaved off the ground, engines roaring, even before the ramp had withdrawn. The ramp mechanism labored, metal and plastic complaining— then jammed on the twisted distortion of the melt.

"Get that hatch sealed back there!" the shuttle pilot's voice yowled over the headset.

"Ramp's jammed," Miles yowled back. "Jettison it!"

The ramp mechanism skreeled and shrieked, reversing itself. The ramp shuddered, jammed again. Hands reached out to thump on it urgently. "You'll never get it that way!" Beatrice, across the hatch from Miles, yelled fiercely, and twisted around to kick at it with her bare feet. The wind of their flight screamed over the open hatchway, buffeting and vibrating the shuttle like a giant blowing across the top of a bottle.

To a chorus of shouting, thumping, and swearing, the shuttle lurched abruptly onto its side. Men, women, and loose equipment tangled across the tilting deck. Beatrice kicked bloodily at a final buggered bolt. The ramp tore loose at last. Beatrice, sliding, fell with it.

Miles dove at her, lunging across the hatchway. If he connected, he never knew, for his right hand was a senseless blob. He saw her face only as a white blur as she whipped away into the blackness.

It was like a silence, a great silence, in his head. Although the roar of wind and engines, screaming and swearing and yelling, went on as before, it was lost somewhere between his ears and his brain, and went unregistered. He saw only a white blur, smear-

ing into the darkness, repeated again and again, re-
playing like a looping vid.

He found himself crouched on his hands and knees,
the shuttle's acceleration sucking him to the deck.
They'd gotten the hatch closed. The merely human
babble within seemed muffled and thin, now that the
roaring voices of the gods were silenced. He looked
up into the pale face of Pitt's lieutenant, crouched
beside him still clutching the unfired Dendarii weapon
he'd grabbed up in that other lifetime.

"You'd better kill a whole lot of Cetagandans for
Marilac, boy," Miles rasped to him at last. "You
better be worth something to *some*body, 'cause I've
sure paid too much for you."

The Marilacan's face twitched uncertainly, too cowed
even to try to look apologetic. Miles wondered what
his own face must look like. From the reflection in
that mirror, strange, very strange.

Miles began to crawl forward, looking for something, somebody. . . . Formless flashes made yellow
streaks in the corners of his vision. An armored
Dendarii, her helmet off, pulled him to his feet.

"Sir? Hadn't you better come forward to the pilot's
compartment, sir?"

"Yes, all right . . ."

She got an arm around him, under his arms, so he
didn't fall down again. They picked their way forward in the crowded shuttle, through Marilacans and
Dendarii mixed. Faces were drawn to him, marked
him fearfully, but none dared an expression of any
kind. Miles's eye was caught by a silver cocoon, as
they neared the forward end.

"Wait . . ."

He fell to his knees beside Suegar. A hit of hope
. . . "Suegar. Hey, Suegar!"

Suegar opened his eyes to slits. No telling how
much of this he was taking in, through the pain and
the shock and the drugs.

"You're on your way now. We made it, made the

timing. With all ease. With agility and speed. Up through the regions of the air, higher than the clouds. You had the scripture right, you did."

Suegar's lips moved. Miles bent his head closer.

". . . wasn't really a scripture," Suegar whispered. "I knew it . . . you knew it . . . don't shit me . . ."

Miles paused, cold-stoned. Then he leaned forward again. "No, brother," he whispered. "For though we went in clothed, we have surely come out naked."

Suegar's lips puffed on a dry laugh.

Miles didn't weep until after they'd made the wormhole jump.

"Jerry Pournelle is one of a handful of writers who can speculate knowledgeably about future worlds. His space program background, readings in science, and Ph.D.'s in psychology and political science allow him to carefully work out the logical development of a world and its societies."—*Amazing*

JERRY POURNELLE

Experience the world-building talents of Jerry Pournelle, co-author (with Larry Niven) of the national bestsellers Footfall, The Mote in God's Eye, *and* Lucifer's Hammer! *The following titles are available from Baen Books:*

THE MERCENARY, 65594-9,
  288 pp., $2.95
KING DAVID'S SPACESHIP, 65616-3,
  384 pp., $3.50
HIGH JUSTICE, 65571-X, 288 pp., $2.95
IMPERIAL STARS (ed.), 65603-1,
  480 pp., $3.95

Send the combined cover price plus 75 cents for first-class postage and handling to: Baen Books, Dept. B, 260 Fifth Avenue, New York, N.Y. 10001. We'll also send you our free catalog!